THE DEBUTANTE
DILEMMA

What Reviewers Say About Jane Walsh's Work

The Secret Duchess

"Ann Brontë's *The Tenant of Wildfell Hall* meets Sarah Waters's *The Paying Guests* in this charming romance by Walsh. …If you are up for a subversion of genre expectations and conventions, especially those promised by the word 'Duchess' in the title, then Jane Walsh will not disappoint you. This book does a good job of balancing a whole number of narrative and thematic elements, going beyond the mere pastiche of Regency era, the set-dressing so to say, and actively explores issues related to class, labor, legal status of women, and feelings of abandonment by the structures of marriage and kinship which were meant to be women's main defense and comfort in the world then. It does all that while delivering a touching, life-like, and sweet lesbian romance without shattering its historical setting's spirit. A strong recommendation by yours truly."—*The Lesbian Review*

"I continue to love how Walsh grapples with the issues women faced in the Regency, especially if they happened to be queer, while providing them both realistic and hopeful paths to an HEA, and this one was no exception."—*Courtney Reads Romance*

The Inconvenient Heiress

"Reading a Jane Walsh novel is a dream with every page. It's a reminder that we have always been here, that we have always been finding community and finding love, that we have always risked it all and been rewarded for our bravery, that queer love is about the quiet moments as well as the loud ones, that we deserve to wear flowy gowns and make our art and find our future, that we deserve to have our love and care returned to us in spades, that we deserve and deserve and deserve."—*The Lesbrary*

"I enjoyed every moment of this. Those forbidden feelings and moments Arabella and Caroline shared were magical, but when everything changed for Caroline and she had to contemplate marriage my heart broke for them both. I was completely invested in them being together and so being on that emotional rollercoaster with them, especially Arabella I could only hope they might get their chance. …[Jane] has a real talent for delivering exciting regency romances that are rich, loving, and deeply sentimental."—*LESBIreviewed*

The Accidental Bride

"…a realistic examination of actually making a marriage work. The meat and potatoes of the story is really [Thea and Grace] learning how to talk to each other and let the other in. It's the 'ever after' of HEA."—*Dear Author*

"The strength of the story is in its compelling main characters. I loved how the dynamics between the two evolved, playing into some common tropes, from the initial passionate entanglement between the two, to a gradual development into something more as the rest of the plot plays out. …Walsh is great at playing with reader expectations, and I was not disappointed in her twists on genre tropes and expectations to deliver a truly satisfying ending."—*Courtney Reads Romance*

Her Duchess to Desire

"One of Walsh's strongest points is her ability to build a strong, positive queer community in a time period that is known to have sometimes been hostile to them. …I love an Ice Queen heroine who melts in the hands of the right person, and Anne is a great personification of that."—*Courtney Reads Romance*

"What a fantastic story. Not like anything I have read before so it was exciting and new and captured my imagination right from the start. Everything is so regal, from the characters, to the lifestyle, to the exquisite designs that Letitia draws up and produces. I just closed my eyes and could picture it all perfectly. It was the element of forbidden romance between Anne and Letitia that had me hooked because it was delicious, came with risks, and none of us knew what the consequences would be."—*LESBIreviewed*

Her Countess to Cherish

"This book was a nice surprise to me in its portrayal of gender fluidity, along with a delightful romance between two sympathetic characters. If you love queer historical romance, you should absolutely check this out."—*Courtney Reads Romance*

Her Lady to Love

"If you are looking for a sweet, cozy romance with grounded leads, this is for you. The author's dedication to the little cultural details do help flesh out the setting so much more. I also loved how buttery smooth everything tied together. Nothing seemed to be out of place, and the romance had some stakes. ...Highly recommended." —Colleen Corgel, Librarian, Queens Public Library

"Walsh debuts with a charming if flawed Regency romance. ...Though Honora's shift from shy curiosity to boldly stated interest feels a bit abrupt, her relationship with Jacquie is sweet, sensual, and believable. Subplots about a group of bluestockings and a society of LGBTQ Londoners add depth..."—*Publishers Weekly*

"What a delightful queer Regency era romance. ...*Her Lady to Love* was a beautiful addition to the romance genre, and a much appreciated queer involvement. I'll definitely be looking into more of Walsh's works!"—Dylan Miller, Librarian (Baltimore County Public Library)

"...it's the perfect novel to read over the holidays if you love gorgeous writing, beautiful settings, and literal bodice ripping! I had such a brilliant time with this book. Walsh's novel has such an excellent sense of the time period she's writing in and her specificity and interest in the historical aspects of her plot really allow the characters to shine. The inclusion of details, specifically related to women's behaviour or dress, made for a vivid and exciting setting. This novel reminded me a lot of something like *Vanity Fair* (1847) (but with lesbians!) because of its gorgeous setting and intriguing plot."—*The Lesbrary*

Visit us at www.boldstrokesbooks.com

By the Author

Her Lady to Love

Her Countess to Cherish

Her Duchess to Desire

Seducing the Widow

The Debutante Dilemma

THE SPINSTERS OF INVERLEY:

The Inconvenient Heiress

The Accidental Bride

The Secret Duchess

THE DEBUTANTE DILEMMA

by

Jane Walsh

2026

THE DEBUTANTE DILEMMA
© 2026 By Jane Walsh. All Rights Reserved.

ISBN 13: 978-1-63679-896-7

This Trade Paperback Original Is Published By
Bold Strokes Books, Inc.
P.O. Box 249
Valley Falls, NY 12185

First Edition: January 2026

CREDITS
EDITOR: CINDY CRESAP
PRODUCTION DESIGN: SUSAN RAMUNDO
COVER DESIGN BY TAMMY SEIDICK

Acknowledgments

Writing a book is more than putting words down on a blank page, and writing a romance novel is more than a meet cute and a happily ever after. It represents months of time and effort, nurturing ideas into plot and character and setting. And it takes more than just the author to give the story meaning.

Thank you to all the authors who write such fabulous books that make me want to continue writing queer romance. Thank you to the artists who pour themselves into cover art and character design and illustration and calligraphy, and who inspire me to create in other ways than writing. Thank you to every barista who ever poured me an iced Americano this year (there were so many, I was so tired).

Thank you to the team at Bold Strokes Books for everything that they do, and special thanks to my editor, Cindy. Thank you for your patience and your encouragement, and for believing in my work. Your words are kind and your critiques are on point, and they all mean a great deal to me.

Thank you to my BSBestie Chelsey for the late-night texts and thoughtful conversations, especially when I was struggling to finish this book. My experience as an author would not be the same without you.

Thank you to the Three Couples for the laughs and all the love. The joy that you share with your partners is a wonderful thing to behold, and I am grateful to witness it.

Thank you to Chris for welcoming me to the Violet Hour and for including me in an unforgettable night at Pulp Books this summer. That invitation came at the exact right moment when I needed a creative boost.

And of course, I could not write romance without the love and support of my amazing wife. Thank you a hundred thousand times over, Mag. Thank you for showing up and cheering me on at every opportunity. Thank you for calming me down when I panic, and for celebrating every win with me. Thank you for your optimism and enthusiasm, and for being so very wonderfully you.

Dedication

For Mag, because I have never belonged anywhere
as much as I belong with you.

CHAPTER ONE

London, 1815

Lady Emily Calloway had not anticipated enjoying her debut Season. She disliked crowds and improper behavior, which appeared to be all the rage in high society. She had only experienced the limited society of her neighborhood in Somerset and was so nervous upon being invited to her first ball in London that she had thrice needed rescuing from her maid in the form of pungent smelling salts.

She was confronted by such a crush of people in the ballroom that she feared for the appearance of her crisp lustring dress, and the evening passed in such a whirl that it was difficult to focus on much of anything. It was fortunate that the gentlemen wrote their names on the sticks of her fan to secure their dances with her, for otherwise she would never have remembered any of them.

But at the end of the night, after her voice had grown hoarse from agreeing with everyone and her feet ached from dancing, after she had given her fan a loving pat and slipped it into her wooden keepsake box, after the dazzling stars had faded from her eyes and she could collect her thoughts, she found reassurance in the proof that she was simply one more lady in possession of the usual accomplishments and elegance of manner and refinement of dress.

Because she was no different in any discernible way, she was greatly admired by the *ton* from the moment of her first curtsy to Queen Charlotte. Within two weeks of her presentation at court, she had received her voucher for Almack's from Lady Jersey, and *everyone* knew that there was no higher honor than dancing there on Wednesday nights.

Unless, of course, one received an offer of marriage from one of London's most eligible bachelors.

Emily was satisfied that soon enough, she would boast of that, too.

"Are you certain that Lord Danfield is the man for you, Em?" Miss Juliet Mayweather asked her after they arrived at Lady Enfield's ball.

Juliet was the dearest of her newfound friends. She was a strikingly handsome woman with straight brows set over dark eyes, the strong features of her face framed by severe black hair. Six weeks acquaintanceship had proved enough time to determine that their opinions were much the same, whether it was a preference for a country dance to a scotch reel, or to choose silk netting instead of silver thread to sew up a new reticule.

"Danfield is the younger son of a duke, has wealth almost beyond compare, and he loves me, Jules. What more could a lady ask for?"

Juliet had shocked Emily by her immediate insistence on using Christian names, but also by using nicknames that Emily would sooner have perished than utter to anyone else. Perhaps it was because Juliet was so exacting in her own way that despite her eccentricities, she found favor with everyone. Only Juliet could scare away half a dozen suitors despite the Season being less than half over and still be considered wholly acceptable even by the sticklers of society.

Emily's stepmother had whispered in her ear that it was more likely due to Juliet's father's enormous shipping fortune.

Juliet pursed her lips. "The *elder* son of the duke would be preferable, if one must marry."

"The marquess? Avenbury is said to be a brooding fellow."

"He has been away from London for so many years." She opened her plumed fan and studied it. "The rumors about him are intriguing and would liven up a dull crowd such as this one. Perhaps your Lord Danfield has said something to you about his brother?"

Emily never found any crowd dull. Intimidating and overwhelming, perhaps, but dull—never. A ballroom could almost be a living thing of its own, heaving with humanity as people either pressed together in chattering groups or paired off in laughing couples to dance. There was always so much happening that her attention shifted from one moment to the next, and it was impossible to remember much before it all began anew the next day. Days had blurred into weeks, and it felt as if she had hardly caught her breath from her very first dance.

"I thought no man intrigued you, Jules. Besides, I have little interest in rumors. The fact of the matter is that Danfield is the darling of every soiree, so there is no question who is the superior choice between brothers. You shall be dabbing at your eyes from the first pew of St. George's soon enough as you witness the grandest wedding of the Season—my own."

"If he proposes."

Emily straightened her back. "He will." She would have bet her best reticule on it if Juliet hadn't told her that she considered gambling to be gauche.

"He is handsome enough." Juliet gazed at Lord Danfield where he stood with a group of gentlemen across the room. "I admit that he does have what every debutante could possibly want. A handsome face and a fine head of hair. A good collection of waistcoats and the shiniest of boots. Each time I see him, fans flutter faster and I notice a truly alarming display of ankles."

"*My* ankles will remain well-covered." Earlier in the evening, Emily had buttoned up her train so she would not trip over her dress when the dancing started. Now she slipped the button free and twitched the fabric so that the flounce of her hem rested at the edge of her dancing slippers.

She was not perturbed by her lack of attraction to the man she wished to wed. It was reassuring enough to know that she captivated *him*. Although entrancing the absentee marquess might have been the coup of the decade, Lord Frederick Danfield—despite having only one estate of his own—was still a most excellent catch.

"His attentions have been remarked upon by my father."

Papa's exact words had been *you should consider yourself the wiliest privateer I've ever encountered if you can land as plump a prize as Danfield*, but she would not repeat it. Her father was a ruddy-faced retired rear admiral who was gentleman enough for their neighborhood assemblies, but Emily had to confess that although he was a baron, he lacked something of elegance in London. He preferred to leave social gatherings to his second wife, Emily's stepmother.

"Go forth and claim him, then," Juliet said, and gestured with her fan. "Danfield is alone now, and ripe for the picking."

"I have more pride than to fawn over him the instant that he is available."

"It is of no matter, for here he comes seeking you."

"Oh! I wish I had time in the retiring room. Am I in looks?"

Was this to be the moment that debutantes dreamed of? Emily wasn't sure how she should feel. This was what she had wanted, after all, so she had assumed she would be more excited. Perhaps the excitement came *after* a proposal.

"Turn the other way and pinch your cheeks, if you wish. But is it not better if you look cool and unbothered by his attentions? I think with such a man, you would be wise to keep your wits about you."

Emily laughed. "I have no such power in the face of nobility."

"A woman always has power. Do not forget it."

Danfield swept into a bow as he arrived. He was a tall man with carefully tousled black hair and a penchant for diamonds in his tie pins. His eyes sparkled with merriment, and he was already smiling.

"Never has a gentleman beheld such a sweet and gentle rose as you, Lady Emily."

She smiled and dipped her head to acknowledge the compliment. He was not a rare wit, but kindness was better than entertainment in a marriage. A man of good humor was always assured of a warm welcome.

"In fact, roses pale in comparison to the fine bloom of your cheek."

He was neither original nor apt. She knew from long acquaintance with her looking glass that her skin was fast to blush, but she felt no heat now in her cheeks.

"You are too kind, my lord," she murmured.

Juliet cocked her head to the side. "Your words do you credit, Lord Danfield. Lady Emily is the most elegant woman in attendance tonight."

"Indeed she is. And may I count on your discretion, Miss Mayweather, if I dare to court scandal by asking Lady Emily if she wishes for some air outside?"

Emily frowned. "Scandal is a courtship that I would never encourage."

She tried not to squint as she scanned the room for her stepmother. Lady Calloway was no favorite of hers, but she could benefit from familial support—although she hardly considered her as family and only addressed her as *Stepmama* to please Papa.

He leaned in close enough for her to inhale his cologne, and she turned her head slightly. Musk was also not a favorite of hers. His smile turned conspiratorial. "Perhaps I have a pressing question that needs answering."

Following him could be an invitation to trouble instead of matrimony, and she had no interest in such trouble with him or with anyone else. And yet how was she to deny him if she wished to wed him? Emily bit her lip and looked at Juliet.

"A lady's propriety is her finest virtue," Juliet said. "You may ask any decent question of my friend right here, or in the privacy of her house with her father present."

Danfield's eyes narrowed. "The gardens are said to be very fine."

"I go to the gardens with no man, my lord." It felt surprisingly good to say *no*. It was not a word she had uttered much since arriving in London. Was this what Juliet meant about power? What an intriguing notion.

The tension left his face, and he bounced back on his heels. "What a jewel of a woman you are! Well, if I am to bear the agony of your potential regret in full earshot of everyone, then so be it. Lady Emily, you would make a fine wife."

Emily waited for her heart to leap and her pulse to race, but instead all she felt was a trifle embarrassed.

Juliet fanned herself. "A declaration is not a question."

Danfield gritted his teeth. "You must have had the best of governesses, Miss Mayweather."

Emily smiled at him. "I encourage you to call upon my father, my lord."

The next day Danfield paid a call to Papa. He kept him in his study for an unmannerly hour, likely filled more with tales of his time at sea than the fate of his only daughter. The men then joined her and Lady Calloway for tea and to announce Emily's good fortune to them.

An elegant evening was planned to celebrate their engagement in a fortnight's time, and Emily was delighted to discover that a gentleman's proposal was quite a bit less painless than she had expected it to be.

❖

Miss Rebecca Tremblay was ready to be delighted with everything and everyone.

The voyage had been a long one, and it had been weeks since she had been in any sort of decent society. Forty-three days on a packet ship from New York to Falmouth was not for the faint of heart, even though the captain had been witty and the dinners were passable and there had been that one lovely night where she had convinced her fiancé to dance on deck with her under the moonlight. She was still shocked he had agreed, given that he was far from a romantic man.

The week of bumpy roads in the carriage to London had hardly been much better than the ship. Then to be told almost before she arrived that she was to be whisked off to her first London soiree!

But this was the life to which she must become accustomed, though it gave her the shivers to think of the grandeur that awaited her. Especially if there was no time to dispatch the wrinkles from her finest pink silk, forcing her to settle for her second-best white muslin.

Marrying a marquess would thrust her into an echelon that she had not even dreamed of while growing up as the daughter of an American gin distiller. The bleak winters and languid summers and the parties of Montreal and Halifax and New York were behind her now. Glittering London society was her future.

"Tonight's event is to celebrate your brother, my lord?" Rebecca asked her fiancé, the Marquess of Avenbury.

Her mother sat beside her in the carriage and her father sat beside Avenbury. The seats were so well-sprung that she hardly noticed the bounce as the horses clopped down the cobblestones. Avenbury had mentioned that they were off to Mayfair. If she had not already known where it was from the society papers that made their way to America each month, she would have still understood that it was a fancy address. She had become adept at picking up such hints from his tone during the sea voyage. He was a man of long stares and few words, his beautiful accent often dripping with censure.

But he would grow to love her, like many had at home. With a sidelong glance at her father, she straightened in her seat. Even with this betrothal, she could not be certain that her parents finally approved of her actions. They adored the idea of a marquess as a son-in-law, of course. But sometimes she thought that if they could have exchanged her for any other girl in New York as a daughter, they would have happily signed the transaction papers and waived the fee.

"Yes, I learned upon my arrival that Danfield is recently engaged."

His voice was as disdainful as ever. What manner of man was he that he was so disinterested in his own brother's betrothal? But given that they were on their way to honor him, Avenbury's voice must be hiding his fraternal affection.

Rebecca had always heard that the peerage was an odd lot. She had the occasion to dance with a younger brother or two, but never before with the heir to a grand title before the marquess had come along and awed everyone.

She wrestled a ringlet into place behind her ear and hoped the fashion plates she had studied at home were not so outdated as to render her appearance as an embarrassment. What did well enough in New York might not at all be the fashion in London.

"I will be pleased to make your brother's acquaintance."

"We shall all be pleased," Mother said. "Any family of our dear marquess shall be treated like our own."

Avenbury glanced out the window and did not reply.

Truly, Rebecca had had enough of brothers. With three of her own, each more tiresome than the last, she would have preferred a sister to visit, but she was resolved to love whoever she was presented to tonight.

When the carriage stopped, Rebecca clasped a hand to her mouth to hide her gasp. Were all the houses in London so palatial? She wished now she had spent more time looking out the window instead of trying to decipher Avenbury's grimaces. Torches blazed along the walkway to guide them to the enormous door of an edifice that towered above the square. Everywhere she looked was white stone and engraved marble beneath the flickering firelight.

The marquess flipped open his pocket watch and held it close to the carriage lantern. "Half eleven," he said with satisfaction. "They will be sitting soon to supper."

Was this his brother's house? His father's? It could very well be the marquess's own, for all Rebecca knew, but she dared not ask. She had learned that he did not enjoy questions. Well, all must be revealed soon enough.

Rebecca lingered in the carriage for a moment too long, earning a brusque order from her father to hurry. As neither her parents nor the marquess made any move to help her, she gathered the skirts of her voluminous white dress in one arm and hopped down the step herself.

No one greeted them as they entered the grand house, but there was an enormously gratifying gasp that thrilled Rebecca to the center of her being when the butler bellowed out "The Marquess of Avenbury!" at the entry to the ballroom.

"Montreal is every bit as fine, and New York even better," Father said, eying the marble balustrade. Rebecca knew he was tallying up the price of the architecture. He was a short balding man with a large moustache that he was fond of stroking when deep in thought, as he was now. He wore a sober black double-breasted tailcoat and black breeches, and Rebecca thought with pride that he looked like a man of some importance among the crowd.

Mother, as always, followed her husband's train of thought. "We had every convenience at home, and as much extravagance as one could wish."

Mother had fretted over her gown more than Rebecca had and had finally dressed in salmon-colored satin with French knots at the hem and neckline. The color set off her graying chestnut curls.

"Then perhaps we should have stayed at home," Rebecca said, intending only to tease but regretting her words when Mother's eyes narrowed.

"Where you got yourself into no end of trouble? I think not."

"I've worked for years to get our gin into Europe, and now you talk of *staying behind*! No business acumen at all."

"I meant nothing by it," she said, long accustomed to smoothing over her words.

"You should be grateful that such an influential and important man as the marquess will have you. He may be the one to finally lead you into sense. If such a thing is even possible."

Rebecca stopped listening. She was so familiar with their disappointment that she could have delivered the lecture herself. There were more interesting things that demanded her attention tonight. Everyone was so beautiful, and as they were all staring at her, it was easy to look her fill. Hair was curled as tight here as it was at home, and the dresses were similar enough. Some of the ball gowns were cut so daringly low on the bosom that she was shocked—and yearned to know which fashion plates she could secure to see more.

Rebecca had known the marquess for several months. He was a fine figure of a man, always smartly dressed, ready with a quip, and engaged of an evening. She had thought he knew the whole world in New York, where hats were doffed upon his approach and drinks and cigars offered in his wake.

But she had not known the true extent of his celebrity. Avenbury in New York had been a popular man. Avenbury in London could have been a king. She was astonished at the depths of the bows that greeted him, the trepidation and awe on the men's faces. The women were almost fainting at the chance to catch his eye, and it was almost unbelievable that she, among all of these bejeweled and glittering ladies, had been the one to win his hand.

How intimidating.

Rebecca knew, of course, that their betrothal was not due to her individual attributes. Had it been offered because of her beauty (of which she had been assured from many a suitor), or her accomplishments (which received dimmer praise than her face, but she thought herself proficient enough at the harp), or her behavior (unappealing to her family but charming enough to society at large), she would have felt humbled.

As it was, she had simply been part of a business deal.

Avenbury moved to the front of the grand ballroom, commanding attention. She followed, each step lifting her spirits higher. The opening of his mouth silenced the crowd in an instant, and she felt a little burst of happiness that she was to be his bride.

"I have been away for far too long, my friends," Avenbury said as he gazed into the crowd, and there was a ripple of laughter. Did they think him funny, or were they polite? Did he truly know everyone here, or was it rhetoric? How delightful to have even half so many friends. She wondered which man was his brother, and how soon she would meet him, then realized that Avenbury had resumed speaking some minutes ago. "I have been busy increasing my fortunes, but now I am ready to be among you once more." At a hard stare from Father, he smirked, and added with a slight bow, "I am particularly delighted to make my fiancée known to you all. I present to you Miss Rebecca Tremblay, the future Marchioness of Avenbury, and someday, God willing, the future Duchess of Northelm."

He gestured to Rebecca. She felt as tall as a poplar tree and as open as a sunflower. The past did not matter now. Tonight was the ending to her fairy tale, and tomorrow would be the beginning of her radiant new life. If Avenbury was like a king to these people, then she would be their queen. She swallowed hard as she watched her parents beam at the marquess as if he were a beloved fourth son.

She was convinced that the roar in her ears was thunderous applause until she realized that no one had moved their hands. The roar was her own heartbeat, pounding loud enough that she thought they all must hear it. Rebecca's smile had been genuine when he had said her name followed by such lovely titles, but now she forced it to stay on her face as the crowd stared at her.

Were they displeased with her hair? Her figure? Her dress? Were the women jealous? Were the men in shock?

What was the meaning of this odd reception?

CHAPTER TWO

Pinpricks of white danced across Emily's vision as her knees buckled. She fished the smelling salts from her reticule with shaking hands, thumbed the vial open with the ease of long practice, and inhaled. Her body shook like a leaf in a storm as the shock of the sharp odor raced through her.

Oh, what a dreadful cure. And yet nothing was as effective at clearing her mind.

After the heady rush and a lungful of air, she was steadier on her feet. *Now* she could focus. Still gasping, she slipped the vial into her reticule. She regained her composure as the marquess proclaimed, "And someday, God willing, the Duchess of Northelm."

What was this nonsense? Had the Marquess of Avenbury returned from years of travel as blithely as if he had been absent for a week's jaunt at his country estate? Was it possible that he had announced a betrothal tonight?

To a total stranger to high society?

At Emily's own engagement soiree?

She wished now she had pressed Juliet for every word of every horrid rumor about him.

Emily had experienced a perfectly normal debut Season, which she had planned to end in a perfectly normal betrothal celebration. She had been prepared for congratulations and a multitude of speeches and toasts in her honor tonight, and to revel at belonging to the wonderful world of the beau monde.

But who among them would speak of Emily now, when the duke's heir had arrived with his own bride-to-be?

A younger brother's nuptials paled in comparison to an heir's.

The triumph of the night was snatched from her, and the hollow confirmation that she was never to be more than second-best settled around her heart like a thorny cage.

Her fingers twitched, but she restrained herself from reaching for the salts again. Once was more than enough of an evening.

Danfield's face was white and his jaw was clenched. "So the black sheep of the family is to be married. He has some sense of tradition left in him, if he showed up with a fiancée and not a bride. How intriguing to be told at the same time as the masses."

Gone was the affable charmer, replaced by a cold-faced stranger glaring daggers at his own flesh and blood. Emily could not speak, but he didn't seem to need any reply.

The marquess and his fiancée were still standing at the front of the room. The woman had frozen like a fox before a hound. She must have been wily indeed to capture Avenbury's attentions and was well caught before the *ton*'s sharp gaze.

Emily had known that Avenbury and Danfield were twins, but it amazed her how similar they were. Avenbury's black hair brushed his starched collar where Danfield wore his shorter, and they favored different styles of cravat and waistcoat, but otherwise Emily thought even the mirror would have difficulty to tell them apart.

Danfield strode over to his brother. Emily bit her lip and straightened her skirt, then rushed after him. His business was now *her* business. Did she not have every right to hear it at his side? Perhaps it was forward of her, but it could not be impolite to involve herself.

The ache in her chest subsided as she clung to clarity of thought instead of the vial. No matter how displaced she now felt, teetering at the edge of security, she *knew* she belonged with Danfield as his future bride. She was cleaving to her future husband's side.

Just a trifle precipitously.

"Avenbury." Danfield jerked his chin at his brother. "A word?"

"I do not take orders from my younger brother." Avenbury's voice was as soft as his eyes were hard.

"You have absented yourself so long that one forgets the natural order of things."

"And so the throne has been warmed in my wake? How obliging you have been."

"Your barbs would be better delivered in private."

"Then by all means, let us talk."

The brothers stalked off, their strides well matched, as alike in breadth of shoulder and length of leg as they were in their faces.

Emily stared at the woman, hardly noticing much more than a riot of chestnut curls framing wide brown eyes. She could not tell who moved first, but there was only a moment of unspoken agreement before they scrambled after the gentlemen.

The brothers had not gained much ground after leaving the ballroom, and Emily caught sight of them turning into a room at the end of the grand marble hallway. The door was closed when she rushed up to it. She itched to push it open, but decorum stopped her. Involving herself was no bad idea, but shoving her way into a private conversation would be unforgiveable. She had not engaged herself to a duke's son to show her unworthiness now, no matter how much she may wish to know what was happening.

But did she belong in the room with them? Or the ballroom, where a thousand questions must await her? Or outside the door, with this stranger beside her?

"Oh, do open it," the woman urged, her voice low and lovely, her eyes shining, and Emily's pulse leapt wildly as she obeyed.

Danfield's head jerked up, annoyance flashing in his eyes as Emily and Avenbury's fiancée stood at the door.

Embarrassment flooded Emily. What had she been thinking? She should never have done such a thing. She *would* never have done such a thing without someone else's encouragement, and she glared at the instigator of the crime. Not only was she unperturbed by Emily's glower, but she seemed unconcerned by the tension that lay thick in the air. They were clearly unwelcome, but she slipped into a chair by the door as if she had been invited.

Avenbury gestured toward her. "You see how Miss Tremblay loves me enough to follow where I go?"

The marquess *approved* such a lack of decorum from his betrothed? He had always been a figure cloaked in mystery whenever anyone spoke of him, but she could not have fathomed any son of a duke to be so lax in manner or propriety.

Danfield laughed. "I do not believe for one instant that this means you have changed. But such a tale is unfit for delicate ears."

"If you are speaking of me, my lord, I assure you that my ears are hardy enough," Miss Tremblay said, beaming up at him.

"I am not too delicate for any news that concerns this family." As soon as the words slipped past her lips, Emily couldn't believe that she had uttered them. Why, her whole life had revolved around cultivating an air of delicacy! And to encourage gossip—but *was* it gossip if it came from the source? Surely the world had tipped over. Never before had she felt so uncertain as to what was right and what was wrong.

"As little as I like to contradict a lady, I beg of you to please understand that neither of you are yet part of this family." Danfield stood. "You must excuse us. We have business to discuss."

"Well, that is another thing entirely. I know my place is not in *business*." Miss Tremblay laughed. "I would be of no use to either of you if you intend to speak of sums or orders or—dear me— negotiations! Do rejoin us at your leisure, gentlemen."

Emily stared as the men filed past and closed the door behind them. All she had wanted was a normal courtship, and somehow it was ending in farce.

"This is absurd," she said, but she wasn't certain if she was speaking to herself or to Miss Tremblay.

"The men will settle everything between them."

Somehow her calmness was not soothing. How was she so unbothered?

"We must return to the ballroom."

"But I told them we would be here," Miss Tremblay said, blinking at her. "We must wait."

Emily was certain that each and every one of her nerves was stretched thin. "This is entirely improper."

"Two gently bred ladies sitting across from one another? There is no man here to besmirch our good names."

"I know neither you nor your name."

"Rebecca Tremblay. Heiress to a gin fortune. Perhaps you missed the announcement in the ballroom?"

Those words from anyone else would have been condescending, rubbing her nose in the fact that of the two of them, Emily was now the one of lesser standing. But this woman's eyes were kind, and her voice was soft. She spoke as if they were already friends.

Her accent was not entirely familiar. She was not from England, and the fact startled her anew. The marquess was marrying an *American*?

"I meant to imply that I do not know your reputation."

"You will be familiar with it soon enough. We are marrying brothers, after all."

That was incomprehensible, so Emily focused on the matter at hand. "This is improper because we are in a private room in a duke's house, where we have no right to be. I do not know how you conduct yourself across the ocean, but this is considered poor behavior here. We must leave before we are found out."

Miss Tremblay tilted her head to one side. "I admit such a thing would also be seen as rude in New York. But are we not to marry these men? Are we not therefore above such censure?"

"Even if we were *already* married, we should not be in their father's private rooms!" Emily shook her head. "This is a duke's house. You are marrying the marquess, not the duke himself. You may remain here if you wish, but I am leaving this minute."

She opened the door, poked her head into the hallway, and then retreated back inside and pushed the door closed behind her. For the second time tonight, black and white sparkled before her eyes and threatened to overwhelm her. "Oh, dear Lord. The Duke of Northelm is in the hallway!"

For a night that began so auspiciously, she was beset by bad luck now.

This would be the end of all of her fine beginnings.

❖

Lady Emily's face was whiter than snow, and Rebecca felt a moment's pity. How delicate these English girls were if the very sight of a man set them to swooning! She knew herself to be made from stronger stock. There was no man alive who could weaken her knees.

The cordial thing to do was to console her new friend. "We have nothing to fear from the duke." Rebecca tried to sound reassuring.

"One word from him, and our betrothals could be over. Do you wish yours to be ended almost before it has begun?" Her eyes were almost wild, if wilderness was something that could be found in such rarified environments.

Rebecca reconsidered the situation. "Oh. Then it appears we have *everything* to fear from this duke."

"What are we to do? There is no way out of this room without him seeing us."

Lady Emily paced its length, her white satin skirts brushing against Rebecca as she passed her. Her blond hair was pinned up so tightly that nary a curl bounced out of place as she walked. Her shoes were hardly more than scraps of embroidered white silk laced to her ankle. Rebecca admired them excessively but decided against enquiring about the best shops to frequent in London. There would be time enough for that later, as they would see much of each other once they married brothers.

Unless Lady Emily was right, and their presence here could jeopardize such an outcome.

Rebecca didn't like that notion at all. It had been a long journey to get here, and she did not wish to return to the Americas. "Perhaps you are worried for nothing. The duke might not even open the door."

"He must be in search of his sons. This could be the first place he looks! It was the first one they sought out, after all."

It was a small room, filled with books and a large desk and several chairs. "We must simply be creative, and the puzzle shall solve itself. Oh! Would you be inclined to hide? You could fit yourself beneath the desk, and I could stand behind the curtains."

"May we leave creativity to the artists of the world? I most certainly would not be inclined. My skirts would be a sad rumple once I came out."

Lady Emily's dress was as fine as her shoes. Miles of soft white fabric caressed her every curve, with a sweet pink posy tucked into her generous decolletage. Rebecca agreed that it would be a shame to ruin it, and yet…"Is rumpling not a small price to pay to avoid detection?"

"Then perhaps *you* would like to hide under the desk and wrinkle *your* dress and *I* can stand behind the curtains?" Lady Emily pressed a hand to her temple. "Listen to us. Reduced by circumstance to argue like fishwives. This is hardly becoming of us. The idea of hiding is utmost folly." She swallowed, and her face paled further. "We shall face the duke and acknowledge our actions."

Rebecca admired the sentiment. It was a romantic stand of bravery. She found much to admire in Lady Emily, in truth. She was a pretty woman. Her face was a perfect heart, with a wide forehead and pointed chin that she lifted high. Her eyebrows were naturally arched and were now halfway up her forehead as she widened her already large dark blue eyes, which sparkled with determination. A little color was returning to her face, pinkening her high cheekbones.

But facing the consequences of her actions was something that Rebecca was loath to do. Avenbury had little enough mentioned his father, so she was not sure what kind of man the duke was. But if there was a chance that this could end her betrothal, she had to find a way to escape.

If Lady Emily would not agree to hide, then there was only one other option.

"I shall leave you to your noble fate, Lady Emily. I, however, would much prefer to return to the ballroom now."

Before Lady Emily could say a word to dissuade her, Rebecca threw open the window and was outside in a blink.

Chapter Three

The very nerve of the woman!

The curtain fluttered in the breeze, moving toward Emily as if tempting her to follow.

How had Miss Tremblay even thought to act so boldly? Had she been climbing out of windows her whole life? There had been a quick flash of her stockinged leg as she had swung herself over the sill, and Emily thought she had even seen an inch of her thigh above where her stockings were tied. Her *bare thigh*, in a duke's study!

Heavy footfalls sounded in the hallway and her stomach plummeted. Oh, dear Lord. Was the Duke of Northelm approaching? Or would she be rescued by Danfield?

Emily had always prided herself on her sound judgment. Before making decisions, she considered all aspects. She recoiled from impulse and had a distaste for the word headstrong.

And yet, as the sound of boots came closer and her heart beat faster, she did something that before tonight she would never have considered possible.

She clambered out the window.

It was a good deal more difficult than Miss Tremblay's demonstration had indicated. Her skirts tangled around her legs, and she had to bend in a most awkward manner to avoid striking her head on the window frame—or worse, disrupting the hairstyle that had taken her maid two hours to perfect. She was heaving for breath as she hopped down to the lawn.

"Finally!" Miss Tremblay cried, her eyes shining in the dark.

"You waited for me?" Emily panted, astonished. She would have thought Miss Tremblay to be halfway to the ballroom by now.

"I wanted to call out to encourage you when I saw you struggling with the sash, but thought you might prefer discretion."

"I always prefer discretion."

"I thought as much," Miss Tremblay murmured.

Her heart was pounding and she was overwarm, despite the breeze that rustled the leaves on the trees. This was utter folly. She may not have been discovered skulking about the duke's study, but was it better or worse to be found traipsing about his shrubbery in the dead of night?

Miss Tremblay seemed to have no such worries. She was grinning as if nothing was at all the matter. Had she no sense of propriety? It would be altogether too rude to enquire, but Emily was flummoxed in the face of her composure.

Emily shook out her skirts, adjusted the posy at her bodice, and cleared her throat. "We shall walk around the house to the terrace and slip inside from there. I remember the doors at the back of the ballroom open up to the gardens, as I stepped outside for a moment of air after I arrived. If we are quick, our absence will be hardly remarked upon." She prayed that it would be so.

"I would be happy to follow you."

They were at the side of the sprawling manor, where no lanterns were hung to guide anyone's path. Emily could not be sure which way to go but did not wish to admit it to her companion. She chose to venture left and hoped they would find themselves among proper company soon enough.

The footing was different on the grounds compared to the pavestones of the terrace or the gravel of the garden paths. Earlier in the evening when she had gone outside, the air had been sweet with gardenias, and her heart had been filled with ambition and success. She had wanted to savor her triumph alone, for who else could understand it? Who else had even noticed the times she had nodded encouragingly to Danfield when she could not find any interest in the conversation, or accepted his request to dance when she had a headache?

Juliet perhaps had kept score, but she had never been as encouraging of the match as Emily had wished. In fact, there were times that Emily felt that she had been against it, but she did not understand why.

Now she trudged across the lawn, her slippers dampening with each step in the late evening dew, hoping with all her might that her skirt was not streaked with dirt from her window escapades. Worst of all was that she was in the company of a total stranger who bore witness to her inelegance.

Who may yet end up as her sister-in-law.

How odd this all was!

"It is a lovely night," Miss Tremblay announced, falling into step beside her. "I don't know what I expected, but I thought the air might feel different from home. This is another country entirely, after all."

Good manners dictated that Emily reply, little as she wished to. "When did you arrive in London?"

"Yesterday."

"You will have plenty of time to discover all the differences between there and here. I am sure there will be many. My father always says that he can tell a new country by the trees, and the difference in birdsong."

"Is your father an officer?"

"A rear admiral."

"You must be proud."

Once, she had been. But why was she speaking of such things? She hadn't meant to mention her father to anyone tonight. Thank goodness he was not at the ball, or she would earn a lecture from him when she reappeared. No midshipman's mishaps had ever escaped his notice. Lady Calloway had not likely noticed anything out of place, as long as her wine glass was full and her friends danced attendance upon her.

Her attention shifted again to her walking companion, but in her own way, she unsettled Emily as much as her family. When else would she have ever barged into a closed room or leapt out a window? It was all Miss Tremblay's terrible influence.

The longer they walked, the darker it seemed. The soft breeze was like a lover's touch, and Emily could smell floral perfume and the grass that they crushed underfoot. It was quiet, except for faint bursts of laughter and music which reassured her that they were walking in the right direction. The moon wasn't enough to provide more than a silvered edge to the house and a glimmer on the hedge and did nothing to illuminate Miss Tremblay. It was as if Emily walked beside her own shadow, and only the sound of her breath and the rustle of her skirts proved that her companion was not some ghostly spirit.

She felt a strange kinship to her. They were two women on the cusp of a new life, with the new moon overhead luring them forward.

But what fanciful thoughts were these?

How private and strange everything had become.

"This is not how the evening was meant to be."

Emily had not realized that she had spoken aloud until she heard Miss Tremblay laugh.

"Did you not have the dinner you desired? Or was the duke's cellar not up to standard?"

Emily thought Miss Tremblay might be teasing, but she was not always certain of such things. The expression on her face was simple interest. Was it possible that she was the sole forthright person in society? Something about her inspired Emily to answer honestly.

"I did not expect *you*."

"Oh!" There was a world of affront imbued in the exclamation.

Emily was chagrined. "I did not intend to insult. But tonight was meant to be my betrothal celebration."

"It still can be."

"Not when everyone will want to speak of the duke's heir, and his beautiful heiress."

"You think me beautiful?"

"Is it common to fish for compliments where you are from?"

"I simply enjoy hearing such things." Miss Tremblay's smile was mischievous.

There were a thousand things to worry about. Had their disappearance been remarked upon? Had the brothers come to blows? Had the duke opened the door and seen Emily as she had dropped out of the window?

But her heartbeat had slowed and her breathing had never been easier. Was something of Miss Tremblay's sanguine nature seeping into her?

"How fun it is to have someone to get into such scrapes with!" Miss Tremblay reached out and took her arm in her own.

Emily yanked her arm away. "I am not the sort of woman to partake in mischief."

"I beg to differ, Lady Emily. This is mischief of the highest order."

"I will never do such a thing again."

"Then this shall be our secret."

"I dislike secrets immensely."

"If it is no secret, then may I tell my brothers?"

"Absolutely not."

"Look, there is the terrace! You have led us to security. Well done."

It was a relief to see the bright lanterns and the abundance of flowers overflowing from their planters and the stately stone balustrades again, but Emily felt a pang of regret.

It must be regret that such exploits had ever happened, *not* that they were over.

"Should we enter together, or separately?"

"Separately, I think." Emily hesitated. "How do I look? Am I in much disarray?"

Miss Tremblay gazed at her. "You could use some attention, if you do not mind that my hands are less experienced than your maid's."

"Go ahead, then."

She did, in fact, mind very much. To allow someone else's hand on her person made her uneasy. To know that she needed it made her uneasier. She hated to appear less than her best, and it rankled that she was found wanting in that respect. But what choice was there? To reappear in the ballroom with her hair and dress mussed would give rise to dark speculation that she would do anything to avoid. What would Lord Danfield think if his betrothed returned with grass stains on her skirt?

Miss Tremblay stripped off her long white kidskin gloves and draped them over her forearm, then stepped close enough for Emily to inhale her perfume. Violets. How sweet. Her touch was gentle as she fixed her hair, brushing away an errant leaf and adjusting a curl, then rubbed at a spot of dirt on her skirt. "You shall do," she murmured, nodding in approval. "You avoided any real danger. There are no tears in the satin, no stains. Your slippers are in dire straits, but if you stand just so and do not dance, you shall draw no attention to them."

Emily cleared her throat. "Thank you. Please allow me to return the favor."

She studied Miss Tremblay as she removed her own gloves. The skirt of her white dress was so full that any smudges from the windowsill would be well concealed within its folds, and that little rent at the hem would also go unnoticed. She straightened her sash and retied the bow at the back of her dress. When she plucked a twig from the lace of her sleeve and brushed against her bare arm, she heard Miss Tremblay's sharp inhale.

The rosy bloom of her cheeks and the sparkle of her eyes had distracted Emily from noticing until now that her lips were slightly too wide for her face, and her upturned nose was a trifle short. But she was so animated and her face was so expressive that she must have been considered the most beautiful heiress in all of New York City.

Emily bent low and arranged her skirts. "You are presentable."

"Go forth, Lady Emily," Miss Tremblay urged her. "I shall follow."

Emily shook off the odd feelings and walked through the doors without a glance behind her.

❖

Rebecca could hardly touch her breakfast. She ached to be away and exploring London, but her parents had no such urgency. Mother insisted on her usual second cup of tea, ignoring Rebecca's sighs, and Father helped himself to a kipper after a plate of eggs.

Her temper was further tried when her brothers entered the breakfast parlor. Her friends at home always told her that they brought charm to life with their presence, but in her own estimation all they ever did was fill a room like a swarm of hornets.

"Yes, of course I will have a cup, Mother. Would like nothing better, in fact."

"Father, did you read the newspaper yet? No? I shall sit here and read a corner over your shoulder."

"Breakfast? I hardly had a chance to eat at our apartments. Oh, and you have marmalade!"

Henry reached over Rebecca for the toast and bumped her elbow when he sugared his tea, and Marvin sat on the arm of her chair to read Father's paper with him. She wished for patience, but a lifetime of prayer had never granted her a single ounce more than what she had been born with.

They had all traveled together on the packet ship, but her brothers had been in another carriage on the journey from Falmouth and had arrived too late to accompany them to last night's ball. Although they would have enjoyed it far more than she had, it was good fortune that they had not been there. Unlike her parents, they would have remarked on her lengthy absence and would have teased the truth from her.

"Becky, you won't mind if I take the last muffin?"

The muffin lay untouched on her plate, but she had only taken it so that her parents would not insist on waiting for her to serve herself before they left for the day.

"By all means, Henry. Please do."

He grinned at her and took a hearty bite. "Everything tastes so much better here than on the ship."

"Excitement whets the appetite, and we have exciting prospects ahead of us indeed." Mother smiled at him fondly.

That started one of their endless rounds of talk about sales and production and distribution and shipyards, all of which had been discussed at great length over the past six weeks when Rebecca had been little able to escape their company.

She slumped forward and propped her chin on her hand. "I had hoped to visit the shops today on Bond Street."

"Here for hardly more than a day, and already my daughter wishes to spend my coin." Father laughed. It wasn't unkind, but it stung nonetheless.

"I am happy to look." She tried to look dignified.

"You're too impulsive to look." Marvin tugged at one of her curls. "By the time you walk out of the shop, half of the draper's wares will be already packed up for the carriage."

If her brothers had bothered to truly pay attention to her, they would know that although she did enjoy fashion, it was the booksellers and the stationers that tempted her. But she could do without shopping. She had read a great deal about the attractions of London and yearned to visit the Tower and walk along the Serpentine and marvel at the statues in the British Museum.

Sometimes it was lonesome to be the only one who enjoyed such things in the family.

"We must visit the banks today," Marvin announced.

"Mother? Are *you* interested in going anywhere with me?" Rebecca tried not to sound plaintive.

"I will accompany your father. Can you not pester the marquess?"

Rebecca rather doubted it, but her father spared her reply. "Avenbury is coming with us today. A sensible sort like him won't wish to be gadding about London when there is money to be made."

Rebecca was not yet sure if the marquess was a sensible sort. She was beginning to think of him as a maddening riddle. She had expected their relationship to change once they arrived in London, and after she was introduced to his family. But the minute she had re-appeared in the ballroom last night, he had hurried them all into the carriage and they had gone home.

She had not danced one step. She had been introduced to no one. She had been denied any pleasure in the evening with the exception of her adventure with Lady Emily, but she suspected she was alone in thinking that it was a pleasure.

Given the unusual circumstances of their encounter, it was no surprise that Lady Emily had been flustered and cross though she had politely tried to hide both facts. There was something intriguing about her that made Rebecca wish she had met her on a different night. She had felt badly when she had learned that they had interrupted an evening so important to her.

Remembering Lord Danfield's expression in his father's study made her wonder what attraction he held for Lady Emily. He was an awful brother to have greeted Avenbury the way he had last night! The less she saw of him, the better.

"You will find friends here soon enough, and once you are married you will have your pick of companions to accompany you to the shops. They will all want to be close to the woman who won the marquess."

Rebecca sat alone for some time after everyone left, until the servants silently cleared the table and she was not even left with a cold cup of tea for comfort.

England was no different from home after all.

Well, Rebecca could find ways to entertain herself. She had not yet explored even half of the rooms of the grand townhouse. There were letters to write to her old friends, describing last night's ballroom and the thrill of being engaged. There was a garden that she had sat in for all of five minutes the day before, and such a garden—filled with roses and Sweet Williams and hollyhocks, with a bench positioned to catch the best of the afternoon light—deserved hours of contemplation and perhaps a book of poetry to fully enjoy it. There must be a library somewhere in the house, filled to the brim with unread tomes and treasures.

But when her parents and brothers had bustled away, her mind busied itself with scores of similar memories.

Warm summer nights when she had scrambled out windows to attend illicit parties with ne'er-do-well friends in New York. Cold evenings when she had begged a groom to drive the carriage through the streets of Montreal to ice skate with the girls who had attended finishing school with her. Early mornings before anyone awoke in Halifax, when she strolled the parks in the morning fog with her maids, and pretended that she was anywhere but there.

Right this moment, Rebecca wanted to be anywhere but *here*. Alone, in the breakfast parlor.

And so she called for the carriage and her maid, and she fled.

CHAPTER FOUR

Emily had never wished for an afternoon to pass more quickly. The ladies and gentlemen who flitted through her drawing room paid her the flattering attention that she had wished for last night at her engagement ball, but their congratulations on her great good fortune was soured by its brevity.

Nothing about herself or Danfield interested them. Her popularity had nothing to do with herself but rather for what she might know. The name on everyone's lips was the Marquess of Avenbury.

Every laugh was feigned, and every smile was forced as Emily did her best to placate them without revealing anything. It was not so difficult, given that she had learned so little of the situation in which she was now worried that she was embroiled.

"Now that the marquess has returned, you must know the details of his betrothal! What is his lady like?"

"How wonderful to have such a dashing brother-in-law! I daresay he must be the wit of the family dinners?"

"Let us ask Lady Emily for her opinion. Lady Emily, is the Marquess of Avenbury more partial to dancing or cards? I am simply dying to invite him to our next gathering."

"I thought you were leaving for the country this week?" Emily asked. It seemed as though quite a few people had changed their plans abruptly to remain in London.

"Oh, this week, next week, next *month*! What difference does it make? The country never changes. You will learn soon enough, my dear. Your future husband will be bothered by his estate manager to travel hither and yon, and there will be questions for *him* forever and a day about planting or reaping or shearing or selling. But *you* do not need to heed the call of commerce. A wife may do as she will and stay in London, provided that her husband's pockets are deep enough."

Was that the goal of marriage? To be forever in separate towns, with Danfield tending to his business while Emily tended to her pleasure? What an appealing notion.

But what was she thinking? She certainly hadn't said yes to marriage simply for an engagement party and a wedding and a life of solitude after the vows were said. Why, Danfield was kind, and wealthy, and…and…

Well. There were plenty of other reasons. They would come to mind after everyone had left, when she had a quiet moment to think.

"Would you care for more tea, Lady Charlotte?" Emily forced her hands to be steady as she poured, but her mind was not on the task.

Was solitude the type of marriage that Miss Tremblay envisioned with the marquess?

There had been so many questions this afternoon about the mysterious heiress that it was no great wonder that Emily could not escape thinking of her. The life Emily would have with Danfield spread before her in sunny splendor, but all she could think of was the look on Miss Tremblay's face as they had tidied each other up at the end of their strange encounter.

It had been unlike anything she had ever experienced before. A hot flush washed over her at the memory of the bewitching look in her eyes.

"We are so pleased by our dear Emily's embrace into the ducal family," Lady Calloway said as she accepted another bouquet of flowers on Emily's behalf. The mantle was resplendent with blooms of every shade and description, but Emily hardly noticed any of it. She gritted her teeth as she smiled. *Our dear Emily.* What farce.

This was the reason to wed which had eluded her.

Danfield was indeed a wonderful prospect for any debutante, but escape from her family and entering into a life of her own was the real prize.

"We had hoped for such success, and of course it is of no surprise that Emily has captured Lord Danfield's attentions!"

Emily seethed to herself as she poured more tea. It was a relief that no one overstayed their welcome, as they were so disappointed in her disinclination to gossip that most people stayed a scant five or ten minutes.

Juliet stayed after everyone else had left, and her stepmama had disappeared upstairs to regale Papa with Emily's popularity. "*Do* you have any gossip, Em?"

She was a woman with a keen gaze, and Emily typically could hold very little back from that steady eye. "I know nothing."

"You know something." Juliet's eyes moved a fraction of an inch to the tea tray, and she swooped a petit four from the tray to her mouth with the elegance of a bird of prey. "You always know something."

"All I know is that Miss Tremblay is an outrageous American."

"Outrageous?"

Emily regretted saying it. She could hardly tell tales of Miss Tremblay without revealing her own behavior. Climbing out of windows! Whatever had possessed them both! She decided to say nothing further of her. "I could not believe my eyes when the Marquess of Avenbury entered the ballroom. I nearly fell to the ground when he announced his betrothal."

"We were all surprised. The nerve of him to deprive London's belles from their finest efforts on his behalf."

"I daresay not even a marquess could tempt you."

Juliet was unmarried and unbothered by the fact. Whenever Emily tried to question her about it, she merely raised a brow and proclaimed herself too interested in too many other things.

Emily could not imagine such a thing. To be married had been her cherished goal since her first dance at her first ball, and she had been flush with success ever since Danfield had asked for her hand.

Said flush was diminishing at an alarming rate.

"I thought Avenbury might never show his face again in London."

"Danfield would not speak of him after his brother left, and I would never question him about so sensitive a subject."

"Ah, you plan to be a biddable wife?"

"There is no other kind, Jules." Emily lifted her chin and raised her eyes heavenward, hoping she sounded virtuous when all she felt was envy toward Miss Tremblay.

"If one must succumb to the lure of a fortune or a pretty face, then one might do as well to remain one's own mistress."

"I did not seek out Danfield for either reward."

"It could have been nothing else. The man's favored topics include his hunting dogs, war, and the blandest of compliments."

"He is a charming conversationalist."

Juliet chose another petit four. "If it was neither his wit nor his face nor the depths of his pockets, then it must have been his position. For that I must congratulate you. You could hardly have raised yourself higher than a ducal connection."

If the marquess had returned a month prior, things could have been different. But such thoughts were shameful. Emily would never have stolen a man from an engaged woman and was not so ambitious that she would have dropped all other prospects simply because the heir to a dukedom had stepped foot on British soil.

These feelings of envy must subside.

If they would not disappear of their own accord, then she would banish them by attending service on Sunday to remind herself of humility and what was owed her fellow woman. Miss Tremblay did not deserve feelings of jealousy.

If only Emily could retain the sermons longer than a day! It never failed that Monday would dawn, and the memory of all the good that she intended had evaporated with the mist.

❖

When Rebecca returned home, her family was gathered in the drawing room in Avenbury's company. She chose to accept the cup of tea that her mother offered, and to ignore her glare by slipping onto the sofa next to the marquess.

"I am delighted to see you here, my lord." She sipped her tea. "You are always a welcome sight amongst my family."

It was true because it meant she could evade their lectures, but he did not need to know that. Perhaps it was not the happiest of families that he was marrying into. Her brothers were currently deriding each other's tailors, although Rebecca was quite sure that they all patronized the same man. Her father was poring over the newspaper again in the afternoon light, after a disinterested nod in her direction. Her mother's face could have been hewn from granite and her eyes could spark tinder, but Rebecca decided that without further investigation, it was possible that it was her brothers who had risen her ire.

Long experience hinted that it was in fact her, but there was little point to fret until she knew for sure.

Avenbury's face was grave as he gazed at her. "I am a man who can tolerate many things from a wife, but I confess that bluestocking tendencies are my limit."

"There now, the marquess is in agreement." It was unfair and yet unsurprising that her mother hastened to side with the marquess instead of her own daughter. "The coachman told me about your adventures today." Mother frowned.

"I don't think it's fair to brand me as a bluestocking for seeing the sights of this fine city. I have not met a single woman to match the description and instead have been perusing architecture instead of ape-leaders. The Tower is a marvel, you know."

"You also visited the booksellers."

She sipped her tea again. "I became lost looking for the dressmaker." She widened her eyes at her brothers, who were harder to convince than her mother, but they were not paying attention to her.

"Do not do it again."

"Of course not, my lord." She would be more careful next time. There was no need for him to be concerned of her whereabouts when all he wanted was her father's money.

"I am here to deliver an invitation. You have been summoned by my grandmother."

"How lovely. I look forward to meeting Her Grace."

"You will not think it lovely once you have met her."

She laughed. "Men have such a droll sense of humor! She is like as not to be as delightful as a sunrise."

"Do stop being so fanciful," Mother snapped. "You cannot speak of a duchess so casually."

"I apologize. I am honored to be so distinguished by this opportunity." Rebecca tried to ignore the sting of her mother's words.

"She will expect you tomorrow at precisely two o'clock. You should be there no later than quarter to the hour, for she considers lateness a great slight."

"Everyone has their little ways," she said. "I quite understand."

He looked at her for some time, and she shrank from his gaze. "You will tomorrow."

After Avenbury left them, Rebecca sank into the chair nearest to Mother. "He is a man of some dramatics, is he not?" She tried to sound as if she admired him. "I am ever so glad that I have always enjoyed the theater."

"He is to be your husband! Speak of him with more respect."

"I do respect him. I simply pay him no mind with his comments about his dear grandmama. He is always saying such humorous things, Mother. Do you recall when he was paying court to me in New York, and he was so amusing when cutting down the length of men's trousers with his eyes? I will be a happy woman to be wedded to a man of such keen discernment."

"Your happiness is secondary." Father raised his head from his papers. "Money is the important thing here. Charm the dowager duchess tomorrow, my daughter, and all will be well with our pocketbooks."

Rebecca struggled to compose herself. The truth was that she felt rather desperate to be loved, and had what felt like an infinite store of love to bestow upon anyone who was inclined to look kindly at her. Why could it not be her own family? "Her Grace will be beside herself when she meets me. I will be sure of it."

Mother inhaled sharply. "Do be less flippant about Avenbury's family. Soon, they will be your own."

She wasn't being flippant. She stared down into her half-empty cup.

"We cannot wait for your marriage," Marvin said, laughing with Henry. "You shall be bothering someone else for chaperonage to the worst plays and most boring historical sights known to mankind."

"And to kill any spider that dares cross your ceiling."

"And to lend you a farthing to pay for tea when you fancy to try yet another new shop."

Rebecca felt a little squeeze around her heart. "I did not realize I had been so burdensome all these years."

"Less of a burden, and more of a…nuisance? An irritation, perhaps?" Henry grinned.

Rebecca would just have to make sure that her new family would love her, starting with the dowager duchess tomorrow.

When the invitation arrived, Emily was grateful that she was by herself in the parlor with her needlework. It would have embarrassed her if Lady Calloway had witnessed her squeak of excitement, or how she clasped the crisp white paper to her bosom. But such a lapse in composure must be forgivable, for to have tea with the dowager Duchess of Northelm was an honor indeed! Satisfaction shivered up her spine and tingled in her heart. Emily must have impressed her at the engagement ball, though she had only received the faintest of nods in her direction when she had dared to steal a glance at the dowager.

Although the summons was for the next afternoon, she set aside her embroidery to stare into her wardrobe for over an hour. Had the dowager been at Mrs. Stafford's soiree the week before? She fretted that she could not remember, as she did not wish to wear the same gown twice in her presence.

A minor detail, perhaps. But one that she was confident would not be overlooked by Her Grace.

Emily had a sleepless night. There were so many variables that she could not control, so many infractions that she could amass in front of the dowager. To take a sip of tea at the incorrect moment. To wear a color that the dowager considered gauche. To voice an opinion that did not match the family's—a true horror.

Unkind thoughts loomed at the edges of her mind. Surely a young lady truly deserving of such an honor would not need to worry about disappointing Her Grace? A deserving person would face no difficulty in front of the highest titles in the land. But the summons *must* be a mark of favor. She tried her best to think of all the compliments she had received in London instead of the flaws that clawed at her heart and finally fell asleep near dawn.

Her worries dissipated once she focused on readying herself for the challenge ahead. First, she bathed in her favorite almond scent, and then in a fit of doubt washed it off and applied rosewater instead. Three maids were tasked with her toilette. It stood to reason that multiple hands were required to perfect her appearance for such an important appointment. One maid worked on her hair, threading ribbons studded with pearls through her curls, and another shook out her ivory muslin and helped lace her stays and ease her into her dress. While Emily was being dressed, the third maid held up each jewel in her possession for approval. She chose pink opal earbobs and a thin pink velvet ribbon to tie around her neck, with a matching pink satin sash to tie around her waist.

The carriage ride was over in a blink. Emily was as lightheaded as if she had held her breath all day by the time she was curtsying to the dowager Duchess of Northlem, her knees sinking as far as she could without toppling over.

After she professed her gratitude for the invitation and seated herself across from the dowager, she noticed two unexpected things.

The first was that Her Grace was scowling. It was no paltry expression of dismay. No, the lines beside her mouth were etched deep into her cheeks, and her brow was heavy over her eyes. She sat straight, authority radiating from every line of her body. Even her tight gray curls seemed to be bristling. Her hands were clasped in her lap, but they might as well have been pointing in accusation.

Emily was wishing that she had not asked her maid to tighten her stays so much when she noticed the second thing.

This was no private audience.

Chapter Five

Miss Rebecca Tremblay was seated at the right side of the dowager and looked for all the world as if she had not experienced a single trouble in all her life. Her shoulders were relaxed as she examined her surroundings with an artless look of wonder in her eyes, and her pale pink lips were parted enough for Emily to see the gleam of her front teeth. She was tracing the pattern on the Aubusson with the toe of her slipper. It astonished Emily that Miss Tremblay appeared to belong to the room despite such casual manners. Her gown was a beautiful pale green silk crepe, a thin wool shawl nestled in the crooks of her elbows like a blanket.

The dowager's scowl deepened as she fixed her eyes on Emily. "How dare you be late? Are you so inconsiderate of me?"

It was still ten to the hour, and she had been asked to arrive at two. How humiliating to be called out in front of Miss Tremblay! She swallowed, and although she was already at the edge of the sofa and her spine was as straight as she could manage, she tried to square her shoulders and lift her chin even higher. "I apologize, Your Grace. It will not happen again."

"It had best not."

The work of three maids had resulted in Emily's flawless appearance, and her reward was the slightest softening of the dowager's lip as she scrutinized her. Triumph surged through her. She had been in the right with her choice of opals after all.

"Lady Emily, your dress does you credit."

Praise, sparing as it was, always lifted her spirits. "Thank you, Your Grace. You are too kind."

She held back a sigh of relief when the dowager's eyes left her and fixed upon Miss Tremblay. Was that *amusement* in Miss Tremblay's eyes, to match the smile on her lips? Emily quailed for her. The duchess would not take kindly to impertinence.

"I gather that you have won the heart of my eldest son." Her voice was doubtful.

Miss Tremblay's smile grew wider. "I very much like to think that I have captivated my dear Avenbury as much as he has captivated me."

The duchess coughed.

"Your Grace," she hastened to add, her lashes lowering over her eyes.

"I have long doubted the existence of such an organ."

"I do not pretend to know all the details of your son's former life. I am of the belief that a wife should leave a husband's business to himself. But it is no great wonder that his heart expanded once he left the shores of England to find adventure awaiting him."

"Adventure." The dowager pronounced the word with some astonishment, as if it were foreign to her.

"Oh yes, Your Grace! The sea voyage itself is a wondrous experience. Have you ever been on a ship?"

There was a pause.

The censure in the dowager's eyes was not directed at her, but Emily wished she could flee when the air around them seemed to cool. Miss Tremblay did not flinch. She spoke as naturally as if she were chatting with the parson's wife about the best way to dress a goose for dinner, instead of questioning the nautical experience of a duchess.

"I have not. Do you recommend it?"

Emily heard the steel in the dowager's words. It might even have edged on mockery, if such a thing was not beneath a duchess. She gathered from Miss Tremblay's reaction that she did not understand the depths of the water in which she swam. Her face brightened as if she had been given a treat, and her eyes sparkled as she clasped her hands in front of her.

"Indeed I do, Your Grace. The sea air is the most bracing in all the world. The vistas could charm the coldest of cynics, and the hardest of hearts would soften to see the amber of dawn break against the horizon. A ship's deck is a wonderful place to gather one's thoughts. Such solitude one might find there!" Miss Tremblay's face turned dreamy.

"I shall endeavor to remember such a thing." She turned toward Emily. "I assume *you* can well understand the dilemma we are in."

Emily felt a rush at being considered a confidante, but it fast turned to dread. Miss Tremblay was as unsuspecting as a lamb trotting toward the butcher. Her fingers itched for the smelling salts in her reticule.

"*Do* you understand, Lady Emily?"

"Yes, Your Grace," Emily murmured.

The dowager Duchess of Northelm turned to Miss Tremblay. "You will not do."

Her smile vanished. "I beg your pardon?" When thunderous silence met her, she added timidly, "Your Grace?"

"You are an exceptionally poor choice for Avenbury. I was mystified when he announced his betrothal, and I am no less bemused now that I have spoken to you. You will be a miserable excuse for a marchioness."

Miss Tremblay was blinking, as if she had not considered such a thing before. Emily wished to comfort her. She had soothed many a debutante in retiring rooms when they had faced rejection from their suitors and consoled them when Emily had won patronage to Almack's, but they had not. It was difficult when one was granted one's heart's desire while others were crushed with disappointment.

She had no doubt that the dowager would scare Miss Tremblay away from her attachment to Avenbury. In a way that she did not wish to examine, she felt it would be a loss for them all. Such a lively person would have improved the family gatherings that she saw in her future.

And yet the dowager was right. There were dozens of ladies more suited to be Avenbury's bride. It would not be difficult for him to find a replacement.

Finally, Miss Tremblay spoke. "I am wondrous glad that my Avenbury did not need anyone's approval before offering me his hand in marriage."

Emily wheezed out a breath.

The dowager turned white. "I beg your pardon?"

Miss Tremblay settled further into her seat, adjusting her shawl around her shoulders like a cozy coat of armor. "If you find me lacking in any way, I would dearly love to rectify my shortcomings. May I count on your help to become the best marchioness that I could be?" Her voice was warm and cheerful, with no hint of mockery or animosity.

The dowager stared at her.

Emily could hold back no longer. "You cannot be serious!"

Miss Tremblay laughed, and it sounded like a thousand tiny starbursts. "Well, the way I see the situation is thus. If you do *not* help me, you risk being brushed with my tar. Is that what you both wish instead?"

It was petty, but Rebecca enjoyed the shock on Her Grace's face.

She had not realized that the invitation was an ambush until several minutes ago when Lady Emily had shifted closer to the dowager and away from Rebecca. She had likely not even realized that she had moved, but it had been clear from that moment that neither woman was a friend to her.

The feeling that came over her was chilly and then hot, the familiar sting of realizing that she did not belong even though on the surface, they were part of the same group. It had happened in her family, time and time again, and in countless social situations, in numerous cities and in her own neighborhood, and even on the ship during their recent voyage.

And yet the pain of it was fresh as ever.

Although she felt queasy and rather like lying down, she smiled at her adversaries. "I think we are all in accord."

"We are not," the Duchess of Northelm huffed.

Lady Emily inched closer to her. "Indeed not."

"I understand that neither of you hold me in high esteem. But regardless of your wishes, Your Grace, I will be your granddaughter-in-law. I am quite sure that you did not raise your grandson to be dishonorable. Avenbury will not break his word to me."

The duchess recoiled, as if Rebecca had done something unpardonable like sworn or spat in her face. Then her eyes narrowed and she looked even meaner. "My grandson is *entirely* honorable."

"Then there is no trouble. And I assure you, I do not come to the marriage with nothing. My fortune is considerable."

It was a fact so well-known to her that she felt no conceit by mentioning it. Money soothed many pains in life, both small and large. The jangle of a pocketful of coins was a universal language and should be understandable to the English. If it took her dollars instead of her affection to win them over, it would be good enough for now. Soon they would grow to love her for who she was, and not for what she brought. By Christmas, she would have the dowager laughing at her stories and Avenbury's sour-faced brother teasing her like he was one of her own. Love would secure her place among them.

Admittedly, the dowager looked like a tough woman to love.

The dowager seemed as irritated as if there were a burr beneath her saddle, and the mare she was riding was being unpardonably willful.

"I suppose I should be grateful that you understand the importance of money, Miss Tremblay. Many young ladies are empty-headed about such things. But what those young ladies understand best is what you are sorely lacking."

"In which ways do you believe me to be lacking, Your Grace?"

"Grace. Decorum. Manners. You behave as if we are equals, where we assuredly are not. Even if you do marry my grandson, do not be so foolish as to believe that you will ever be my peer."

Rebecca thought about that for a moment. If the present duke died, and Avenbury ascended into his place and she herself became a duchess, would she not be the same standing as the dowager? But perhaps she was speaking metaphorically. This sounded the same as her mother's lectures—it would not matter what she said in reply to any of it. She must simply endure the words, and sail forward as she wished.

"Your social skills are too unmannered. Too...open. There is a certain freshness about you that is not unappealing, but it lacks sophistication."

Rebecca brightened. *Not unappealing* was the faintest of praise, but praise nonetheless.

"Miss Tremblay, you need more help than you can imagine. My grandson is not an easy man."

"He has made his choice, and I have made mine."

Her father would be outraged if she cowed and broke the engagement. No amount of persuasion from the dowager could sway her.

There was a long pause. Rebecca knew it would be inappropriate to leave before she was dismissed, but she was starting to wonder how long she would be expected to sit here in silence when the dowager spoke again.

"If you insist on marrying Avenbury, then I must insist that you learn his ways before becoming his bride."

"I have no objection to learning."

"Thankfully, Lady Emily is an exemplary young lady. She will guide you through society." She nodded, a look of satisfaction in her eyes. "Lady Emily will not disappoint me."

Lady Emily had been quiet during the dowager's pronounce-ments and looked surprised to be spoken to at last. "I will do my best," she said, her eyes darting between the dowager and Rebecca.

"Miss Tremblay, I expect you to follow Lady Emily everywhere. You shall become constant companions."

Lady Emily's lips pursed for a moment before she smiled. "I would like nothing better, Your Grace."

Rebecca did not believe it for an instant. She was hurt more by Lady Emily's reaction than by the Duchess of Northelm's statements. She had expected there to some common feeling between them, given the similarity of their situation.

But she realized now that they were only similar on the surface. Lady Emily was a paragon, and Rebecca was an urchin tugging at her hem for favors.

"Miss Tremblay?"

"I will do as you wish, Your Grace."

Rebecca was willing enough to parrot whatever the ducal family wanted her to say. She did not owe them her thoughts. Once her outward behavior was to their liking, they would approve of her. Meanwhile, she would continue to do as she wished in private.

By the time she was home, she had convinced herself that the summons could not have gone smoother, her life would soon be improved in every conceivable way, and she and Lady Emily would soon be the best of friends.

In a testament to true friendship, Juliet presented herself at Emily's townhouse a mere half hour after Emily had sent a servant with a missive for her. She ensconced herself in an armchair with a cup of tea, her bright eyes following Emily as she paced the room.

"How could the dowager ask me to present myself as friendly with Miss Tremblay? Would anyone even believe us to be friends?"

"As I have not yet met the woman, I cannot say. But why would anyone doubt it?"

Emily thought about Miss Tremblay. She was friendly, sincere, and had an effervescence that was most attractive. But there was also the slyness of her eyes, hinting at thoughts that did not match her agreeable words. The pertness of her manner. The unrepentant curiosity, and what some might even call defiance. "The dowager herself implied that she was unmannered and unsophisticated. Would I befriend such a person?"

"You would if you were engaged to brothers. Which, I may point out, you are." Juliet gazed at her thoughtfully. "I do not understand this reluctance of yours. You are exactly the type of person who would befriend a marquess's fiancée."

"What is that supposed to mean?"

"Are you not interested in the highest of titles? Have you not hung around earls and viscounts and ladies of wealth and prestige all Season?"

"I am interested in many people," Emily said stiffly. "Including yourself."

Juliet sipped her tea. "I may not have a title, but I am much in demand as a friend. *You* intrigued *me*, my dear Em."

The truth of it gave Emily pause. "I am no snob."

"Is it so terrible if you are?"

Emily did not care for the assertion. "There is nothing wrong with wishing to fit into good society and caring about who one befriends. Friendship should not be forced from duty! And what a difficult duty this shall be." She sighed and pressed her fingers against her temple.

"Oh, dear me. Have I interrupted a tête-à-tête?"

CHAPTER SIX

Emily spun around to see Miss Tremblay herself standing in the doorway, her smile lighting up the room as if the sun were peeking out from behind a cloud.

"Miss Tremblay. I was not expecting you."

"I can't imagine why not. I gathered from our audience with Her Grace that we are henceforth to become one another's shadows. I thought it most appropriate to call upon you as soon as I could get away from my own home."

Juliet's face betrayed her fascination. She rose from her chair and offered her hand. "I am eager to hear all about this. I am Miss Juliet Mayweather. At the risk of being presumptuous and engaging in the height of gauche behavior, am I to assume that you are Miss Rebecca Tremblay?"

"I am indeed."

Emily's face burned. She should have introduced them as soon as Miss Tremblay entered the room, but shock had chased away manners.

"It is a pleasure to meet you. Now please do sit down and tell me absolutely everything about yourself." Juliet guided her to the sofa and patted the cushion beside her.

Emily could not find it in herself to be happy to see her, and yet envy seeped through her heart as she watched Juliet and Miss Tremblay's evident interest in one another.

"This is exactly the type of warm encounter I wished for when I came to your country," Miss Tremblay told her, and even went so far as to clasp Juliet's hand. "There can be no greater felicity than finding oneself among true friends at last."

"It might be early days to consider yourselves to be devoted friends," Emily said, sitting by herself in the armchair that Juliet had abandoned.

Miss Tremblay reached over and patted her knee, leaving Emily staring at her. Her leg felt unaccountably warm, then cold as she removed her hand. "*You* will become my dearest friend. There is no other way forward."

Her certainty rankled Emily. "We will not see much of each other after the weddings. Danfield and Avenbury do not have estates anywhere near to each other."

"Oh, that is no matter! I plan on spending a great deal of time in London. I would welcome your company anytime at Northelm Manor. There shall be no need for ceremony between us!"

"I would not mind some degree of ceremony to be kept."

Miss Tremblay's unexpected arrival in her drawing room mirrored her unexpected arrival in her life. But their close association must end with their respective marriages. She would squire Miss Tremblay about the *bon ton* until the ringing of the church bells subsided and the wedding cake was all eaten up, and then they could part ways.

Emily could tell by the way that Juliet tried to hide her smile behind her teacup that she was enjoying herself immensely, which tried her patience.

Juliet gazed at Miss Tremblay as if they had known each other for years. "This all sounds delightful. I would be honored if I were to be included in such an open invitation to visit."

"I would not have it any other way," Miss Tremblay assured her.

Emily was disquieted as envy stirred again inside her. If she did not wish to call upon Miss Tremblay, why would it bother her if Juliet did?

Miss Tremblay seemed as comfortable on her sofa as she was in the dowager's drawing room. She took stock of her surroundings and appeared to find everything satisfactory, her smile fixed on her face.

Of course it was satisfactory. Emily had no love lost for her stepmother but could not fault her impeccable taste in address.

"Have you received any invitations for the coming week?" Juliet asked Miss Tremblay. "I do hope I shall be seeing you about London."

She laughed, a happier sound than the practiced trills of delight that Emily was accustomed to hearing in polite society. "My dear Miss Mayweather, I have received so many invitations that it would almost be better if I had received none at all! How is one to choose? I must admit that it is the greatest good fortune to be so in demand."

"We can help you." Juliet raised a brow at Emily. "We would like nothing better, should we?"

"I am honor bound to agree," Emily said, thinking of the dowager. There was no choice to be made, if she wished to remain on good terms with her future grandmother-in-law. She sighed. A task worth doing was only ever worth doing well. "If you notice an invitation from Lady Brookshire amongst your cards, you would do well to accept it."

"Em and I would love to see you amid the crush, Miss Tremblay."

"Em! How delightful." Miss Tremblay looked at her. "Such an exemplar of female friendship to see women so familiar with one another."

"I would be happy to call you Becca, if you were inclined to call me Juliet. Some of my intimates even call me Jules."

A flame of indignation burned in Emily's breast. She hadn't been aware that Juliet was so cavalier about who she invited into her inner circle.

Juliet seemed to understand her, for she added gently, "You and Em are the only two in London at present who are included among such intimates."

"I am honored to be among them!" Miss Tremblay cried. "Lady Emily, may I be so bold as to presume that you hold me in such esteem as well?"

It would be unmannerly to refuse, much as she wished to. Oh, *damn* Juliet for putting her in this position! "Of course," she said between gritted teeth. "Do call me Emily, my dear Rebecca."

She refused to stretch the bonds of fragile friendship to include nicknames. Christian names would be more than sufficient.

Rebecca gathered up her fan and her reticule, crammed her bonnet on her head, and bid them a dreamy adieu.

After Rebecca returned from visiting Emily, she went to the wrought iron bench in the back garden beneath the birch tree and sat until the sky grew dusky. It was peaceful and quiet, with birds chirping overhead—Emily had been right the night they met, the birdsong was delightfully different in England—and the rich scent of the pink and purple Sweet Williams was most soothing.

She had always prided herself on her optimistic outlook. But every so often, she was confronted with the reality that it was a *choice* to be happy.

She had not expected to come up against such a reminder today.

It was not unexpected that the dowager duchess had disparaged of her. Rebecca had hoped to meet a pleasant, kind lady who doted upon her grandsons and who would welcome their beloved betrotheds with open arms, but she recognized that a glowering iron-willed woman with more reserves than the British banks was admittedly better suited to be a member of Avenbury's family.

It was Emily who had disappointed her.

Even though Emily had sided with the dowager during their appointment, Rebecca had expected that once she talked to her on her own that they would laugh about the absurd encounter. After all, they should be natural allies, joining the family together at the same time. She had been filled with high hopes on her way to visit her.

Instead, Rebecca had overheard her claim that her friendship would be mere duty, which made her cheeks burn to remember it.

What an unkind thing to say.

But she had looked chagrined to see Rebecca, and she had agreed to use her Christian name. She was not so naïve to think Emily would have done so without Juliet's urging. If only Juliet was engaged to Danfield! Her warmth of manner was everything Rebecca could have hoped for in a friend.

At least Emily had been helpful enough to recommend a soiree, and Rebecca in turn urged her mother to accept the invitation from Lady Brookshire. Avenbury was unlikely to bother to escort her, and she was so very eager to dance.

"If Lady Emily vouches for this party, then we cannot do wrong to attend. We must align ourselves with the right people, and it is difficult to sleuth out who such people are without guidance." Mother's face was pinched. "It is a good deal of trouble."

"I apologize if my engagement to a marquess has inconvenienced the family," Rebecca murmured.

Mother's eyes narrowed. "None of this cheek, now! I won't have it, after all we are doing for you. It is a great expense to rent a house in London, and those dresses of yours cost a pretty penny. We are all putting forth our best efforts for your success."

It would do her no good to wait for her mother to tell her that she was proud of her, or happy for her, so Rebecca lowered her head. Since they had moved to New York, Mother had always spoken more of *their* efforts instead of *her* happiness.

The ballroom held so many people that Rebecca could hardly believe there would be sufficient room for dancing, but she was most gratified when the crowd parted and ample space for two dozen couples was cleared.

She was even more gratified when their host introduced herself and Mother to Lord Reynold Fitzgilbert, who claimed her hand for the first set. Lord Reynold was a slender man with tousled blond curls who sported a tremendous waterfall cravat that Rebecca thought was dashing.

"This is my first dance in London," she informed him as she took his arm.

"I am honored. But where is your beau? I thought I would see the marquess snarling from the corners at any who dared come near his bride-to-be."

"Oh! Avenbury would never."

He would not care enough to even glance her way if he had been in attendance, but she did not add that part.

"The deuce he wouldn't! I beg your pardon for my language, but if you're engaged to *him* then I imagine you have heard far worse. You must know he is always dogging the heels of London's beauties. He's a changed man if he hasn't kept you on a tight leash. You're beautiful enough to break a man's peace of mind. It's little wonder that you baited him to his fate."

"I prefer to think of our union as a love match."

He guffawed as he swung her around the room, and Rebecca lost herself in the joys in dancing. It was a wonderful thing to swing about the room with little care!

After the set ended, Lord Reynold tightened his grip on her upper arm. "The stars are very fine outside," he said. "There is a quiet vantage point that I can show you from the balcony. You won't hear a peep from anyone. Ideal for gazing at the heavens."

He wasn't giving her much of a choice, as he was already walking them to the back of the ballroom.

"Miss Tremblay! I am so glad to see you."

Emily approached them. How beautiful she was! It was not possible to tire of looking at her. Her dress was most becoming, a delightful filmy froth of white muslin settling as gentle as a cloud over her full pink skirts. The flounce at her hem was embroidered with green leaves and little red roses, lined by rows of thin satin ribbons. Matching ribbon was sewn into the edge of her puffed sleeves, tied into a neat bow at the elbow. She had a little freckle on her collarbone, charming Rebecca more than the symmetry of her bright blue eyes and the perfect curl of her blond hair.

Who needed a fiancé when she had Emily to glower at her prospective beaux?

"Now that everyone has admired your dancing, you cannot deprive them of an equal opportunity to admire your graceful form as we turn about the room together. I must insist. It is a most gentle exercise, and a wonderful restorative after so lively a dance."

Emily tucked Rebecca's arm into the crook of her arm as naturally as if she had done it a hundred times or more. As they both wore their gloves fashionably below the elbow, their bare arms pressed together. Emily's skin was smooth and warm, and one of her ringlets brushed Rebecca's shoulder as she turned to her.

Rebecca realized that she had not yet said anything. "You took the thought from my mind."

They had not moved more than ten paces from the spluttering Lord Reynold before Emily pulled her even closer. "What did I interrupt?" she whispered, her voice low and urgent. "What were you about to do?"

Rebecca was startled to see the alarm on her face. "Lord Reynold told me that the stars were pretty tonight."

"And you followed him as if you have never seen stars before in all your life?"

"I thought I ought to relook in case there were any differences to see them from London. How interesting to think of it."

"He was behaving like a scoundrel." Her voice was flat.

"He said he knew Avenbury," she protested. "No friend of my fiancé would dare do me any harm. All the world must know how much my sweet marquess loves me, with how rapturously I have spoken of him to any who would listen."

"You are overly trusting. It will not serve you well here. There is no accounting for what the nobility does to each other. Friends are not always so friendly."

She sighed. "I am not so naïve as all that. I did not intend to go further than the doorway to peek up at the stars. Not one step past the threshold. But even so, I refuse to believe so ill of Avenbury's friends."

"You must be careful, Rebecca! Cads abound."

"Thank you for your attention to me." Rebecca paused. "Is your concern a pretense on the dowager's behalf?"

"I beg your pardon?"

"I heard what you said to Juliet yesterday. You are less than pleased to befriend me."

"That was ill-mannered, and unkind of me. I am sorry." They walked half a dozen paces in stiff silence before Emily added, "This is difficult for me to admit, but I was jealous." She looked away.

"Jealous!"

"But I shall not give such a petty emotion one more inch of space in my heart. You deserve better from me, and I promise that you shall have it." Her face was determined.

"You are forgiven."

Rebecca thought she might forgive her anything, and the realization made her stomach plummet. She had vowed to leave such behavior behind her, and yet she hardly had been in England long enough to unpack her trunks, and she was already falling into her old ways.

But this time would be different. She had always latched too quickly to female friendships, and it had caused her no end of trouble. But Emily was not an unsuitable friend who lured her to drink too much at parties to spite their mothers. And nor was she a sophisticated and mysterious older woman beckoning from a shadowy corner, a knowing smile on her painted lips.

Rebecca was in no possible danger from a porcelain doll of a debutante who seemed overly fond of rules, regimen, and…oh, the loveliest almond perfume Rebecca had ever inhaled. It was faint but intoxicating, light and almost floral with a hint of mystery. Was it a scent only found here?

"Would it be odd if I enquired for the name of your perfumier?"

"I patronize several shops on Bond Street. I could give you a list so you could choose what pleased you best."

"Perhaps we may go together sometime."

"I have no immediate need of scent." She sniffed at Rebecca. "And neither have you, if you have a full bottle of what you are wearing presently. Violets, and honey. It suits you."

"Then we could visit the draper's instead. Your dress is beautiful. You walk in a veritable cloud of muslin."

She admired the way their skirts brushed together, her ice blue and Emily's pale pink complementing each other.

She had always enjoyed being among a bevy of girls at home, playing doubles on the pianoforte, pinning up each other's dresses to practice their dance steps in the lazy winter afternoons, brushing out their hair and trying the newest styles as they crowded together in a shrieking pile in front of the looking glass in the parlor.

Could she find such friendship here? She glanced at Emily and could not imagine her curled up in an armchair in her sitting room, laughing over last night's gossip. Perhaps Juliet Mayweather would be willing to take the role. She seemed to have the same curiosity that burned within Rebecca, and which did not seem to plague Emily.

But although Emily may be lacking in curiosity, there was something intriguing about her and the way she brushed her ringlets from her face with her gloved hand, and the way she moved her head to look at the crowd.

And yet these were not really things to admire, so Rebecca remained silent with her confusion of feelings.

CHAPTER SEVEN

When Emily glanced at Rebecca as they rounded a corner, she noticed with a start that Rebecca was gazing at her with a dreamy smile on her face. What an unusual woman she was! Emily would not have been surprised if she were to clasp her hands to her bosom and claim it had been the best day of her life, when she had danced but one dance and then walked the length of half a ballroom.

Some women were taken by fancy more than others.

More and more, she seemed an unusual choice for the Marquess of Avenbury, but Emily supposed she may yet possess charms enough to attract such a husband.

She was resolute in doing her duty by Rebecca. She was ashamed of her behavior with Juliet and should never have complained of the dowager's edict. Emily owed it to the dowager to help Rebecca and vowed to do nothing less than her best. She would become Rebecca's best friend in truth, if that is what it would take.

She nudged Rebecca toward a group of women in conversation beside a marble column. "There is always safety among the sticklers of society. Seek them out if ever you are in trouble again." As they approached, she raised her voice. "Lady Jersey, you are looking well tonight. And, Lady Sefton, it is always a delight to be in your presence."

Emily sank into a curtsy but didn't unlink their arms, so Rebecca was forced to follow suit.

"What a charming display of unity." Lady Sefton peered at them. "Have you practiced such a thing?"

"We are in natural harmony with one another. May I introduce Miss Rebecca Tremblay to you?" Emily patted her hand. "Miss Tremblay is engaged to the Marquess of Avenbury."

"There is nothing so tedious as three-day-old news, Lady Emily." Lady Jersey smirked behind her fan.

Emily kept a smile on her face through a round of pleasantries, and then managed another unified curtsy before resuming their turn about the room.

"Are all of your acquaintances so rude?" Rebecca asked after they had walked for a moment.

Emily could not reply at first. Had she embarrassed herself in front of Rebecca? Did she see Emily as lacking now that her social standing may not be as secure as the dowager had seemed to think? She almost squirmed but restrained herself.

"Lady Jersey is an exception," Emily said finally. "Good manners cannot always be expected from her. But I assure you that she is a powerful woman and one with whom you must ally yourself. She is one of the patronesses of Almack's, and I hope that she will find you suitable enough to permit you entry through its hallowed doors."

"I gather that this is something to be desired?" There was a teasing smile on Rebecca's lips.

Emily straightened her back. "Everyone of importance is there on Wednesday nights. It is a place of utmost propriety, and the dancing is lovely."

"It sounds like a bore."

She was stung to hear her beloved club so roundly dismissed. She had thought that Rebecca would be pleased with the introduction. "To be accepted there is to be accepted everywhere."

"I thought my engagement to a duke's heir was enough for me to be accepted everywhere."

"Well, that is true enough. You shall not want for invitations nor entertainments, as long as you are affiliated with the Northelm dukedom."

"Then why do I need Almack's?"

Emily struggled to form a reply. "Perhaps you do not. But it is a mark of high honor, and the marquess must want you to be distinguished by the patronesses."

"Ah. Did the dowager ask you to do this?"

"She did not. I simply thought it would be a good experience for you."

"Then I appreciate it," Rebecca said softly, and Emily's heart was full and warm.

As soon as Emily had done her duty by Rebecca, she sought out Juliet.

Perhaps it was the vestiges of panic from when she had witnessed Rebecca walking toward the balcony with the deplorable Lord Reynold, but she felt overwarm and out of sorts. She had never met another woman who elicited such a strong reaction.

Of course, she had never met an American before. It was possible that they were all charismatic and beautiful and made one's stomach flip. She vowed never to cross the ocean, if this was the daily discomfort she could expect to endure.

"I am in dire need of a friend, Jules."

"Did I not see you arm in arm with a woman who has volunteered to be the very friend you are seeking?" Juliet's brow was raised, so Emily knew she was teasing.

"We may be friendly, but we certainly are not confidantes."

"Soon you will be. After all, we are all intimates now, calling each other by Christian name."

"*You* were the one to agree to such a thing, and so precipitously!"

Juliet laughed. "There is something unique about her, is there not?"

"Yes, the fact that she will someday be a duchess."

"Can you blame her for being so lucky? Wouldn't you have set your cap at Avenbury if he had been here?"

"Of course I would have. Wouldn't anyone?" She pushed aside the fact that Danfield didn't seem to like Avenbury, and as a general rule he liked everyone.

"I am not so certain," Juliet mused. "But it is no matter. I have noticed that your new friend is quite taken with you."

"She is quite taken with the sky for being blue and with silk for being soft and sugar for being sweet. I declare that I have never met a girl with so much to say about so little."

What Emily did not add was that Rebecca's candor was refreshing.

"It can't be easy for her, arriving in a foreign country and having to contend with the dowager duchess. There are high expectations for her."

"There are the same expectations for me."

"But you knew what they were. Becca may have been better off staying in New York."

"It is likely that she was duty-bound to wed, as was I."

"Yes, but you also *want* to wed."

Emily was prepared to wed. She was willing to wed. But did she want to wed? She had never thought about it before.

Juliet frowned when Emily did not reply. "You do want to, do you not? You chose Lord Danfield."

She still couldn't bring herself to utter the word *want*. "Yes, I chose him."

Juliet looked unconvinced.

"Love has nothing to do with it. I do not love Danfield, and I doubt he loves me. I will endure, Jules, as thousands of women have done before me. I would hate to marry someone I love." Life was safer without the threat of love.

"I have never heard such an unromantic notion in all my life."

"Love turns people into fools, and fools into bores. There is nothing less interesting than a man in love, and nothing more pitiful than a woman pining after a man who wants nothing to do with it."

"That is a grim assessment of married life."

"I shall maintain my freedom after my wedding day, and I fully expect Danfield to do the same."

Juliet stared at her. "You don't mean you would be unfaithful?"

"Of course not! I mean that I will retain my composure and my good sense and I will not endlessly pester him for favors and permissions."

"You chose him because you do not love him? Do you love someone else?" Her voice lowered. "Someone *unsuitable*?"

"Of course not. I have never been in love. No one has yet inspired such emotion in me, and I doubt it will ever come to pass."

"Do you think Becca is in love with the marquess?"

"She has proclaimed little else since I met her."

It was plain as day that Rebecca was head over heels in love, and Emily had vowed to have nothing to do with such reckless emotion. She could be her friend, and show her kindness, and introduce her to all the right people.

But of her marriage to Avenbury and the outpouring of emotion that went with it—well, least said was soonest mended.

❖

Rebecca was not pleased to learn that she was expected to present herself at Northelm Manor for comportment lessons with the dowager Duchess of Northelm.

"This is unnecessary," she told Her Grace at the first one, where she learned that the depth of her curtsy was incorrect in the presence of a duchess, and that one was not permitted to sneeze at court even if desperately needed.

"I was considered a very eligible prospect in New York," she said at the second, where she was told that her smiles were too wide and too freely given to be considered elegant.

"I would do better in society without so many rules forced upon me," she said at the third, where she thought she had finally tried the dowager's patience to its limits.

"The rules are forced upon everyone," the dowager said. "You are nothing special in that regard."

Rebecca had resigned herself to endure the dowager's words, but enduring them did not take away their sting. She had indeed felt special since the night of her engagement, even while knowing it was impersonal. It was rare for a girl to wed a future duke, was it not? And given that their marriage was inevitable, why did she need lessons at all?

"You will not embarrass this family," the dowager continued. "One vulgar comment from you, and all of society will turn from you in disdain. It would be a dint in our sterling reputation."

"I do not swear, Your Grace. I keep no coarse habits."

"You are excessive in your compliments, and you have no delicacy in your manner. You are forthright and too earnest by half."

"I shall endeavor to restrain myself."

By the fourth lesson, the dowager was reduced to rubbing her temples with rosewater as she lectured her. She said it was to soothe the headache that Rebecca brought with her wherever she went.

"My mother says much the same thing," Rebecca admitted before she thought better of it, but she was rewarded by the tiniest smile on the dowager's face as she turned her face away.

By the fifth lesson and the end of the first week, the dowager struggled to maintain her composure. "Is it such a difficult concept to grasp? Miss Tremblay, you must behave as if you *deign* to patronize the shops on Bond Street instead of *desiring* to spread your custom there."

"But what if they have the exact thing I desire? If I need a new bonnet, should I not be enthusiastic to find one?"

"You should never be enthusiastic about anything that catches your eye in a shop window. A marchioness desires the best. As the best can never be achieved, a marchioness can rarely be satisfied. Therefore, a ready-made bonnet can never be something to enthuse over."

"That sounds rather like misery."

"One of the highest ranks in the land, and you compare it to misery?" The dowager considered this with a slight smirk. "Perhaps you are learning discernment after all. But it will not do to ever say such a thing outside of this room."

"Of course not." At the duchess's raised brow, Rebecca hastened to add, "Your Grace."

After the dowager left the parlor at the end of a long afternoon, Rebecca had a headache of her own and no rosewater to relieve it. She pressed her fingers to her temple and massaged it. Ought a marchioness-in-training experience fatigue? The dowager had not yet covered that topic, but Rebecca assumed it fell under the category of weakness and therefore should be given a wide berth.

"Miss Tremblay! How do you do?"

She looked up as Emily swanned into the room as if gliding on the frozen pond that she and her brothers used to slide on during the frigid Montreal winters. Her dressmaker must be the most talented in all of London, for every time Rebecca saw her, Emily appeared to have stepped directly from a French fashion plate. The palest blue muslin clung to her bosom and fell in deep gathers from the velvet sash at her waist. Delicate lace peeped from the edge of her sleeve and the hem of her skirt and lay between the linen folds of the fichu tucked into her neckline. Rebecca didn't need her mother's avaricious eye to know that the fineness of that lace had cost a small fortune. Emily had all the natural grace and delicacy that everyone expected Rebecca to possess, as if it were so easy to wake up one morning and be someone completely different.

Emily should be marrying the Marquess of Avenbury. That seemed to be the common conclusion, and who could blame them? Rebecca herself thought Emily better suited to the role.

"I am coping. I can say no more than that, as I have been strongly cautioned toward discretion and I must practice it."

"I have heard that the dowager Duchess of Northelm frightens debutantes half to death each Season. I daresay she would be proud to see her effect on you."

"Proud is not how I would interpret her assessment of me," Rebecca said with feeling. "Disappointed would be more apt. Perhaps with a touch of enmity."

"My carriage is here to take me home. If you are also ready to leave, please do come with me, and my coachman can bring you to your address."

Emily was not only beautiful and graceful, she was *kind*.

Rebecca considered declining the invitation. It was difficult to face the embodiment of womanly perfection after being criticized for her own shortcomings. But the fact of the matter was that Rebecca liked Emily as much as the rest of the beau monde did.

"Thank you. My brothers are due to arrive in the curricle in another hour, but I would prefer to leave now. They are rarely on time and may well forget all about me." She smiled as if it were a jest instead of the truth.

"You seem in low spirits." There was concern in Emily's eyes as they settled themselves in her carriage.

"Would you not be, if you were told that everything about yourself was lacking?"

"The dowager means to help." Emily's brow creased as Rebecca laughed. "Truly, she does. It is better to be cut by her tongue than to be lashed by all of society. Once they turn on you, you shall never be in their good graces again."

"I should think that would be an ideal outcome. It would give the dowager good reason to banish me to a faraway estate in the country." Rebecca shrugged. "I am told that there are several to choose from. Including a castle, if you can imagine it."

"That would be a lonely fate."

"You would be more than welcome to visit me, and take pity on your poor, languishing sister-in-law."

"I might even be tempted to move in with you."

That gave her pause. "You are in no danger of ostracization, so what would be your cause of banishment?"

She looked away. "I meant nothing by it."

"I am famished," Rebecca announced. "There must be somewhere that we could stop for refreshment." It would do Emily good to talk, and Rebecca was interested in listening to her vent her spleen if need be. She seemed to be a person who kept things to herself too often for her own good.

"Did the dowager not offer you tea?"

"Of course she did, but it comes with so many caveats and instructions on correct behaviour that I can hardly ever partake in any of it. Do let us find somewhere so that we may talk, my dear Emily!"

CHAPTER EIGHT

Emily had not set foot in Kelligrew's Tea Emporium in years, but she rapped the roof of the carriage and gave the address to the coachman as easily as if she had been there yesterday. When she stepped across the threshold it was as if she stepped back in time, and she almost stumbled when she heard Rebecca's voice instead of her mother's.

The shop was exactly as she had remembered it.

"I find it difficult to believe that someone as elegant as you spends much time here," Rebecca announced. The chairs were upholstered with velvet that had faded to white near the seams. There were chips in the paint near the door, and the iron sconces on the walls were crooked. It was a charming establishment for all its shabbiness, with bright curtains in the windows and clean swept floors. "Why did you choose this place?"

"It was the nearest shop for refreshments." Rebecca's unfamiliarity with London meant that she would never know that it was a lie. "Besides, they have the best baked goods in all of London." Her mouth watered as she thought of the delicate orange flavor of the Savoy cake. It had been her favorite as a child.

"I do like immediate satisfaction." Rebecca beamed at her, but then turned bashful. "I can tell that it is unlikely that we will encounter anyone from the nobility. I understand if the true reason that we are here is because you are as embarrassed by my manners as the dowager."

How was it that Rebecca always appeared so comfortable in her surroundings, as if nothing was easier than slipping into any situation that presented itself to her? She tugged her thin white leather gloves off as soon as she sat down, too eager for tea to be strictly polite, but it charmed Emily. Her cotton dress was the color of a daffodil and flattered her waist and hip as the fabric draped against her body. She was as welcome a sight in the teashop as she was in a duke's manor.

Emily never went anywhere anymore that reminded her that for every step she danced in the most elegant ballrooms of London, she was from humbler origins on her mother's side. Her grandfather had been an impoverished clergyman, a distant cousin to a gentleman in Somerset who had introduced her father to the family. Her mother had been graceful and elegant, and although she had never severed the connections to her family, Emily had been raised to understand that she did not belong among them.

Sometimes it felt like a betrayal of her past.

"I am not embarrassed by you." Emily locked eyes with her. "You are my friend."

Rebecca lowered her shoulders and settled back in her chair. "I confess that you are the best part of my new life."

The words crept into her heart and settled there like a nesting bird. She didn't know why it felt so good to have Rebecca's approval when she had already earned accolades from the highest ranks of high society. But although a great many kind things had been said to her, Emily suspected that most of them were gilt, and hollow at the core.

Rebecca's words felt true as gold, and eminently bankable.

"Besides, we have so many secrets between us."

"Secrets?" Emily paused as she poured the tea. "I have no secrets."

"The window was a common occurrence for you, then?"

"I try not to think about that night."

"I thought it was great fun." Rebecca sipped her tea and took a Shrewsbury biscuit dusted with cinnamon from the tray of confections that had been placed before them. "That was not my first window."

"I did wonder if you had experience."

"Not only have I climbed out of them, I have also climbed *into* them. I went to a great many parties in my past with no invitation." She brightened. "I would be happy to show you how I did it, if you know of any forbidden soirees that you are dying to attend."

"Absolutely not! I beg of you, do not bestow such confidences upon me."

If Rebecca revealed her misdeeds, would Emily be honor bound to confess them to the dowager? Or worse, to the marquess? Best not to hear any of it. She dropped a chunk of sugar with too much force in her tea.

"Bestow! What a grand word. My confidence is not a gift, it is a matter of life. I am much in the habit of speaking my feelings and thoughts aloud, where they do more good than remaining in my head. Besides, you and I must not stand upon ceremony with each other."

"It may be unwise to share *all* of your feelings."

"Then how will we ever know if we have the same ones?" Rebecca leaned forward and gestured with her biscuit. "The dowager is a hard woman with hard words, and I shall have trouble adjusting to her presence in my life. Is that so wrong to say?"

"I do not pretend to have any understanding of the society in which you previously found yourself. But such sentiments will be unwelcome here."

"About in-laws? Or does this apply to all family members? I have even more to say about my parents and my brothers, if you are interested to hear any of it."

"A duke's family has taken notice of you, and you are to join their ranks. You will be seen as ungrateful to utter anything except kind words about any of them."

Rebecca considered this, and then nodded. "I have found myself in my share of trouble in the past but have vowed to start my life fresh here in London. I am willing to try my best to make the family happy."

"If only the family wished for *us* to be happy in return," Emily said, then gasped at her own treason. Did confidence beget further confidence? She was too comfortable when she was beside Rebecca and fretted that it did not bode well.

Rebecca set her biscuit down. "You are the perfect person to marry into the family. I am the one who does not fit in."

Emily picked up her cup and swirled her tea, trying to decipher the leaves at the bottom. "My mother loved it here at Kelligrew's."

"What a wonderful reason to visit."

"I have not been here since I was a child. She died three years ago."

Rebecca reached across the table for her hand. "Is this difficult for you? We do not need to stay."

Her hand was surprisingly comforting, and Emily gave it a tentative squeeze. She was unaccustomed to being touched. "Every time we came to London, we visited my grandparents and congregated here. They had little enough money, but they always found the means to purchase tea and a biscuit for me. Good-hearted, generous, wonderful people."

"They sound lovely."

"After Mama died, it took Papa hardly any time at all to marry my stepmother. Lady Calloway is an earl's daughter, and very fashionable. They never speak of my mother. Her portrait was removed from the parlor. They want me to forget."

Emily's throat was dry, and she gulped the last splash of tea dredged from the porcelain pot.

"You will never forget her. She is your mother, now and always." Rebecca's eyes were rimmed with tears. "Do not allow them to destroy your peace and your memories."

"What if I belong *here* more than I do in Mayfair?" Emily had never said the words out loud before. "I have had the best of governesses. I attended finishing school in Bath. I should feel secure in my place, especially since my betrothal to Lord Danfield…and yet I doubt myself. Somehow, I do not feel like I belong among them."

"A little time is all you need, and you will be happy where you are. What more could we ask for than wealthy, titled, handsome husbands? We belong alongside the best, no matter where we once came from. If nothing else, money grants our upward passage."

Emily stared into her empty cup. Was she no better than her father, seeking titles and prestige, discontented with her past? To leap from admiral to baron and then to marry the daughter of an earl was not so unlike her own summit toward ducal ranks.

"I have faith that there is at least the tiniest amount of rebellion in you." Rebecca smiled. "We are not so unalike after all."

"Well, I am here with you instead of returning the carriage straightaway to my father. Does such a thing count as rebellion?"

"Not as great as my own. After all, I am the reason my family left Montreal for New York." Her face tightened. "But that is enough chat! Let us be off, so you may return your carriage in good time, and before my brothers start to worry about my whereabouts. It would take them a good long time to fret, but once started, they might well tear London apart."

"Thank you for taking me sight-seeing." Rebecca turned to smile at Henry as he drove the curricle. "There is so much to see in Hyde Park, even though it was not the fashionable hour to stroll."

This was what she had looked forward to when she had agreed to marry the marquess and move to England. If she had known that her engagement would mean so much studying—but there was no use fretting over the choice she had made. She would endure twice as many of the dowager's lectures if it meant finally earning her parents' approval.

"Visiting banks and shipyards is getting tiresome, I must admit. Once you have been to one, have you not been to them all? Besides, I love an excuse to drive the curricle. The roads make the carriages faster here. Or maybe there are better horses in London."

"You like so much to go fast that you are imagining reasons out of thin air."

"Maybe so! But I have to say that I do like England."

"More than home?"

"Where was home?" he asked with a laugh, cracking the whip as they rounded a corner. "We spent so much time in different cities while Father set up his business in every shipping port he could find, I could not say where I liked best. Was it growing up in Montreal, or was it the past few years in New York? Or the time we spent in Halifax when we were children?"

Rebecca had not realized that any of her brothers might have shared her feelings. Did he ever feel out of place? She longed to ask but knew he would tease her if she was to say something sincere.

"I liked Montreal best," she said finally.

She had been young enough then to be truly carefree. In New York, she had been old enough to partake in the grand array of social engagements and parties that she loved. But she had a special place in her heart for the town of her finishing school days, when the weeks had been measured in nothing more substantial than daydreams and wishes.

"You had best change your tune and say London is your favorite, if you want the British to like you."

"I want everyone to like me." She thought she said it under her breath, but he jostled her elbow.

"That's your problem, Becky. It is not possible to be liked by everyone. You should have accepted it years ago and then you wouldn't have become such an old maid."

She rolled her eyes at the unmerited insult. "I am two years younger than you. Would the marquess have proposed to an old maid?"

"With the size of your dowry, I expect he would have proposed if you were a crone."

It was likely true. Avenbury had been keen to invest in her father's business. She wasn't sure why he had been so passionate to bring the Tremblay gin to England, but he had spoken as if a world of opportunity awaited them in England.

"Let us walk for a while," she said. She was not ready for the afternoon to come to an end.

"Hey now! What's that line for?" Henry's eyes brightened. "I like the looks of this."

He threw the reins and a coin to a lad in the street, then took Rebecca's arm and walked toward a gathering of people. A man in a bright red frock coat was standing beside a wooden box with a cloth draped over its top. Another man was bent over with his eye up to a peephole in the box, and an impatient line of people were laughing behind him, urging him to finish with his lollygagging.

A sign propped up against the box declared it to be *Mr. Graham's Fantastical Moving Mechanisms*.

"You will all have plenty of time!" the man who Rebecca presumed to be Mr. Graham cried out. "No rushing. Curb your impatience and you shall look your fill when it's your turn."

"He's been ten minutes already!"

"Aye, give him a swift kick in the pants to hurry up!"

"Whatever is it?" Rebecca asked as they drew closer.

"It's a peep show," Henry said. "Had you never seen one at home? There are painted slides inside the box, and see how the man is turning that crank? He moves the slides, and the images leap to life inside the box. It's impressive. You cannot imagine how realistic it is, even knowing that it's no more than daubs of paint at different depths to create the illusion."

"Oh, may we look?"

"Why not? I've got a few shillings burning a hole in my pocket."

"Come one and come all!" Mr. Graham bellowed. "Such marvels as you have never seen before await you. The best sights in all of the kingdom can be found right here in this box, at such low cost that you will be astonished!"

When they did get the opportunity to look, Rebecca was transfixed. It was extraordinary that by putting her eye up to the glass, she was transported to a busy marketplace, with haggling merchants standing over baskets of goods. She gasped when Mr. Graham moved the slides to show her a palace filled with fantastical creatures prowling the hallways. And now she was in France, at court!

Why couldn't life be so simple? Painted ladies and gentlemen, moving in charming harmony in a tiny room filled with wonder.

But perhaps it *was* so simple. Was this not the world she was moving into now? A little thrill bubbled up in her chest. She would be stepping into each of London's ballrooms like Mr. Graham's slides clicking into place.

"If you enjoyed that, then you have a curious mind," said a lady who had been in front of her in line, and who had taken a leisurely time to view each slide. She was some years older than Rebecca, with a sharp chin and deep-set eyes, well-dressed with a dashing hat and an elegant sapphire shawl. "Perhaps you would be interested in talking more about such natural philosophies?" She murmured an address and an hour, almost so quietly that Rebecca could not hear her. "The salon that I patronize is a most edifying place. You may well enjoy yourself there. We have many scientific demonstrations, and our members enjoy a robust dialogue around a great many topics."

"I am intrigued," Rebecca breathed, gazing into her eyes. "I have never been to a salon before. I am new to London, you see."

"I guessed as much from your accent. My name is Miss Sophia Cantrell. I would be pleased to further our acquaintanceship, if you are of a like mind?"

"I am Miss Rebecca Tremblay, and I am always happy to meet a new friend."

"One can never have too many of them."

"Becky, come on!" Henry was already several paces ahead. "The horses are restless."

"My brother awaits me," she said, and rushed away.

CHAPTER NINE

Papa frowned at Emily. "Why are you so glum this morning?"
"A lady never admits to being glum," she said.

"Spare me such nonsense! You are at breakfast with your family, not trying to impress old Lady Sefton or to please a duke."

"My future family may well prefer pleasantries with their tea."

Papa laughed. "True enough. That dowager duchess looks like she could split a muffin through its middle with her eyes alone. You've got yourself into a pretty enough situation, but it has its costs."

"As anything does."

She buttered her toast and wondered what was on the table at Northelm Manor. Did the ducal family enjoy extravagance for breakfast, or was it merely that their cutlery cost thrice as much as her father's? What a silly thought. It was more suitable for conversation with Rebecca. And after all, it was Rebecca who was more likely to bear the brunt of a breakfast interrogation from the dowager, as Avenbury was currently in residence there. Danfield had a smart apartment on Pall Mall and seemed the sort of man who would pay more attention to his newspaper than to Emily once they were wed, so pleasantries should be perfectly acceptable to him.

Lady Calloway entered the parlor, humming a little as she paused to re-arrange a vase of flowers on the sideboard.

Emily tensed and slid her plate away. "I have a great many errands, Papa. May I take the carriage?"

Lady Calloway raised a brow. "Errands? What kind of errands?"

"Lord Danfield has told me to expect an invitation from the Duke and Duchess of Northelm to dine in a few weeks' time, and I thought I should have a new dress for the occasion."

"I would like nothing better than to visit the draper's myself. Have the carriage brought around at half past one and we shall be on our way."

Emily clenched her jaw. "You are far too busy to accompany me. I would never dream of taking up your time."

"You cannot go unchaperoned."

"I will take as many maids and footmen as you deem appropriate. Besides, I was planning to go with a friend."

She hadn't been, but anything would be preferable to spending the afternoon with Lady Calloway. She could not sit beside her without thinking of her beloved Mama, cast aside when a new wife had joined the family.

Love was a terribly cruel infliction between spouses. One could never be safe from it, not even from the grave.

"Which friend? Not that dreadful Miss Mayweather, I hope."

"Miss Mayweather is an entertaining conversationalist."

"She is an odd woman! Turning down five offers of marriage. In my day, we had a different sort of word for such a woman than *entertaining*."

Papa laughed. "A girl can be as choosy as she wants to be. Plenty enough men on the market, especially with the size of her fortune."

"I have never liked the association," Lady Calloway said. That sentiment alone would have been reason enough for Emily to pursue the friendship had she not liked Juliet so well of her own accord. "You shall write to her and tell her that you will see her at the next ball, but that you have a previous commitment to the draper's with me."

"It is not Miss Mayweather who I promised to meet," Emily blurted out. "I am to go with Miss Tremblay."

It was an outright lie, but Emily thought it would not be difficult to persuade Rebecca to visit the shops with her. After all, hadn't she wished to visit her perfumier?

"She can come in her own carriage to take you, then. I hear her father is worth a pretty penny. Honestly, I cannot imagine why you would have committed ours when you had not even asked us for it!"

Emily opened her mouth, then shut it again.

"Here, I will ring the footman myself for a paper and pencil. Be quick about it now."

Emily obediently took the paper when it arrived and went to sit at the escritoire in the sitting room that adjoined the breakfast parlor. She wrote the words *My dear Miss Tremblay* across the top of the page and paused. Ought she have written *Rebecca* instead? It still felt inappropriately intimate to say her name, and even more so to write it. Besides, what if someone were to see the letter? What if Avenbury truly was besotted with Rebecca and read her missive over her shoulder? Would it reflect poorly on Emily if she wrote *Rebecca*? Would they laugh at her lack of manners?

Oh, she was thinking too much of such nothings. She could not imagine Avenbury enjoying a casual at-home with the Tremblays. It was more likely that Rebecca was enduring another comportment lesson from the dowager and would not even see the letter today.

"Come now, the servant is waiting to deliver your note. He has several others that are quite pressing, so hurry up!"

The tension felt like a physical force against her chest, and her mind went blank.

"Emily!"

Her pen flew as her face flushed, the words on the page cramping together in a less than elegant example of penmanship. What had all those years of finishing school been for if she could not even pen a letter properly? But it wasn't worth wasting another sheet of paper to rewrite it when her thoughts were so scattered. She could not find the wax seals, and Lady Calloway was calling out to her again, so she folded the page into a series of squares and triangles until the edges were neatly locked together, her fingers moving swiftly from the memory of dozens of letters she had folded and passed to her friends at finishing school. She scrawled Rebecca's name on the outermost square, with her own along the back, before giving it to the waiting footman.

She hoped it had been a coherent enough missive.

Comforting herself that she was unlikely to receive a reply, she settled down to clear her mind by applying neat, even stitches to patch up a white linen handkerchief.

Rebecca had been in London for a month, but each day could have been a week with how exhausted she was. Such late hours everyone kept here! She struggled to keep her eyes open until half three every morning, when normally she would have sought her bed by midnight. Each day brought a new commitment of some kind, and her mind whirled with names and unfamiliar titles that were difficult to match with so many faces.

She had woken up this morning with a resolve to keep today for herself.

There was nothing easier than settling down with a book to forget all about her situation. She was grateful for everything, despite Mother's barbs suggesting otherwise. But surely even a marchioness-to-be deserved rest? Despite her efforts, society's attentions had proved tepid thus far. She considered it encouraging as long as no one refused to speak with her, which she had feared from the dowager's dire predictions.

Avenbury had squired her to a Covent Garden theatre the previous evening and had even pressed a kiss to the back of her hand. His friends were a trifle too crass about such behavior to be considered droll, but she was pleased that it gave evidence to their passion for one another. He had meant it to be in jest, but Rebecca was more than happy to spin tales to whoever asked her.

Rebecca had pled a headache this morning when her mother had left for a Venetian breakfast. Her father and brothers had gone to a luncheon with their new business associates.

The house was so quiet that all Rebecca could hear was the occasional footfall of the servants in the hallway. She was in her favorite sitting room—the one with the windows thrown open to the back garden and the cheerful pink paper on the walls—and she had gathered all the pillows she could find and was reclining in a nest of them on the sofa.

She had not read more than a dozen pages when the servants' footfalls were replaced by her brothers' banging boots. Rebecca closed her book on her chest, shoved her head deep into the pillows, and prayed for peace.

"She's in here!" Marvin hollered down the hall when he entered the room.

"I am sleeping," Rebecca said, her eyes screwed shut.

"Nonsense! Who sleeps away the afternoon? No one in this household."

"I do."

"You've never in your life had an afternoon nap."

"It is a recent habit, and one I am unwilling to halt."

"Wake up then. You've got a letter."

Rebecca opened her eyes. "A letter?"

Henry dangled a folded square of paper in front of her, and she sat up and snatched it.

"Who's it from, then?" He shoved half the pillows to the floor and sat beside her.

"That is my business, as it is my private correspondence."

"Well, it can't be a love letter, so what's so private about it?" Marvin plucked it from her hand and studied it.

Henry laughed. "Quite right! Avenbury is not the sort of man to muck about with flowery prose to please any lady, and certainly not our sister."

"I could be the recipient of a love letter!"

It proved the wrong thing to say when Henry's head came up like a pointer looking for a fox. "I say, so it *is* one? I can see well enough it is folded like a puzzle letter. Damning evidence indeed, Becky. No innocent girl is the recipient of such a thing." He clucked his tongue. "We ought to investigate this further. Can't have our man Avenbury being misled down the aisle!"

"He deserves to know if he's being made a fool of."

"We owe it to him to read your letter."

"I have not yet read it," Rebecca protested. "And I can assure you it is not from a lover."

Henry unfolded it and squinted. "That handwriting is not from a lover. Terrible."

"Bad handwriting? No, it must be a beau, beside himself with love." Marvin took it from him, then tossed it aside after the barest glance. "How disappointing. It's from some lady."

Rebecca stared at him. "Would you have *preferred* for me to be unfaithful?"

Marvin shrugged as he threw himself back onto the sofa. "I am willing for honesty amongst siblings. Avenbury is not the man I would have chosen as a brother-in-law."

Rebecca sighed. "Of course you are thinking of him as a prospective brother-in-law, and not whether he is a worthy husband for your sister. Tell me, does he not shoot often enough for your liking? Or gamble deeply enough?"

"Gambles *too* deep," Marvin said. "Hard to keep up with him. But he's a decent man."

"Wealthy," said Henry. "Hence the gambling."

"Handsome, too! He's got all the ladies looking at him, no matter where we go."

"Which ladies?" Rebecca frowned. "Who is looking at him? And where?"

"Everyone looks at a marquess, Becky. It's like walking beside a magnet with the number of eyes that are drawn to him. But a man can't help how he was born."

"Just like you can't help that ugly mug of yours," Henry told him, then howled as Marvin slugged his arm for his trouble.

Rebecca looked down at the half-forgotten letter. To her surprise, she saw it was from Emily. It was not how she would have imagined Emily's writing to look. She tugged the paper loose from its folds and smoothed it over her knee. She had not received a puzzle letter since her school days and had not expected Emily to have gone to the trouble of folding it instead of sealing it. The missive was also not what she imagined Emily would write. The thoughts on the page were scattered, half-written sentences that did not make much sense.

She asked if Rebecca would be interested in frequenting a well-known draper's, and if so, then Emily would be happy to accompany her, but although it would be a great inconvenience to suggest today, she would be free if Rebecca herself was free, which of course she likely was not due to such late notice, which would be perfectly understandable and they could always find another time to go, and she was very apologetic that they would need to use the Tremblay carriage if they were to go at all, and she remained hers faithfully, etc., etc.

It was almost as if she were trying *not* to invite Rebecca anywhere, but such a thought was absurd.

Rebecca's mood lifted.

She recognized the address that Emily had scrawled on the page.

While her brothers argued over who was to drive the carriage to collect Emily and to bring the ladies to the draper's, Rebecca changed into a smart pelisse.

Emily did not appear delighted when Rebecca called upon her.

"I did not mean to bother you," Emily said as she settled in beside her.

It was close quarters in the carriage. Marvin was happy to be driving, and Henry sat across from them in the seats with Rebecca's maid.

"Becky loves to shop," Henry said. "Nothing could be less of a bother to her. Besides, we like Piccadilly well enough."

But when they arrived at the draper's, Marvin cracked the whip and Henry leapt back into the carriage.

"Two hours will be time enough for you, won't it?" Henry called out to them.

"I beg your pardon?" Emily stared at him.

"We have things to take care of, but you'll be safe enough here amidst the fripperies that you ladies like to look at."

Emily turned to her. "Your brothers are leaving us?"

The horses raced away from the curb.

"I don't recall you inviting *them* to shop, and trust me when I tell you that they would be a hindrance instead of any help."

"I suppose they do not know the first thing about dressmaking. I wish to arrange for a new dress, you see."

"Excellent. Because I find I don't wish for anything after all. You may stay as long as you like, but I forgot to mention that I also have something else to do. You are all right here, are you not?"

Emily stared at her. "You forgot what?"

"I shall return in a short while! Long before my brothers return, do not worry. They think I love to shop, but I confess they do not know much about me in truth. I hope you find the dress of your dreams, Emily."

Rebecca darted out the door without a second glance.

Before Emily could understand what was happening, she was through the door herself and was haring after Rebecca.

"Wait!" she cried, dodging passersby in the busy street, straining her eyes to catch sight of her. The shops on Picadilly were the height of fashion, but they were no place for a lady alone.

Rebecca whirled around at the sound of her voice. "Oh! I didn't expect you to want to come with me."

It was unmannerly, but Emily grabbed her arm and pulled her to the side. There were far too many people around them to be comfortable. "Where are we going?"

"We? Well, I thought you might prefer to stay at the draper's, but when I was walking with my brother last week, I met someone interesting."

Emily's stomach plummeted. "Oh no. Not a man. Please tell me, *not a man*." She could not bear witness to infidelity. Why, she would need to tell Danfield, and Avenbury! She quailed at the thought of confronting the marquess.

"Not a man. A lady."

She blinked.

"A *bluestocking*." Rebecca's eyes were wide. "I've always wanted to meet a bluestocking! She told me that there is a salon for like-minded people at three o'clock on Wednesdays. I thought I should never have the right opportunity, as my parents would never approve. When you asked if I could bring you to the draper's and I saw that it was one street over from the salon, and that today of all days is Wednesday—I realized it would be the perfect day to attend. I wasn't going to tell you, because you said the other day that you did not wish for so many confidences from me. What you do not know will do you no harm, except now you have decided to come with me of your own accord. And now we have yet another secret between us."

Rebecca was beaming as if she had solved a riddle.

"Come with you?" Emily cried. "A bluestocking's salon is no place for either of us. The dowager would faint dead away to even hear a whisper of such a thing."

"But who shall whisper to her? As long as we return before my brothers, then no one shall be the wiser. Are you coming with me, or not?"

A salon would be the death of her good reputation. But Rebecca's face was shining and her eyes were so encouraging. Maybe she belonged in such a place, but Emily could *never*. A spark of envy surprised her. "I cannot." She stepped back.

"Very well, I shall return in an hour's time," Rebecca called out over her shoulder.

Emily pressed a hand to her heart, then grasped a handful of skirt and rushed to catch up. "I cannot stay at the draper's alone, with no maid and no chaperone."

"If that is all it is, then I am happy to leave my maid with you."

"And *you* go on alone!" Emily was aghast.

"There are plenty of people around us."

"Anything can happen, and I would be distraught if anything did happen to you. We must stay together, and we really ought to stay at the draper's."

"You care about me," Rebecca said suddenly, her eyes locking with hers.

"I care about propriety. And decorum. And my own reputation, of course."

"If you did not care, you would have let me walk away. By leaving well enough alone, you would have been sure to keep your propriety and your decorum and your reputation."

"We are friends," Emily said quietly. "I care about my friends."

In a moment of clarity, she realized Rebecca was her truest ally in all of London. More so even than Juliet, for Rebecca was earnest about their marriages where Juliet had always been skeptical. If Emily were honest, she had been resigned from the moment that Rebecca had used her Christian name. She would not have chosen friendship with her, but the die had been cast and this woman was to be part of her future.

If that meant attending a scandalous salon…her fate was sealed.

CHAPTER TEN

Rebecca knew that Emily was right. Everything she had learned at the dowager's comportment lessons pointed her back in the direction of the draper's. But her curiosity had been roused from the instant she met the dashing Miss Sophia Cantrell at the peep show. If she never went, then she would never *know*, and if she never knew, she would forever wonder what was discussed at such a place as a natural philosophy salon. And what kind of people did the discussing? Her ignorance could be banished with one simple visit. Why, she could even be satisfied with a scant quarter hour.

Emily adjusted her bonnet as they approached the worn wooden door, pulling the brim further over her face. "Is this the address?"

"If it isn't, then another adventure awaits," Rebecca said, laughing. "Let us find out either way."

An older gentleman welcomed them inside the door. He was a small man with a trim gray beard and natty black trousers and looked dashing indeed.

"I thought this was a salon for bluestockings," Rebecca blurted out. She had not expected to see a gentleman.

"Salons can take many forms, and old dandies such as myself can often be found at such places. Miss Cantrell invites people due to their interests. I am Mr. Boyd and pleased to meet you."

An older woman, striking in appearance, joined them at the door. Her black hair was pinned up in a haphazard pile atop her head, with silver tendrils at her temples curling around her face. She wore a loose morning gown of green satin trimmed with gold braid, and a shawl trailed from around her shoulders. "I am Miss Abigail. I do not recognize you. Are you new to the Empyreal Fellowship?"

"We have never been here before," Rebecca said. "We are not members."

"We are an informal group, but we welcome those interested in natural phenomena, scientific experimentation, and botanical study. All things heaven and earth, you might say. Oh, and magic, of course."

"Magic," Emily repeated, her voice heavy with doubt.

"There is much that is not explained in our everyday world."

"We are interested to learn what we can," Rebecca assured her.

"First may I learn your names?"

Rebecca introduced them.

"And how did you find out about us?" Miss Abigail was not smiling as she gazed at them, and Rebecca wondered if they would be denied entry after all.

"Oh, Miss Tremblay!" Miss Cantrell approached them and embraced her in a cloud of perfume and blue silk, her russet curls touching Rebecca's cheek as she kissed it. "I had hoped you would come."

Rebecca was startled at the show of familiarity. "I am surprised you even remember who I am, our meeting was so brief."

"Miss Cantrell never forgets a face," Miss Abigail declared.

Mr. Boyd winked at her. "Especially not such a pretty one."

Rebecca blushed. People were a good deal more forward here than they were in high society.

"Do not embarrass my new friend," Miss Cantrell chided them. "She is here because I thought she was interesting. Pay them no mind, Miss Tremblay. And the same goes for you, Lady Emily. All are assured of a fine welcome here at the Fellowship, as long as you enter with an open mind and spirit."

Rebecca and Emily followed Miss Cantrell to a room where two dozen men and women were talking in small groups. Her spirits lifted when she heard laughter—real guffaws, not polite trills or sarcastic chuckles. There were raised voices and broad gestures, and so much energy that the room almost seemed to hum with it. They were introduced to artists and poets and journalists and singers.

It was not so different from places she had attended in New York, and Rebecca found herself relaxing into conversation.

Emily nudged her arm. "Is there some sort of demonstration going on over there?"

"Are you intrigued? This is encouraging. I had thought you a person sadly bereft of curiosity."

"I have my share," she said with dignity.

They crossed the room and watched a man presiding over a small audience, a sovereign piece in one hand and a black rock the size of his fist in the other. "When I hold up this coin, it will leap from my hand to the lodestone! Watch the wonder before you."

He took the coin between his finger and thumb and held it aloft as he walked back and forth, then stopped in the center of the crowd and brandished the coin before the lodestone. After he brought it almost close enough to touch, he withdrew his hand with a flourish, and the coin was drawn to the lodestone with a dull clunk. The crowd clapped as the coin remained stuck fast.

"Perhaps a coin is not so impressive, but shall we test it with something larger?" He brandished a serving fork, and it too clung to the lodestone with ease.

"How amazing!" Rebecca exclaimed.

"It is no more than simple science," Emily murmured to her.

"Have you seen such science before your very eyes?"

"My father spent his life in the navy. Of course I am familiar with such things. A compass uses the same method."

Rebecca shrugged. "We shall simply have to return to see a demonstration that you are unfamiliar with, so that you too may marvel at something. It does the soul good to be astonished every so often."

"We should return now to the draper's. Is it not close to the hour of your brothers' return?"

"Has so much time passed already? Perhaps that is the magic that Miss Abigail mentioned when we arrived."

"It was a pleasure to meet you," Rebecca said to Mr. Boyd and Miss Abigail as they passed them on their way out.

"The pleasure is ours," Mr. Boyd said. "The elderly among us will always look out for the young folk. We were you once."

"I see," said Emily politely.

He pursed his lip and examined their faces. "I see more than you think I do, and more than perhaps you see within yourself."

"You speak in riddles, sir."

"It's often safer to do so."

"Oblique phrases and sly winks will do us no good here," Miss Abigail said. "We must be more blunt so that we are understood."

"Well, I don't know about that." Mr. Boyd hedged. "There will be time enough for plain talking later, if the right questions are asked."

Rebecca had certainly come to the salon with questions, but found she was leaving with even more of them chasing each other in her mind.

❖

Emily did not feel entirely herself again until later that evening at Almack's.

Here, in the ballroom on King's Street, among the prettily dressed women, in front of the long mirrors and the gilt columns, she could breathe deeply. She took pride in the fact that she was one of the select few chosen to dance away her Wednesday nights and to make polite conversation with other like-minded ladies and gentlemen.

How often in her youth had she imagined herself dancing in front of the likes of Lady Jersey and Princess Esterhazy? How many dresses had she selected and discarded from her wardrobe each week? There was ritual in every step of her preparation.

Tonight she wore white silk, decorated with pale pink rosettes and plenty of gold braid to complement her hair, which her maid had spent an hour pinning into rags the previous night so that it would curl most becomingly today. Her white kidskin gloves were tied above her elbow, and her dance slippers were pristine. Her hem was an exact quarter inch from the floor to maximize the appearance of gliding across it when she walked.

The details of her dress were inconsequential, but the impression that was created out of such details was paramount.

Once Emily was confident that she did not stand out in any way, she believed herself to be a satisfactory addition to the club, capable of enduring the harshest scrutiny. Lady Calloway likewise fit among the chaperones and proud mamas, her silver gown and painted fan as pretty as anyone's in the crowd.

Her own mama would not have liked it here. She had been a woman of simple tastes but had been so proud of all of Emily's accomplishments when she returned each quarter from her finishing school. She had wanted so much for Emily to have every opportunity that she had not experienced. If only she could have seen her wild success this Season!

Although *wild* was not an apt descriptor of anything related to Almack's.

The sole decision of any importance was whether one preferred ratafia to orgeat. There was a great deal of comfort in the familiarity of a crowd who made all of the usual observations, as predictable as a sunrise.

As soon as Emily saw that Danfield and his grandmother were in attendance tonight, she and Lady Calloway went to pay their respects to the dowager.

"It is a great pleasure to me to know that one of my grandsons behaves with enough propriety to have earned his voucher." The dowager nodded to Danfield, who inclined his head at the compliment. "Avenbury would be neither welcomed here nor would wish to attend."

"I had the pleasure of introducing Miss Tremblay to Lady Jersey and Lady Sefton recently, Your Grace," Emily said to her. "I do hope that she too will be given a voucher before the end of the Season. She would love nothing more than to join us, I am sure."

If Rebecca were to attend, she would see it for the cherished haven that it was. Much preferable to a natural philosophy salon!

There were no dangerous ideals within these walls, no exuberant recitations of poetry, and *certainly* no bluestockings.

She forced her mind away from the Empyreal Fellowship, lest her face betray the curiosity that still burned inside her. Some of those people had been most intriguing.

The dowager bestowed a nod upon Emily, who sank into another curtsy the moment her head moved. "I confess that I still have my doubts about Miss Tremblay, but you, Lady Emily, are a credit to the family."

"I chose the best for my bride." Danfield beamed at her.

"You are too kind," she murmured.

He went to fetch them both a glass of wine.

"Soon we shall need to decide where your wedding is to take place," the dowager said. "Here in London, or at Castle Beaufort. There are merits to both."

"Oh, I had no thought of it being soon. With all the excitement of the marquess's return, I know the family has much to do. It is right that his marriage to Miss Tremblay will take precedence."

"It is no effort at all to plan a wedding. I can order the gloves to be given as gifts at a moment's notice, no matter how many people are in the church that morning. Danfield could have a new carriage fit for his new life in a trice." The dowager accepted a glass from Danfield when he returned to them. "In fact, perhaps there should be a double wedding. Both of my grandsons, married on the same day. We shall host a grand ball to celebrate."

Emily almost dropped the glass that Danfield handed to her. She sipped, hardly knowing if he had chosen ratafia or orgeat. "The same day?"

She knew jealousy was a sin. She knew it, she had prayed for it to be stricken from her heart, and yet still it twisted up her insides. Even her own wedding day would not truly be hers if it was to be shared.

Rebecca would be a beautiful bride, though. Emily could almost imagine her in her wedding finery. She grew warm and swallowed more wine.

"I don't know that I care much for that idea." Danfield frowned. "What if Avenbury and I came to blows?"

"Do not be facetious. You both know better behavior than that."

"I would never wish to take away from the importance of the marquess's marriage." Emily tried to sound pious, but the nauseating truth sat like a rock beneath her breastbone. She, who had plotted and planned for her engagement, was not looking forward to her own wedding.

"Nothing will show greater family unity than a double wedding," the dowager declared. "The Beaufort family in perfect harmony. You and Miss Tremblay are the best of friends, and the gossip rags will love you for it."

Lady Calloway clasped her hands together. "This is the best decision in the world! Our Emily, part of a ducal ceremony. There would be no greater honor. We cannot wait for her to join her hand to yours in matrimony, Lord Danfield. The admiral and I have been in alt since your proposal."

Emily supposed she should be grateful that someone was in alt, for it certainly was not her.

She found relief when the dancing started, and she could clear her mind by thinking about her posture and the position of her arms, counting her steps so that she appeared graceful, poised, and effortless.

When it came time to waltz with Danfield, her joy ebbed away. She had been approved to waltz by the patronesses some weeks ago and enjoyed the steps very much. But it felt odd as she held tight to his arms and he swung her across the hardwood floor, as if she were watching them both from afar instead of experiencing the moment. This man was meant to be her husband. She had wanted nothing else since the moment she had stepped into her first ball and locked eyes with him from across the room.

She had known he was well-born and wealthy, and she had decided that there was nothing easier than determining that he would be the one for her.

So why did he feel like a stranger to her?

Why did she herself feel like a stranger?

"You are quiet tonight," Danfield said.

"I am counting my blessings along with my steps, my lord," she said, and added a laugh that she had long ago rehearsed to sound light and carefree. "What a wonderful thing it is to be here with you."

It did elicit wonder, but it was because she was suddenly wondering *why*.

He smiled. "I know Grandmother can be determined to have her way, but I hope that talk of the wedding did not trouble you. I agree that I would not prefer to be married on the same day as my brother."

She relaxed. "I am content to have a long engagement."

"Oh, I don't know that we need to wait long. I am eager to be your husband."

His smile was intimate and yet she felt as untouched as if he were an actor upon the stage. Perhaps they were both no more than actors following the duchy's script, handed down through the generations.

But was it to be farce, or tragedy?

CHAPTER ELEVEN

"You must be careful," Lady Calloway told Emily. "Vauxhall can be a dangerous place. There is something in its air that is not always seemly. Unexpected things can happen in such a place, and it is best to be on one's guard."

Papa snorted. "Oh pah, it's easy enough to avoid trouble. Stay with your friends and navigate your surroundings with a clear eye, and you'll find Vauxhall is filled with innocent enough amusements. The fireworks are not to be missed. If there are acrobats, I recommend watching them. Nothing is more impressive than human ingenuity!"

"I promise never to stray from the paths," Emily said. "Lord Danfield shall escort me everywhere, and we will be in respectable company with his cousins."

She looked forward to the evening until the carriage arrived and Danfield and his cousins, Lady Henrietta and Lady Elizabeth, greeted her.

"Avenbury is meeting us at Vauxhall later, but we are bringing Miss Tremblay so that she might enjoy dinner with us," Danfield said.

Emily had not expected them to be in attendance. With each encounter, she was flustered by Rebecca's enthusiasm for flouting convention, which was difficult given that Emily *liked* convention.

"Avenbury is so droll," Lady Elizabeth said. "I do hope to hear his legendary witticisms tonight."

"Those witticisms are not fit for lady's ears," Danfield said tightly. "Not even his cousin's. I would recommend not listening to a word he says."

Emily had long wondered at the source of tension between the brothers. Perhaps it was no more than a dislike of his manners and his taste.

Rebecca scrambled into the carriage and laughed as her skirts were almost caught in the door when the servants closed it behind her. She nestled herself beside Emily and plopped her reticule onto her lap. "What a lovely party!" she exclaimed. "I am looking forward to seeing everything."

"Vauxhall will offer you anything you may be looking for, though I do not recommend going in search of *everything*." Lady Henrietta smirked.

"Oh, do you mean it is a place where mischief abounds?" Rebecca shook her head. "I assure you that I have not the least interest in it. I will be content with a glass of champagne and to laugh at the jesters, nothing more."

"Such common amusements can indeed be had," Lady Elizabeth drawled.

Rebecca's smile dimmed as she recognized that she was being mocked.

Emily lifted her chin. "I too am looking forward to such things. It shall be a grand evening of enjoyment."

She was rewarded when Rebecca pressed the tip of her shoe against her own beneath their skirts, and her eyes sparkled in the lamplight.

It was Emily's first time at Vauxhall, but she knew in her bones that she would not have enjoyed it as much if Rebecca had not been at her side. It was gauche of her to exclaim her wonder at the pavilions and porticoes, and the clever lights disguised as stars tucked among the tree branches. Her enthusiasm showed her lack of town bronze, but it made Emily look at her surroundings with fresh appreciation. It was far more enjoyable to observe and appreciate the details of the evening, which Emily so often failed to notice in her attempts at presenting a calm veneer of ennui to those around her.

The ham tasted better after Rebecca marvelled at how thinly it was sliced, and the champagne was exceedingly frothy and delightful when Rebecca giggled with her at the slip of cold bubbles down her throat.

How could something as fragile as another woman's friendship result in such happiness? Friends had drifted through her life in a pleasant enough manner, but they were tied to other times and places. Her memory of them paled beside Rebecca's vibrancy, and her insistence of grasping onto moments instead of watching them pass by.

The mood changed when Avenbury strolled up to them. His cousins fawned over him, but Danfield did not rise to greet him.

"Fashionably late," was his only comment, after making a point to flip open his fob watch.

"Avenbury always knows how to make an entrance," Rebecca said, smiling at him. "Shall we walk? It is a perfect evening, and the weather is clement enough for every pleasure."

He raised a brow. "How fortunate. There are many avenues to choose beneath the stars."

Emily didn't like the look in his eye and determined that Rebecca was not to be left alone with him. "We shall all benefit from a change of scenery."

Danfield harrumphed but got to his feet and stuck out his arm. "I am happy to escort you anywhere you wish."

Emily felt a flutter of nerves beneath her breastbone. Her betrothed was a perfect gentleman, and he certainly looked the part with his dove gray waistcoat and well-pressed trousers. She knew she should reach out and take his arm—there was nothing in the world simpler—but she could not.

She did not understand her own reticence.

Emily turned to Rebecca. "I hear that the acrobats are worth viewing. Perhaps we could watch them together?"

None of the party seemed interested, but Emily tucked her hand in the crook of Rebecca's arm and hoped they would all follow. Heeding her father's advice, she did not wish for any of them to be separated. She trusted Danfield, she *knew* she did, but Avenbury not at all.

Avenbury and Danfield jibed at each other during the tumbling act, while Rebecca exclaimed at every movement the acrobats made. Emily was distantly aware that her arm ached after the dozenth time that Rebecca gasped and grabbed her tight. She was numb to her surroundings, removed from the party after all in spirit if not in body.

Was this to be her future? Caught in a family drama that she did not understand? Did Rebecca have any more inkling of it than she did? She seemed unaffected by the tension, absorbed in the scene before them.

The brothers were exchanging heated words now, too low for Emily to hear, but she was aware of people turning to look at them. She swallowed. What was her role? Was she meant to be a peacemaker between them?

She found all she truly cared about was shielding Rebecca from it all.

"There is a group of people over there who seem to be marveling at something," Rebecca announced, straining to see through the crowd.

"Shrieking is more apt." Emily tried to keep her voice calm. She did not like the sound of the commotion. "I do not think we ought to investigate."

"There is only harmless fun to be had here," Lady Henrietta said, laughing. "Do let us see what the fuss is about."

Emily hesitated. The unknown fracas held no appeal.

Avenbury shrugged and pushed away from Danfield. "There is nothing better than amusement. Do let us go in search of it."

When Rebecca pulled at her hand, Emily felt bound to follow, and they found themselves among a crush of people. In the center of the crowd was a large box, and a man dressed in smart tweeds. "Who next shall partake in my marvelous experiment?" he cried out. "I am Mr. Florencio, and I invite you to experience a strange and wondrous thing. Who among you is brave enough?"

"I am," Rebecca announced, her cheeks flushed. She stepped forward and tugged at Emily again.

Alarmed, Emily drew back. "We do not even know the nature of such an experiment! I make no claim to bravery."

The crowd laughed, and Mr. Florencio doffed his hat and smiled at them. "Ah, we welcome an ingenue to our midst. Ladies who know not what trouble they get into can be a delight unto themselves."

"I do not wish to get in trouble."

Emily's heart was in her throat, but Danfield stood beside her with an affable expression on his face. If he were willing, should she not stay with him?

"It is theatrics, nothing more," Lady Elizabeth said with a little yawn, and ushered them all into the center.

"Is there anyone else who can be tempted to partake in the mysteries of science? We are about to begin, do not be shy!"

Emily swallowed. It could not be so dangerous, as long as they remained together. Moment by moment, this evening would come to an end, like every evening did, and she could slide into the next day where a fresh set of invitations awaited her. She need never to return to Vauxhall again.

Except she thought it might be seared in her mind. The flash of the lights overhead and the heat that they emitted, the push of people around her, warm bodies jostling for space, the laughing and hollering of the crowd. Everything was too bright, too overwhelming.

She fought to steady her breathing.

Endure, endure, endure.

"These willing souls shall soon be connected," Mr. Florencio announced.

"What fun!" cried Lady Henrietta, and Emily struggled to smile through her nausea.

But then Rebecca was there beside her, so close they almost touched. "What an evening," she breathed, and it was like a cooling breeze rolling over Emily's overwarm cheeks.

Mr. Florencio arranged them so that they stood in a row— Avenbury, Rebecca, Emily, Danfield, their cousins, and three strangers who had volunteered themselves. He maneuvered the box in front of them, fussing over it until it was placed to his liking. From the box he produced a long piece of white string. One end remained inside the box, while the other end was slack in his hand.

"The laws of attraction are strong here at Vauxhall, and we shall prove it this very night! Now, one of you at the end must hold this string, attaching yourself to the box. Hold it tight, mind you, and do not let it go, no matter what transpires."

Avenbury grasped the string and looked at it. "It appears to be nothing remarkable."

"And yet great things are produced from humble origins," Mr. Florencio cried. "All of you in this line, you must hold hands for this to work. Hold them tight, all nine of you. Your fates are now linked."

Emily took Rebecca's hand, and after a moment Danfield reached out for hers. At least she would be well supported if she were to faint, as it was impossible to reach her smelling salts.

"On the count of three, I shall turn this crank, and you shall all experience something wonderful!"

Emily gripped Rebecca and Danfield's hands. Cold sweat dripped down her back beneath her chemise.

"Do not worry," Rebecca whispered, leaning in so close that her ringlets brushed against Emily's neck. "Nothing bad will happen."

Her smile was so warm and so comforting that Emily almost believed it.

"Our participants must now ready themselves for this once-in-a-lifetime experience!"

Emily looked at Danfield, but he wasn't looking at her.

She closed her eyes.

Then she felt a sharp spark run through her body, cracking heated awareness from fingertip to fingertip, her whole body energized. Even her hair felt alive, and her heart raced. She wrenched her hands free with a gasp, staggering away. "What was *that*!"

Avenbury was laughing so hard that his eyes were watering. "What great fun!"

"An electricity machine!" Mr. Florencio boomed, flinging his arms wide. "Such a marvel produces a great spark in the box that passes through the string and then travels through each and every one of you, from hand to hand. The connection of humanity!"

Emily's flesh trembled with the spark's echo, and the hair on her arms was still raised beneath her sweat-dampened gloves.

"Did you not feel it?" Rebecca cried out, grasping her arm. "How exhilarating!"

"I feel it still," Emily whispered, hating the tremor in her voice. But was the spark from the machine?

Or was it from her heart?

What did it mean that she yearned for Rebecca's hand in hers again, and that she was breathless when she stared into her eyes?

"We have been entertained enough," she said to Danfield, striving for a pleasant tone. "Papa and Stepmama will be expecting me."

He nodded, then jerked his head toward Avenbury. "I trust you will find your own way home."

"I have many friends here. Of course I shall."

Danfield shoved past him, and Emily and Rebecca lagged behind him, Lady Henrietta, and Lady Elizabeth on their way to the carriage.

But they exchanged not one word the entire ride home.

After Rebecca had dismissed her maid for the night, she sat in the chair next to the open window and stared up at where the stars ought to have been if the skies had not clouded over. Life always dangled something nice to cling to, even if the offering was meagre, but she felt flat and dull tonight, unable to reach out for a sliver of happiness. She pulled her knees up to her chest and hugged her arms around them.

Vauxhall had been ethereal. Lanterns had glimmered from all the tree branches, little delicacies had awaited them for supper, and then there was the delight of fizzing champagne and the burst of fireworks and the sheer magic of the electricity box. She could have been walking on the air and courting the clouds.

And yet the experience was so *earthy*.

It was unlike the staid and proper environment of the London ballrooms. Was it the night air that inspired such liberty? Or was it the opportunity afforded by the vastness of the pleasure gardens?

Men and women all around her had exchanged looks so heated that they could have sparked fires, and she had seen couples disappear down dark alleys in either fits of laughter or longing stares. The crush of people had been overwhelming. Why, Rebecca didn't think she had been more than two feet away from another body the whole evening.

She had yearned to lose herself in the dizzying spectacle, to give herself up to the uninhibited nature of the night. It had nothing to do with impropriety, and she had not wished to wander the paths in search of a kiss. But there was so much to see, and she had been thwarted by the snobbish and condescending company she kept.

That was her recurring problem in London. Interesting opportunities abounded, but the wrong people ruined her enjoyment of them.

More and more, Rebecca was realizing that the worst offender was Avenbury.

Rebecca had not cared for his behavior tonight.

Instead of becoming more comfortable as their engagement progressed, she liked him less and less. She had been awed by him in America and had been willing enough to marry him. After all, she had to marry somebody at some point, and her father had presented the engagement to her with little choice.

On the ship, she had found the marquess caustic but entertaining. He had dozens of witty stories, and he had even indulged her one night by dancing with her. What a beautiful memory, with nothing but the sea around them, moving smoothly to the rhythm of the rolling waves, with no music except for his humming and the tap of their shoes against the wooden boards. The heavens had been studded with diamond-bright stars, and a moon so low and full that it could have inspired odes in its honor.

Avenbury had kissed her that night, after waltzing with her so close that it would have shocked the chaperones in a proper ballroom. It had been the one time in their courtship that he had looked at her with any sort of carnal longing. His lips had been warm and his breath had been fresh, and she had slid her arms around his neck and pretended to enjoy every moment of the embrace.

His kiss had left her colder than the sea breeze, but she had consoled herself that attraction would come with time. Once he was nicer to her, she would find him more desirable.

Now Rebecca questioned if he had simply been bored on the packet ship, with so few people to talk to and with herself and her mother and their maids the only women aboard. Would he have danced with anyone, in an effort to pass the time?

He never had become nice, and tonight he had been so angry and abrasive with his brother. What history lay behind them that caused such enmity? She had assumed that their aggravation had been resolved on that first night in London, for she had not seen them in the same place since then. Perhaps it was naïve of her to think that such emotion could be handled in one night.

Now when she thought of the most romantic night of her life, she didn't think of dancing on the ship. She thought of tumbling out of a duke's window and walking under the new moon across the damp grass toward Emily's ruined betrothal party. There had been something in the air that night, some element of change and impulse and something she could not quite name.

Emily would likely have called it havoc, but Rebecca was starting to wonder if it had been *magic*.

At least Vauxhall had been an opportunity to spend more time with her. Emily had been so pretty in her spangled dress, glittering beneath the fireworks. Rebecca's heart sped up as she remembered the hot press of her hand when they took part in the electric demonstration. She had not cared that Avenbury was to her left side, as long as Emily stood with her to her right.

Whatever the experience, whether fair or foul, she wished to share it with her.

Rebecca dropped her forehead to her knees.

She was not afraid of much, but this pull between them made her nervous. It was a magnetism that she did not fully understand, and yet she worried she understood it far too well. After all, she had felt it before.

Desire.

It warmed her veins and left her breathless. It brought tears to her eyes to think that such yearnings must go unfulfilled. For all that it felt holy and sacred, she dared not speak of it. But desire fell far short of the totality of her emotions. It was kinship and understanding.

She did not need to know her long to be loyal to her and to be faithful to her.

Emily was a good, proper debutante.

She was poised to become a good, proper wife.

Infidelity would be out of the question.

But would it be infidelity if neither of them were yet married?

Could Emily ever share her desire?

Rebecca had known such feelings before. They were far sweeter than anything she had ever felt for a man. To love another woman was idealistic and cerebral as well as deeply, shockingly carnal.

Maybe Avenbury would never like her, and she would never like him, and that would be fine. As long as she had these feelings for *someone*, this scorching joy.

Her secret life must be kept quiet inside of her, like a garden forever in bloom with herself the sole visitor to its glory.

CHAPTER TWELVE

Emily rubbed at her chest where she swore she could still feel the effects of the electricity machine. She had dosed herself with willow bark tea the night before and lain in bed with a cold compress on her forehead all morning to banish any lingering malaise.

Now it was time to ready herself for tonight's dinner. She chose her dress with care, settling on a lilac silk evening gown with a demure neckline and small puffed sleeves. She fastened her amethyst earbobs while her maid tied a purple velvet ribbon round her neck, embellished with tiny pearls. Her hair was curled and tucked into a pile atop her head, fixed with silver pins.

Her family was dining with the Duke and Duchess of Northelm, and she must appear the picture of perfection as their future daughter-in-law. She had met the dowager duchess on multiple occasions with Danfield, but had seen the duke and duchess once at her engagement ball.

Her face burned at the memory of traipsing around outside with Rebecca that night. It was a wonder that they had not been caught by the duke! There was something about Rebecca that inspired her to take risks that she never would have dared before.

After she slipped her lace fan into her reticule and stepped into her soft white leather shoes, she went downstairs to join Papa and Lady Calloway.

"The carriage will be brought round in a quarter hour," Lady Calloway announced. "We shall be precisely on time. I would not dare arrive a moment late to such a prestigious evening. But our dear Emily will soon be used to such rarified air. Why, it would be no wonder if you were to be seated at the duke's dinner table every fortnight in a year's time."

Emily smiled. "I am lucky."

"Luck! Pah, luck has nothing to do with it." Papa laughed and puffed on his pipe.

She was inclined to agree when she thought of her efforts to draw Danfield in despite her disinterest in him, but it was unladylike to bring up her own attributes.

"If we could all rely on luck, what a world we would live in! But that's not how the world works. I have had my share of fortunate sailings and close calls at sea to know that luck can be fickle. Now, what is a good deal more reliable, of course, is coin."

Lady Calloway nodded. "Money is the surest path to success."

Emily stared at Papa. "But money has nothing to do with *my* success."

"Are you so naïve that you thought that was true?"

"Lord Danfield asked me to marry him, did he not?"

She had earned this engagement. She had done everything that had been expected of her and had proved herself worthy of belonging to high society by winning the heart of a duke's son.

"Of course he asked you. *After* he came to see me. Because we had played cards and he had lost, you see, and he had to give me his vowels. It didn't matter to me that a fine lord didn't have the blunt to pay his debt of honor straightaway—plenty of gentlemen have their fortunes tied up in land! Well, right there and then I saw my opportunity to do right by you, my girl. When he came with the money the next week, I sweetened him up. I told him how pretty you were, and how much you would bring to the marriage, which is always welcome news to a second son, you know. Even the second son of a duke has reason to be concerned with wealth, and I've amassed a goodly share of my own through my years at sea. And it's a good thing I spoke to him when I did, because he told me he had planned to pay court to another lady."

Papa looked proud as anything, but Emily felt sick. "I thought he wanted me."

"He does want you! Any peer in the land would want my daughter as his bride. As accomplished as you are, as elegant, as pretty as any other lady out there."

But Danfield didn't want her more than anyone else. She could have *been* anyone else. She had wanted so much to be like any other debutante, but it hurt to realize just how interchangeable they all were.

The Season seemed a tawdry affair now. The glamor of late nights with the nobility and dancing at Almack's faded. Dining with a duke seemed a senseless achievement, and she wished she could stay home.

Why had she fought so hard to join the matrimonial ranks? She should have listened to Juliet and remained unwed.

"The carriage is here," Lady Calloway said brightly.

She collected herself, gathering her shattered feelings close to her chest.

At least some comfort awaited her, for Rebecca would be there tonight.

The crystal beads hanging from the chandelier twinkled like starlight in the drawing room at Northelm Manor, reminding Rebecca of Vauxhall. This evening was a good deal less fun, but she could always find something to make herself smile. The paintings that hung on the walls were beautiful, and she lost herself in the swirls of pastoral landscapes as she sipped wine before dinner. Rebecca would have been pleased enough to exchange banal compliments with the Duchess of Northelm, but she was being ignored in favor of Emily.

The dowager duchess was as fearsome as ever, a cross look on her face, but her son and daughter-in-law were some of the most beautiful people that Rebecca had ever seen. The Duke of Northelm had a distinguished swatch of silver at his temples, with an overset eye and a strong jaw. The duchess had soft features with a straight nose and full lips and glossy blond curls, and cut a generous figure in her bronze satin gown. Every movement they made was elegant, and even their voices sounded rich and luxurious, their accent so refined that Rebecca wished she could listen to them speak all day.

"We have not been much in London this Season. There has been a great deal to do in Hertfordshire at the estate this year," the Duchess of Northelm said once they were all seated around the dining room table. "Tell me, how are my sons' betrothals being perceived?"

"I am met with constant congratulations," Lord Danfield boasted.

Rebecca resisted the urge to roll her eyes and concentrated on the trout in parsley and rosemary sauce that had been placed before her.

The dowager sighed. "I have continued meeting with Miss Tremblay, but I cannot say there is much improvement."

She was startled by the baldness of the statement. "I have tried my best, Your Grace."

Mother clasped her hands in her lap. "Under your tutelage, Your Grace, we do not fear that she will succeed."

It was as close to praise as Rebecca could remember hearing from her. "I assure you that you need not worry about me. Especially with Lady Emily's shining example before me."

"Another Lady Emily is exactly what this family needs." The dowager glared at Avenbury. "Why could you not have returned three months ago?"

Danfield squinted at her. "You are not giving away my bride-to-be, are you?"

"The heir deserves the best." Avenbury smirked.

"Of course, we always wished that your brother was the heir." The Duke of Northelm sipped his wine as if he had not issued a withering set down to his eldest son.

Rebecca decided that she did not in fact wish to listen to much more from the duke and duchess, if these were the words that came from their mouths. She looked at Emily. Her smile never wavered, but Rebecca knew her well enough by now to know that she was upset. There was the tiniest movement at the corner of her lip, with a flick of her eye toward the duchess.

"You will never hear me deny that Lady Emily is the better choice," Rebecca said cheerfully. Best not to acknowledge the comment about her fiancé. Such a horrid thing to say! Why, it was no wonder that Avenbury was so taciturn. He had little enough example of familial love. "She is everything that is lovely and good. But you may be assured that neither of us shall disappoint you, once we are all well settled in our places."

The Duke of Northelm gazed at her. "I would not be too certain of your permanence at this table, Miss Tremblay."

Rebecca did not understand and was impatient when silence settled over the table while the footmen cleared the fish away and replaced it with platters of quail and veal.

After the servants retreated, Avenbury glowered at his father. "Whatever did you mean by your statement? I am betrothed to Miss Tremblay."

"Indeed you are, and all of society knows it. But there are ways to break an engagement."

"I would not dishonor myself and cry off," he snapped. "No matter how you feel about the union."

"Of course you would not. But Miss Tremblay could."

There was silence, except for Danfield's knife scraping his plate as he cut into his quail.

Avenbury smirked. "Although a lady has every right to end an engagement, you would do well to remember one thing. Miss Tremblay loves me."

She did not, but had spent a great deal of time telling everyone that she most certainly did, so she forced herself to beam at him. "Why would I do such a silly thing as break our engagement?"

"Women change their minds all the time."

"I am not so fickle."

"If you knew your soon-to-be husband as well as you think you do, you could be persuaded into fickleness."

"Perhaps this is a conversation that we should not be privy to," the admiral said stiffly.

Emily's stepmother had looked rapt until her husband spoke, and then she turned pink.

"Nonsense. If we are all to be related, then why should we not break scandal at the same time as we break our bread?" The duchess smiled at him.

Rebecca had difficulty swallowing and pushed aside her plate. "I still do not understand what you are implying, but I am an honorable woman who has taken part in no scandal. My word is good."

"You see? My bride does not scare easily."

"Your bride should be home in America. You cannot possibly care for her. You will be happy enough when she is gone."

"This is beginning to cause offense." Father's face was turning red above his shirt points.

"That does not trouble me," the Duke of Northelm told him. "Was it money that you offered my son? Coin in exchange for a title? We see such things all the time. I can offer you more than Avenbury did, if you will keep your silence and leave England with your daughter in tow."

The duchess smiled, but there was no warmth in her eyes. "We do not need to waste our coin, when the truth shall be enough for Miss Tremblay to turn tail."

Rebecca's blood ran cold. Her first impulse was to shake the truth from whomever held it, but she reminded herself that tonight seemed to be a test of her behavior. She must behave like a lady. Like Emily would. "I am always happy to hear the truth, Your Grace." Her lips were numb as she forced the words out, but she thought she did a credible job at appearing calm.

"Your fiancé killed a man."

CHAPTER THIRTEEN

Rebecca lurched back as if she had been pushed.

The Marquess of Avenbury had committed *murder*? She gripped the table as if it would save her from falling, and stared at her fiancé—but surely she had misheard the duchess's words, for he continued to sip his blood red wine as if his conscience was clear.

Silence reigned. Rebecca caught Emily's eye and saw the horror reflected back at her.

"My grandson has a penchant for dueling." The dowager duchess's mouth was twisted with disdain.

Father and the admiral both looked visibly relieved.

Rebecca forced herself to smile. She knew what Avenbury and her father would expect her to say, even though dread coated her throat so thick that she could hardly speak. "Duels are terribly romantic."

Emily looked at her with censure, and she shrank in discomfort. She didn't think they were romantic, she wanted to assure Emily. She thought they were foolish. She wanted her to know, but she couldn't very well whisper the truth behind her hand.

"A man of honor! There is no shame in a duel. The ladies don't always like it, but you would always be welcome at my table, my lord," Father said.

"And mine," added the admiral. "Honor is to be prized, not made into a penance. No need to wear a hair shirt around me."

"Avenbury is a lamentably excellent shot." The duke's look at his son was pride mixed with annoyance. "It has caused quite a problem."

There was a pause, then the admiral cleared his throat. "How good of a shot?"

"Two men," Danfield said, leaning back in his chair.

"And the reason?"

"He was fornicating with their wives," Danfield said bluntly. "I beg the pardon of the ladies in the room to hear such a tale."

"Your soul is not so clean," Avenbury said to him coldly.

"It is not I who earned the moniker of the Murderous Marquess."

"There you have it," the Duchess of Northelm said with great satisfaction. "Miss Tremblay, no one would blame you for breaking an engagement for such a reason."

Rebecca swallowed. "But no one knows of this. No one has said anything to me, and we have been welcomed everywhere."

"*You* have been welcomed everywhere. *I* have merely accompanied you to Vauxhall, where any fool with a few shillings can gain entry, and the public theatre, and a stroll through Hyde Park."

She felt as if she were seeing things in the sunlight for the first time. She was a fool. A naïve, optimistic, dreamy-eyed fool. She had been courted in a different country for her money, for no decent woman here would have him.

"Our Rebecca is no weakling," Father declared. "You may do things differently here in England, but in America, a woman stands by her husband. Why, she loves the man. She's been telling everyone she meets about how wild she is about him."

The business deal. Her stomach twisted. His bloody business deal was more important than her happiness. Her honor.

Rebecca hadn't realized how far Father would go to bargain away his soul. Her parents resumed eating, as blithely as if the dowager had spoken of the weather instead of a man's life.

Four more courses were served, with a good deal more wine. Rebecca assumed it was to wash down the news more easily. Comportment lessons be damned. She knew it was inappropriate to drink to excess, downing glass after glass and beckoning to the footman to pour more with a liberal hand.

Did the footman know the truth? Did all the servants know?

All of London must know. It was only herself who had been played for a fool.

"After all the excitement, Your Grace, I believe I am in need of fresh air," Rebecca said after the Duchess of Northelm rose after dinner to guide the ladies to take tea in the parlor.

She could not possibly engage in idle chatter, nor could she sit quietly while they tried to persuade her to break her engagement. Her mind whirled. She didn't need a comportment lesson to know that it was improper not to follow the duchess, but the family could not think less of her than they already did. What did it matter if they thought her rude as well as gauche?

To her surprise, Emily stepped away from her stepmother and stood beside Rebecca. "A turn around the gardens would do me a world of good."

The dowager duchess gave them a measured look, then sighed and dismissed them with a flick of her hand.

Rebecca grabbed Emily's arm and hurried her down the hallway, past portraits of ladies and gentlemen who in all likelihood had held even more sordid family secrets, until she reached a door that led them outside.

The stones of the terrace were cold beneath her thin-soled shoes, but she didn't care. Away from the prying eyes and snide manners and arch looks of her future family, she gulped the air as if she was drowning.

"Here." Emily rummaged in her reticule and thrust a small vial at her.

Rebecca examined it. "What is this?"

"Smelling salts, of course. It is exactly what you need."

"I am no danger of fainting."

Emily shrugged. In a practiced move, she flipped open the stopper and brought the salts to her nose. She closed her eyes and inhaled deep. Her whole body shuddered violently enough that she almost stumbled. After a minute or two of gasping for air, her eyes wide and wild, she nodded and straightened her skirts. "Nothing like it to take the edge off a shock."

Rebecca eyed her. "I shall take your word for it. I would rather anything than that."

"I am never without them. And now that you have had your first taste of high society scandal, you won't be either."

Rebecca hopped up on the wide ledge of the wall enclosing the terrace. What did it matter that the rock would catch the delicate silk of her dress, or that dirt would smudge its hem? What did it matter if she scuffed the palms of her kidskin gloves when she gripped the stony edge? Here, beneath the twinkling stars in the soft summer air, all she knew was her own animal vitality.

She was young, she was alive, she was *here*, and everything else—society, its rules and customs, the trappings of the ducal title—must be secondary.

When Emily joined her on the ledge, Rebecca's heart swelled. She knew how she hated to muss her dress. She moved closer and pulled some of the lilac silk of Emily's dress onto her own lap to protect it as best she could from the stone, but her dress was so full that the fabric spilled over both of them in a purple froth. She could hear each deep breath that Emily took to clear her nose and lungs from the aftermath of the salts, and watched her slender throat move beneath the thin velvet ribbon tied round her neck as she swallowed. The acrid scent lingered in the air.

"That was an interesting dinner." Emily spoke quietly.

"Was it interesting to you?" Rebecca looked up at the stars. "We have very different interests."

"My apologies, I am too accustomed to the company that we just left. My stepmama would have scolded me if I were to use a harsher word, even if it is merited." She considered for a moment. "It is less polite, but I must speak the truth. That was a bloody horrid dinner."

"I am sick unto death of proper behavior masking things that are most improper." She closed her eyes to stop her head from spinning. Maybe she should ask Emily for her vial after all.

"I suppose you will break the engagement." Emily's voice was small.

"It would be justice well served if I married the Murderous Marquess and they gained an Atrocious American as a daughter-in-law."

There was a moment's pause, and then they both broke into laughter.

Rebecca wiped tears from her eyes. "There is nothing humorous about any of this, is there?"

"No."

The warm breeze ruffled her hair like a lover's touch, and she tipped her head back. Oh, the wine had been a mistake. It was easier to blame the drink instead of the terrible choices that had brought her here.

What if she had said no to her father when he had told her that she would marry Avenbury? Would daughterly disobedience have been such a crime? They could still be in New York if she had the courage to breathe out the word.

And yet, if she had stayed in New York, she would never have met Emily.

The night air was more beautiful for her presence.

God help her. Come what may, but she was grateful to be beside her tonight.

"They will be looking for us," said Rebecca, but she made no move to go back inside.

Emily laughed. "They do not care one whit for either of us, do they? We could be doing anything we liked out here, and they would be happy that we remained out of their sight."

"That is not true in the least. They love you," Rebecca said. "Everyone loves *you*."

"I am afraid the Beaufort family loves no one but themselves."

Emily could not believe that she was saying such a thing when yesterday she would have defended them to anybody. How was it that she was finally gaining understanding when it was too late?

Emily had braved the dinner and its aftermath but crumbled under its pressures now. How could she bear to tell Rebecca the truth? She was flawed and imperfect. The ducal family didn't care for her any more than they cared for Rebecca. Currency ran in their veins instead of blood.

Papa had *bought* Danfield's affections.

It made her sick to think of it. How naïve she had been! How foolish to think that her charms could have been enough. Young women like herself were the means to finance the noble lives of terrible families. Proper behavior and decorum were a ruse, nothing more than a way to guarantee her acquiescence. Her obedience.

What if she no longer felt obedient?

Emily squeezed her eyes shut for a moment. Oh, if she could afford the luxury of time to understand how she felt!

Tonight was the first occasion that Emily saw Rebecca defeated and robbed of her optimism. She, who was always so cheerful and energetic, was somber under the silvery moonlight.

Emily wanted to do everything in her power to wake her up and breathe life back into her.

Her head was still rushing from the impact of the smelling salts. It couldn't possibly be because of that indecipherable look on Rebecca's face, that little smile on her lips. It couldn't be related to the heady scent of her perfume, or the closeness of her leg where they sat next to each other on the cold ledge. She could see the lace flounce of Rebecca's petticoat and a glimpse of her leg beneath Emily's own skirts, which she held so carefully and so gently in her arms away from the ledge. Had anyone been so thoughtful, so considerate of her?

Oh, but this warmth between them was so inviting.

Emily licked her lips and looked away. Any romance was due to the summer air and nothing more than that. It couldn't be because she felt truly *alive* for the very first time. Her body felt loose and free in a way that her mind never was. The night was filled with the scent of gardenias and the fresh cut lawn, the sound of nightingales and owls, and all she could see was the shine in Rebecca's eyes from the moonlight.

"I'm afraid," Rebecca said, her voice almost inaudible. "I am afraid of this dreadful family and their power. I am afraid of the marquess, murderous or not."

Oh. Rebecca *was* going to break off the engagement. It was the right choice, but Emily felt a keening pain cut through her. She didn't want to do this without her. She thought about Christmas, and the long winter ahead, and every spring and summer without her by her side. Marriage to Danfield would be hollow and lonely without Rebecca's laughter.

Emily feared she may have made an enormous mistake by accepting Danfield's proposal.

"You are the only one I can trust."

"I trust you too," Emily said softly.

She stared deep into Rebecca's eyes and knew she would follow her anywhere.

And then Rebecca's lips were pressed against her own, warm and exciting in the best possible way. Who had moved first? Did it matter, as long as they moved together?

This was the harmony that Emily had not realized she was missing.

Rebecca's lips were so soft, so inviting, caressing hers with such delicacy. Emily sighed and leaned in, wanting nothing as much as their closeness, the sounds that they shared between the movements of their lips. She rested her hands on Rebecca's shoulders, wanting to hold on and cradle the memory of tonight between her hands forever.

Oh, this was everything that she had never dared to even think of before.

This was a gentleness and tenderness that had existed only in her dreams. And then...it wasn't either of those things anymore. Emily shifted on the bench, and found herself pressed breast to breast, lip to lip, and sweat broke out all over her body as the kiss deepened into something fiery and tumultuous and uncontrollable, their mouths urgent and hot, their tongues teasing each other, the imprint of Rebecca's hands on the small of her back and the back of her head, jolting her awake and alive and impatient.

If only this moment could never end.

When they drew apart, she was overwhelmed by the shock of it all. "What was *that*?"

"I think it was the best kiss of my life," Rebecca whispered, her eyes wide.

Emily's head swam. It was the *first* kiss of her life! But wait—how was it possible that they had *kissed*? Surely it had been meant as a friendly exchange, a token of warm sentiment, a courteous declaration of trust.

Emily tried to collect her thoughts, but they did not make sense to her through the swirl of raging passion. "I cannot—this is not—"

Two women! Kissing!

And one of the women was *herself*!

She watched Rebecca gaze up at the sky, then around the terrace at the flowerpots and orange trees, lit by lanterns as well as the lustre of the full moon. She shivered when Rebecca turned to look at her, her eyes darkened with desire.

"I want to remember every detail." Rebecca's voice was low and urgent. She breathed deep. "Every scent. Every stitch of your gown, every tendril of your hair. The smudge of dirt on your skirt, that leaf in your hair. Everything."

Emily touched her hair, feeling where her curls had slipped from their pins. "I must look disastrous."

"You are in the best looks of your life." She slid from the ledge, then gently put her hand on Emily's knee. "Good night, sweet Emily."

And without another word, Rebecca slipped back into the house and left Emily to her confusion.

CHAPTER FOURTEEN

When Emily thought about last night's kiss, she burned. She attributed some of the heat in her cheeks to shame. Panic twisted her insides as she stared at the pristine white paint of her bedchamber ceiling. What if she and Rebecca had been seen from the drawing room window? She could hardly believe that they had ended up in a passionate embrace.

How would Danfield react if he found out? What would her father do?

It was unthinkable.

But what was even more unthinkable was that she burned with *lust*.

Emily, who had never before known a single pang of desire, found herself ravaged by such carnal fever that she could think of nothing else for an entire day after her lips had touched Rebecca's. She could not bring herself to leave her bedchamber. She did not dress. She waved away her maid when she hovered at the door and accepted only tea when her throat grew dry.

Who could think of physical sustenance when her mind was filled with the ephemeral?

How could she step a toe into polite society when such shocking passion might beset her body at any given moment?

Emily had always enjoyed the shelter of chaperonage, happy to prevent undesirable advances and impropriety. But she had not imagined what a desired advance would feel like or how much she might enjoy impropriety!

The frustrations of her fellow debutantes suddenly seemed sensible. They had longed to be held closer by their suitors while dancing, pleading to anyone who might listen for permission to waltz. Emily had considered it a great honor to belong among the chosen few who were allowed to do it, but all that yearning to be held a few inches closer to one's dance partner had seemed silly to her.

But oh, if it could be *Rebecca* to hold her close and whirl her around a ballroom!

How she would have begged.

Emily pushed aside her cold tea and collapsed again onto her bed.

With feelings like these, it would be utmost folly to ever clap eyes on Rebecca again. The moment she entered the same ballroom, Emily was certain that the sticklers of society would single her out for misconduct. At least of the mind, if not of the body.

She grasped the looking glass and pressed her fingers to her lips. Despite their first foray into misadventure, the act had changed neither their shape nor color. Her hair was unbrushed and her eyes were wild, but there was no mark of her indiscretion. Although the Emily of yesterday stared back at her, she felt like a different woman. Her limbs were achy and restless. Her pulse was quick, and her mind would not slow, even when she squeezed her eyes so tight that she saw spots, trying to will herself to sleep.

Emily pled a megrim to avoid leaving her rooms that evening. It meant eschewing a fine dinner with the Beckett family that she had been anticipating all week, but how could she sit among her family and her acquaintances, knowing what she had done?

Kissing Miss Rebecca Tremblay had been transcendent and wonderful.

But she didn't know herself anymore, and she trusted herself even less.

What if such feelings had been dormant her whole life and would now be unleashed no matter who she saw? She would be mortified if she were to dissolve with desire while dining with Miss Flora and Miss Diana Beckett.

But sensible Miss Flora did not have Rebecca's charmingly frank speech. And Miss Diana, though lovely, did not have eyes that sparkled like the stars or hair as soft as a kitten.

Only an exuberant American could transfix her.

The first crackle of awareness must have been born at Vauxhall. That sultry summer night had been tense and unnerving, and she could not deny that hot sparks of desire had rippled across her skin. Even now she could almost feel the lingering effects of the electricity machine, linking her to Rebecca, their palms tingling.

What if there had been magic inside the box, instead of electricity?

Maybe the shock that raced through her body had fixed her heart and finally made it work like everyone else's did. And yet her aching fervor was for another woman. What curse was it that Emily could not share the experience that was held so common by everyone?

Could the patrons of the Empyreal Fellowship help her to reverse this spell?

This was Rebecca's true effect on her, questioning if magic existed!

After a fitful night had passed, Lady Calloway knocked on her door and slipped inside her room. "Are you feeling any better?"

Her voice was gentle and caring, and for a moment Emily wanted to cry in her arms and be soothed like a child. "My head continues to ache."

"I shall call for the physician to come and see you. I do not like this pallor of yours."

Her concern felt genuine despite the strain in their relationship, and yet another foreign emotion stirred within Emily. Was this... familial affection? Had her heart been so damaged at Vauxhall that it had cracked apart, allowing dangerous feelings to seep inside?

Oh, what utter nonsense.

Emily sat up. "There is no need for the doctor. He is a busy man, and I would not wish to cause extra expense."

"You have a delicate constitution. I have seen how often you reach for your smelling salts! There is no price for health, and I have seen too many girls lose their bloom and wither to nothing. It would break your father's heart to see such a fate befall you."

Would it break his heart to know what she had done with Rebecca? She must make sure that neither he nor Lady Calloway could ever guess. She flung the sheet away, sprang out of bed, and started loosening her hair from its braid. "I am in no such danger. I have plenty of energy. In fact, I am well enough to attend Mrs. Pemberton's garden party with you this afternoon."

She brushed her hair with such vigor that it crackled and stood on end, and Emily stilled. Was the electricity *within* her at the mere thought of Rebecca? Was that the true curse of Vauxhall?

"Fresh air and a healthful stroll among the flowers will be just the thing to return the roses to your cheeks!" She hesitated, then patted her arm. "I am happy that you are so much improved. I was concerned after everything that transpired during dinner at Northelm Manor."

Emily lost her balance and sat back down on the bed.

"Your future husband is an upstanding young man, but his brother! I knew nothing of his exploits. The family is much more complicated than I imagined." She sat beside Emily and looked into her eyes. "If you have any hesitation at all about your betrothal—"

"Of course I do not!" Emily said, inching away. "There is no reason for me to be uneasy. Danfield is not his brother. We cannot judge him on another's misdeeds."

"I want to assure you that you have my support, Emily. Your papa wants this match and thinks nothing of duels, but you and I may have a different sensibility from the gentlemen regarding this matter."

Lady Calloway was blinking hard, and her pulse was visible at the base of her throat. It must have taken courage for her to talk plainly, as Emily had never known her to cross Papa in even the smallest regard.

The foreign emotion ached in her breast.

Oh, Papa. In the aftermath of dinner, she had almost forgotten his deceit. Her betrothal was owed to him, not to her own accomplishments. The flirtations she had employed with such vanity toward Danfield had been nothing but silly schemes. What was real, and what was not? What was of her own doing, and what had been done for her?

Was her attraction to Rebecca part of the upheaval of her life, a misplaced affection for the kind of person she wished to marry?

Maybe it had nothing to do with desire.

She could not tell if she was disappointed or encouraged by the thought.

"You have nothing to worry about. I will marry Danfield, and all will be well," Emily said.

Danfield was a disappointment, like every other man Emily had met. He was guided by his pocketbook and by his baser emotions. There was no true admiration of her. Her onslaught of lust for Rebecca had brought her relief on one important matter. It proved to her that she could never have such base desires for Danfield.

Last night's kiss had as good as guaranteed that her future would be bright and happy, as it would be devoid of the dangerous love that could exist between a husband and wife.

Emily hid her agitation during the carriage ride to Mrs. Pemberton's estate outside of London. All that was needed to convince Lady Calloway that she was in good health were a few measured remarks about her anticipation of the beauty of the gardens, and her stepmama continued the conversation almost by herself.

After greeting their hostess, Lady Calloway waved to her friends and joined them. Emily stood by herself for a moment before walking over to a group of women with whom she had become friendly over the past few months.

It had been Emily who established such a routine early in the Season, citing the importance of being among the young marriageable ladies to encourage suitors. It had been a ploy to avoid Lady Calloway's company, and she was ashamed now of such behavior. Hurt by her father's rapid remarriage, Emily had been desperate to cast aside her past and join herself to her new husband's family, whoever they may be.

She had done her a disservice by turning from her, and now perhaps it was too late to make amends.

The debutantes welcomed Emily into their fold, not knowing she was now a lost sheep. There was nothing to fear in the face of dozens of pretty eyes and laughing pink lips and fetching hairstyles. Remarks about her appearance were limited to the color of her dress and the pattern on her reticule, and certainly not about any change in manner or behavior.

Emily recited the usual phrases—asking after their health and commenting on the weather, the pleasantries coming naturally enough after so many weeks of rehearsal—trying to recall if it was Lady Alice's father who was doing poorly, or if it was Miss Sarah's brother—but her eyes kept straying to Lady Calloway. *She* had real friends among the ladies of society, women she welcomed with warmth and laughter. Her conversations were genuine. Emily had not permitted herself to envy it until now.

Had that same warmth once been extended to herself, and she had not seen it? She had been so caught up in the pain of losing her mother and her anger with Papa that she could not remember.

Juliet came up to her and eased her from the flock. "How was your evening with the duke and duchess?" she asked after they had taken a few steps down the path, twirling her lace parasol and studying the flower bed in front of them.

Emily glared at the tulips, bobbing in the breeze. Juliet was being kind and considerate to ask after Emily's experience with her future in-laws, and it was far from her fault that Emily had no desire to speak of anything that had occurred that night.

The flowers must bear the brunt of Emily's displeasure, instead of her friend.

When she did dart a glance at Juliet's face, she found herself quite equal to looking at her dark eyes without floundering.

The sight of her lips caused no surge in her pulse or flutter in her breast.

The unusual feelings she had discovered within herself seemed to be contained to Rebecca alone.

Emily could not let down her guard, for it wasn't only Rebecca's kiss that must remain hidden. She now shouldered the burden of the Beaufort family secrets, and they were heavy indeed.

"I remain the luckiest girl in all of London," Emily said to Juliet. "The duke and duchess wish for the weddings to be soon."

"I never knew that sublime bliss could appear so calm until I saw it demonstrated before me on your face."

"Is tranquility not part of happiness, in your estimation?"

"I suppose this is the reaction I should have expected from you."

"You know I am not the sort to fawn over any man. A marriage should be anchored in good sense instead of passion." She angled her parasol to better shade her face. Emily might be safe from the notice of the average society woman, but it would only take one glance from Juliet for her to uncover everything.

"And what of the mysterious marquess?"

"Avenbury behaved as anyone might expect him to."

"You are not very forthcoming."

Emily wondered how Juliet would react if she revealed that Avenbury had fought several bloody duels, all of them over other men's wives. "The marquess is a man who eats his steak with a fine enough appreciation for the chef and prefers cherries to pears at the end of a meal. That is all I learned of him."

"Our friend must have paid stricter attention, as he is her fiancé. I shall simply ask her." Juliet waved, and Emily whirled around to see Rebecca beaming at them.

She had not expected to see her so soon.

Not today, when she still felt so unsteady.

Not with Juliet laughing and taking her by the hand and complimenting Rebecca on her pleated walking dress and stylish lace gloves, bringing her so close that her perfume dizzied Emily's senses more than a thousand flower beds ever could, and did not

Emily agree that Rebecca's straw bonnet was the most charming they had seen all afternoon?

"Charming indeed," Emily said faintly.

"Em had not two words to spare about your future husband, Becca, but I am eager and willing to hear any exultations you have about the marquess. I am most curious about him."

"Avenbury is a man with a fine adventuring spirit," Rebecca told her. "He is unlike any man I have ever met."

"I have yet to see him this Season." Juliet studied her. "But perhaps the lack of a male escort does not bother you? He is very much his own man with his own interests, is he not?"

"He is so busy these days! We Americans have infected him with our enterprising spirit. Perhaps he feels less suited to evening entertainments when now he can trade them for early morning appointments at the docks and afternoon rendezvous with the banks."

"How intriguing." Juliet's eyes had a faraway look.

"This is a gorgeous hibiscus." Rebecca stooped down and snapped the stem, bringing the blossom to her nose as she stood. "Intoxicating! I have never known its like."

"Mrs. Pemberton may not like us to pick her flowers," Emily said, darting a look around them from under the safety of her parasol.

"Oh, were you presented with a list of dictums upon your arrival? How wonderful that I was spared such constraints. I cannot understand a flower without touching and smelling it." She rubbed her thumb against a pink petal and sniffed it again. "This one is wonderful. Did you know some people call them rose mallows? What a pretty name!"

"I am not sure our hostess would agree with your method of appreciation."

"Well, how would you go about choosing a favorite?"

"By its blooms," Juliet said. "One may study from afar."

"Ah, but that only allows for partial admiration of its beauty. To engage all the senses and bring one's face right to the petal is a truer test."

Juliet smiled at her. "It might be prettier from a distance. Flaws are too easily uncovered by such proximity."

"A little lack of symmetry or an imperfection may make it all the more charming."

Emily was quiet. These fiery feelings licked at her insides, like a hunger that she didn't understand. She was powerless in their wake. If she closed her eyes, she was on the terrace again with the night breeze in her hair and Rebecca's unsteady breathing in her ears, her blood hot and urgent, the crackle of something alarming between them.

How could Rebecca look so cheerful and unbothered? She waved the hibiscus in her hand as she laughed with Juliet. When had Rebecca become so adept at hiding how she felt?

Or had their encounter meant so little to her?

CHAPTER FIFTEEN

Rebecca watched Emily from beneath the brim of her bonnet while she continued to speak of nothing at all of importance to Juliet. It was impossible not to stare, not when she was so captivated by her smallest movements.

Emily's eyes flickered from the garden to Rebecca, and then to the crowd strolling past them to the greenhouse. She gripped her parasol so tightly that it was a wonder she did not break the delicate wood handle. She wore a gossamer silk shawl around her shoulders for no other reason than it was elegant, given that it could provide no protection from the sun or warmth from its sheerness. Her morning dress was the color of the sunrise from a ship's prow, pale gold and full of hope for a new day.

Before Rebecca was forced to make up any new stories about her love affair with her darling marquess, another group of ladies accosted them with shrieks of laughter and exclamations. Her ears rang with praise for a perfect afternoon and the marvelous floral wonders spread out before them in such abundance. Rebecca eased her way to the outskirts of the group and beckoned to Emily to follow.

"Are you well?" she asked Emily as they fell into step.

"I am *unchanged*," Emily insisted, her tone holding the hint of a threat.

Rebecca smiled. "Are you indeed?"

"Oh, damn it all. Is it so evident?" She pressed a hand to her throat, as if checking for her pulse. "I thought my feelings were well-guarded."

"I have always considered you to be relentlessly constrained."

"Thank you. But that was before." Emily lowered her parasol to better shield them from view. "Now I do not know myself."

"Perhaps you know yourself rather better than you did."

"But I'm a debutante!"

"Maybe you are something more."

"Oh, Rebecca. How is one to live with these feelings?" She moved her gloved fist to cover her heart. "When I look at you, I am undone."

Rebecca wasn't sure if Emily's agitation was because she liked such feelings, or if it was because she did not. Could she have mistaken the longing in Emily's eyes the night that they had kissed?

"Have you never been attracted to a woman before?"

"Never!" Emily cried, her face white. "Never to anyone at all. I have never felt so bewitched in all my life."

"It is no enchantment."

"Then why am I so enchanted?" Emily's voice was no more than a whisper. Her teeth caught at her lip and her brow was low across eyes that were wider than the Thames, with depths that Rebecca wished she could sink in. Her hair was not in tight ringlets today, but fell in soft golden curls that touched her shoulders.

Gone was her reserve and her cold exterior. In its place was a warm, vibrant woman, and yet a very distressed one. Rebecca glanced around them. She knew Emily would not want to be seen in such a state. She took her hand and guided her down a winding path away from the gardens, and finally found a bench secluded beyond a hedgerow.

"I feel much the same." Rebecca sat down and tugged Emily next to her. "I have thought of little else than our kiss."

"This is new to me. But have you felt this way before?"

"Now we are talking about secrets again." Rebecca had wanted to keep the truth in her past, but everything felt different now. "My family has lived in several cities, increasing my father's business.

For years, we lived in Montreal, but we had to leave…because of me."

It was difficult to admit it. Here was the root of her parents' displeasure. The seeds had been sown from her own misdeeds, and in their eyes it could never be uprooted, much as Rebecca was trying to mend her ways with her engagement to Avenbury.

"What happened?"

"I had an indiscretion."

Emily's lips parted. "With another woman?"

"With another woman," Rebecca confirmed. "Mother found us kissing in a park. We were not discreet. Before the week was done, I was whisked away to New York. It became a family mission to find a husband for me, in order to eradicate such terrible tendencies. In the end, they had to *fund* a husband for me instead. And now here I am, engaged to the Murderous Marquess."

Every time she thought of Avenbury, her optimism failed her. Had he truly killed those men? Could there be another explanation? Was it worth marrying him to prove to her parents that she had changed?

When she looked at Emily, she knew she was the same woman she had been in Montreal.

"Did you think such tendencies were so terrible?" Emily's voice quavered.

"I did not. And I do not now."

"Do you feel this way for men, too?"

"I thought in time, perhaps, with Avenbury—but no."

"Promise me that we are not the only ones to ever feel this way."

"It seems impossible to think that God created so few like ourselves," Rebecca said slowly. "We cannot be so unique."

"Because I already feel so alone. I cannot bear to endure such longings in solitude." Her eyes were rimmed with tears.

"You are not alone. Not as long as I am here." Rebecca brushed a curl from Emily's heart-shaped face, then took the hibiscus she had plucked earlier and tucked it into her reticule so that the bloom was peeking out. "The duchy might think me a weed invading their garden, but I will struggle to thrive in it as long as you're planted there too."

"What are we to do? We must pretend like we do not have this fierce attraction between us."

"Perhaps we need to take one day and one experience at a time and ask no more of ourselves than grace and patience."

Emily was a cautious woman who fretted endlessly over what others thought of her. Rebecca wanted to catch that adorable face in her hands and kiss the worry from it, for it was Rebecca who leapt without looking, who rushed into fool's errands, and who lost her heart at a moment's notice.

She could only hope that she had not lost hers already.

Rebecca was not certain whether or not her comportment lessons were meant to continue. Perhaps she could have figured it out if she had paid better attention during the previous lessons, but she suspected that such a unique conundrum had not yet been covered. On the one hand, Rebecca had received no instruction to stop coming to Northelm Manor. She knew that the family still considered her in desperate need of education before becoming a marchioness. On the other hand, they had also tried to dissuade her from pursuing matrimonial bliss with the marquess.

Only the dowager herself could resolve the riddle, and so Rebecca asked Henry to drive her to the manor, where she had not stepped foot since she had attended the dreadful dinner and then kissed Emily senseless.

Instead of being brought to the drawing room where the dowager Duchess of Northelm preferred to hold court, she sat in a small parlor at the back of the house and waited for the footman to ascertain whether or not the dowager was at home to visitors.

She recognized the slight as she knew she was meant to. But would she be turned away after the dowager had made her point? She hoped not. She had told Henry to return in an hour, which would likely be closer to two with how little attention he paid to the time.

Enough time passed for Rebecca to wonder if she had been forgotten about, and not merely chastised, but then the footman returned and whisked her to the usual parlor.

Rebecca curtsied as soon as she saw the dowager. "Good afternoon, Your Grace."

"I did not imagine I would see you today, Miss Tremblay."

"I received no missive that your summons had ceased. I remain as ever at your disposal."

"Obedience is a good trait in a marchioness," she conceded. "You should take this as a lesson to be less willful, though that may take more time than I have here on earth to teach you."

It had been curiosity instead of obedience which had spurred her to the ducal doors, but she refused to admit it. The illusion of obedience would serve her further with the dowager. After all, it was an altogether different sort of lesson she wished to learn today.

She wanted to know more about her future husband.

"I would think wilfulness and stubbornness might be good qualities to keep, with a husband such as Avenbury." She managed not to choke on his name.

The dowager's eyes narrowed.

"Are the duke and duchess still in residence? Perhaps they could help teach me and take some of the burden from you."

The dowager's lips pinched. "My son and his wife have a great many obligations. I would state the obvious and tell you that you could not possibly comprehend the constant work it takes to manage a dukedom, but regrettably it falls to me to force such understanding on you."

"I will learn," Rebecca said.

And she did. For once, the lessons were not about her behavior or her shortcomings. Instead, she listened as the dowager talked of the role of the duke as magistrate, and the responsibility of good stewardship of the land, and the great many livelihoods that depended on ducal custom.

Rebecca made the appropriate replies when she thought it expedient to do so, and after an hour, she witnessed the slump of the dowager's shoulders as her voice thinned and then cracked. She might not understand all of the responsibilities that one day would be hers, but she saw clearly enough that she ought to learn to lead instead of to follow, and so she decided to ring the bell for tea.

"Presumptuous." But the dowager's voice had no heat in it.

"I am thinking of your comfort," Rebecca told her. "You will be in a far better state to denigrate me if you are refreshed. I doubt you have more than two insults left in you before your lips are parched beyond measure."

"Insubordinate." But was there the trace of a laugh?

When the tea arrived, the dowager dismissed the footman with a flick of her finger and then gestured at Rebecca. "You shall do the honors. If you are so beset by ambition that you cannot even wait for the ink to be splashed over the marriage licence before taking undue precedence here, then by all means, preside over the teapot."

Rebecca poured according to her best memory of the dowager's preference. Half a cup of weak tea, with one lump of sugar and the thinnest slice of lemon.

She earned a huff for her efforts, and they took their tea in silence for some time.

"Your backbone will indeed be important," the dowager said. "If you insist on your fool's errand of marrying my grandson, then you must have a will of iron."

"I do not know if I have such a thing," Rebecca admitted. "But I will marry the marquess regardless."

"You seem more sober today, Miss Tremblay. I detect the absence of your usual humors. Are you finally cultivating an air of ennui?"

"Not at all." She bit her lip. "But I am troubled by this talk of the Murderous Marquess."

The dowager laughed. "Do you finally prove fickle? Are you ready to give up your ambitions now?"

"It is love, not ambition." It was lies, and she tried to keep her voice steady.

"Love." She laughed again. "If you believe that, then you have not listened to one word that I have uttered to you. You should know by now that love is not a currency with which our kind choose to barter. Besides, what manner of man do you profess to love? You would be happy with a husband who has no qualms about adultery?"

"Do you not still love your grandson, despite his flaws?"

"Ah, but I cannot break the bonds of primogeniture, where you have the choice not to enter the bonds of matrimony."

"Are you thinking to spare me?" Rebecca stared at her. "I thought you were trying to protect your family *from* me, as ill-suited as I am to the rank."

"He will ruin you, Miss Tremblay. Without even a second thought. And you shall be embittered, and disappointed, and he will suffer no consequences. But you are correct that your comfort is not my primary concern. I want the duchy to go to Danfield, of course. We have a spare for a reason."

Rebecca gasped. "You cannot remove him from the succession. Even if the banns are not cried, he could procure a special license. Or we could elope in Gretna Green. My parents do not oppose the match, and I am of age."

"He will see no money if he does any of those things. Oh, you did not consider such a thing? Yes, we have done all we can over the past years to adjust things to Danfield's advantage. I didn't think Avenbury would return. If he did come back to England married, I thought I would not trust his choice of bride."

"I cannot believe the duke capable of such a thing against his own son."

"Every man in this family has the Beaufort pride," the dowager said. "Avenbury will stop at nothing to crush his brother beneath his heel and to take everything back. His father will support him if he can do it. He did not raise weak boys. He pitted them against each other since birth. This is an amusement to him, to prove who is worthiest."

Rebecca stared at her. Those poor children, scrapping and fighting for attention all their lives. "That sounds terrible."

"Avenbury doesn't want to marry you. He wants to embarrass the duke and force his hand. My son doesn't want the title to be associated with an American tradesman, no matter how rich he is. The duels pale in comparison to the disgust the duke has for trade.

Avenbury wants the duke to restore his original fortune, which is a great deal more than your dowry, and then he will discard you with a snap of his fingers. He is playing you for a fool, my girl."

"He does not need to do any of this. My family has plenty of money."

"He might yet need it. If the duke does not acquiesce, then you are nothing more than a very pretty banknote."

"I have always understood my role," Rebecca said. "My father explained it well to me."

Father would never let her hear the end of it if she broke the engagement. It was an impossibility. But with each passing day, it was harder and harder to stomach the thought of her upcoming nuptials.

As she had suspected, she was ready to leave Northelm Manor long before Henry arrived in the curricle to escort her home. Rebecca walked along the gallery wing, her mind wandering instead of studying the ducal ancestors. Long faces and modest dresses and dour backgrounds blurred her sight when she was interrupted by a vision in sprigged green muslin practically floating down the staircase down the hallway, blond curls piled high on her head.

Emily.

Rebecca's spirits lifted. She may be unwanted by her parents and her fiancé, but not by Emily. Her presence was the balm to every hurt.

Emily rushed to her side. "I didn't know you were here! I was taking tea with Lord Danfield and his mother upstairs."

Rebecca absorbed the sting. "So the duchess is home?"

"Why, yes. I have been told to join her for tea weekly now that she is in town."

"Ah. She is not at home to me. I suppose I must endure further lessons before I may gain entry to the duchess's drawing room."

It hurt to know that Emily was so beloved by the Beauforts, even though Emily deserved every ounce of adoration. She was lovely, and kind, and gracious, and—oh, so kissable. Her day dress was mint green and entirely respectable. Her white muslin fichu covered every inch of her chest to the base of her throat, which was circled with a delicate string of pearls. Her pale skin was almost entirely encased by fabric, but Rebecca was aflame with desire at the scant amount she saw.

She wished to peel the gloves from Emily's hands and press her face against her palms. She wanted to toss Emily's skirts to her waist and discover all of the secrets that lay beneath her linen petticoats. She yearned to pull her bodice down and expose her breasts to her adoring gaze.

She wanted to forget all about marriage, lineage, heritage, and progeny. All she wanted was right in front of her in Emily's blue eyes.

"Perhaps I have lessons of my own to impart," Rebecca murmured.

Emily stared at her. "Here?" But there was excitement in her hushed voice, tempting Rebecca closer.

"The only onlookers have painted faces, and I think they will tell no tales."

"I have dreamed of this," she whispered. "I have dreamed of you."

"So have I."

"I want to be kissed again."

CHAPTER SIXTEEN

Rebecca felt a burst of joy at Emily's confession and leaned forward until her lips brushed Emily's, softly and then again with more urgency. She tasted sweet, like peaches and tea, and her mouth was soft and gentle. She kissed without experience, but fit her body against Rebecca's own as if she had done it time and time again.

Rebecca pressed her lips against her jaw and her cheekbone. "You are so lovely," she breathed, like a creature helpless and caught, yet eager for the net that bound her close. She smelled so good, and she was so beautiful, her lashes fluttering against her cheeks and her breast heaving with emotion. "You would tempt the devil himself."

"Would I?" Emily looked delighted. "Truly? I have never thought of myself as a temptress."

"I would follow you into the practice of the darkest arts." Rebecca nodded. "Were you ever inclined to practice witchcraft, I would be your holiest observant."

"Now you blaspheme. I would never go against God in such a way." She looked away, her brow knitted low over her eyes.

"We do not go against God now." Rebecca took her chin in her hand and angled her face so that they were looking each other in the eye. "I cannot believe that this is anything less than holy."

Emily gestured at the wall behind them. "All of these men and women. Were they not in pursuit of something other than... whatever this is?" Her eyes glistened, and she stepped back. "Are we not honor bound to be in pursuit of the same?"

"There is nothing wrong in what we do. In how we feel." Rebecca kissed her again, hoping beyond measure that her lips would be more convincing than her words.

"Could it be so easy?"

"Does it need to be so hard? Does it not feel natural to you?"

"That is what frightens me. It is as easy as taking breath. As easy as walking. I feel like I have been born for no other purpose than to seek safe harbor in your arms! And yet not even one week ago, I had no idea such feelings existed."

"It is not so unfamiliar for me…and yet it is as if I feel them for the first time." Rebecca looked up, and up, and up. The roof soared four stories above the gallery with its homage to the past, but the light that shone through the glass ceiling bore witness without judgment to their passion. No lightning struck, no plague befell them. "Can we not enjoy a moment of peace together? I fear we will have little enough of it with our husbands."

At the mention of husbands, the spell broke, and Emily wrenched herself away. "I cannot. I *must* not." Her face was pale and resolute.

"I will never push you further than you are willing."

"It is not a matter of will! My will is nothing in the face of what I feel. Every craven, base emotion is exposed. Every sordid word— no, every *thought*."

Her words echoed in the cavernous hallway. Was it soiled with whispers and looks of longing? But how could it be? Was it not sacred, instead? The halls and lawns and gardens of London had been their confessionals instead of the churches, words spilling forth without more urging than a raised brow and a beckoned finger.

"Then I do not feel the same as you."

"You do not feel this passion?" Her eyes were wide and frightened.

"I feel every ounce of passion that you do. I *throb*, Emily. I *desire*. My blood runs hot, and I have such impulses that might frighten you. But I do not fear it. I welcome the reminder that I am who God made me. I was made for this moment. And maybe you were too. Who are we to go against His purpose?"

Rebecca thought Emily might flee at her words. Instead, she took a deep breath, took one last look at the paintings beside her, and made her choice.

She grasped Rebecca close, slipped her arms around her waist, and pressed her hands against the small of her back. Her mouth moved with ardent fervor across Rebecca's lips. She touched her tongue tentatively against hers, then with more confidence.

She chose Rebecca. She chose passion, and emotion, and uncertainty.

Rebecca let her head tilt back and was rewarded when Emily kissed her neck and licked at a spot near her collarbone. "Now perhaps I have need of those smelling salts of yours," Rebecca murmured, and heard Emily laugh before they drew apart.

"God help me, but I need more." Emily swallowed. "I cannot understand this need, this wanton desire. But if you share it... I am willing to embrace it too."

"Someday, if you are willing, we will have more," Rebecca said. "I cannot predict when...but I want as much of you as you are willing to share."

"I want every intimacy that you can give me." She spoke as if uttering a solemn vow.

Rebecca left Northelm Manor as the luckiest girl in London.

The Theatre Royal on Covent-Garden was so full that even though Emily sat in a box high above the masses, she felt uncomfortably crushed. Deep in her heart, she suspected that she would have found it crowded if there was even one other person in attendance, because what she wanted was to be there alone with Rebecca.

Rebecca leaned forward in rapt attention with her hands resting on the railing, breathlessly reciting the words along with the actors on stage. It was charming to see her wide eyes and parted lips as she chanted sonnets alongside Romeo. *"My lips, two blushing pilgrims, ready stand to smooth that rough touch with a tender kiss."*

Emily could hear every sound Rebecca made. Every rustle of her skirts, every time she licked her lips, every beat of her heart. With her emotions so clear on her face, if Emily listened hard enough she thought she might hear every thought that crossed her mind.

She was privileged to witness such a private performance. It would have annoyed her from anyone else, as it was improper theatre behavior. And yet from Rebecca, earnest and sweet and open, such heartfelt actions touched her.

Emily slid her foot over until it pressed against Rebecca's underneath their skirts. She was rewarded by a wide grin when she turned.

"This is glorious." Rebecca sat back in her seat and gazed into Emily's eyes. "Captivating."

A shiver ran up her spine.

"Few others seem to think so, judging from the inattentiveness of the audience." Avenbury stood, yawning. "I can't blame them. I like Shakespeare well enough, but I am in no humor for a tragedy tonight."

"Your presence is tragedy enough," Danfield muttered.

Emily lowered her gaze. Danfield had explained brusquely in the carriage that his grandmother had insisted on the four of them attending the theatre together. Emily understood the intent well enough. The dowager wanted them to present a unified front to anyone who perused their box, and indeed they were being well examined tonight. The glare from so many quizzing glasses pointed in their direction was almost dizzying as the glass and jewels caught under the lights.

She pressed her foot harder against Rebecca's and shifted in her seat so that their thighs touched. The heat of her leg through her silk dress was comforting. Emily wished for nothing more than to nestle against her and rest her head against her shoulder.

But she was trapped. On her other side, Danfield draped his arm along the back of her seat, and his gloved hand was perilously close to touching her arm. Even with layers of fabric, she didn't wish to be touched by him. He moved, and his hand brushed Emily's arm.

"Are you cold, Lady Emily?" Danfield asked, his brow creased.

Her shudder had nothing to do with the temperature. "Not at all, my lord. It is quite warm in here."

She must learn to endure intimacy between them. Truly, it was a relief that she felt none of the wild passion for him that she felt for Rebecca. She would guard herself from misery in her marriage, and if he ever had occasion to duel with someone, it would never break her heart.

"Dreadful hot, I should say."

As he spoke with her, he was studying his brother. On Rebecca's side, Avenbury was leaning a hip against the railing at the front of their box. He was talking with his cousins, Lady Elizabeth and Lady Henrietta, both of whom Emily had met and disliked at Vauxhall.

"Would you pass me your lorgnette, my dear Emily?"

Rebecca's voice in her ear was soothing, and her shoulders relaxed. "Of course."

She drew out the lorgnette from her reticule and passed it to Rebecca. As she took it by the mother-of-pearl handle, Rebecca trailed her fingers against Emily's hand. She snapped open the hinge and brought the spectacles to her eyes, scanning the audience.

Was this to be every summer of their future? Emily's skin was aflame with yearning for someone she could never publicly embrace, or claim with any more familiarity that what they experienced right now.

"I am off to fetch refreshments," Danfield announced, and left the box.

Avenbury glowered into the crowd below. "I believe I see an acquaintance of mine. Hetty and Liza, do let us find more entertaining pastures."

Without further ado, Emily and Rebecca were left alone.

"That was so easy that I think next time we ought to orchestrate such a thing ourselves," Rebecca said, closing the lorgnette. "It's much pleasanter without them."

"That may well work in London, but what about when we remove to their estates?" Emily thought about being alone with Danfield, and her heart sank. She had bartered happiness for fortune and security, and she had to console herself with knowing that she had chosen this.

Her father may have paid his dues, but Emily had said yes when asked.

Would being alone in the country be better or worse than sitting beside the woman who plagued her thoughts and her dreams, but could hardly touch?

"I cannot imagine Avenbury will pay any more attention to me at Castle Beaufort than here. But how am I to act?" Rebecca sighed. "I cannot forget that he killed two men, Emily. It weighs on me more with each passing day."

"You must act normally. Our fathers applauded him, and we must honor our mothers and fathers."

"And embrace a murderer? I do not know if I can do it."

"Would you care for the smelling salts now?"

Rebecca pushed her proffered reticule away. "What if they are here tonight?" She stood and gazed into the crowd through the lorgnette again.

"Who?" Emily started. "The ghosts of the men he duelled with? You are thinking too much of Shakespeare. Life is neither *Hamlet* nor *Macbeth*. There are no such apparitions. Not here, nor anywhere."

"Not the ghosts. The *wives*."

Emily sucked in a breath.

"What if the women Avenbury seduced are here? Do you think they are staring at me?" Rebecca leaned further over the railing, her hand twisting the cameo hanging from a thin black ribbon at her throat, her face pale but determined. "Do they think I measure up to his usual affairs? Or are they laughing at me where I stand?"

"Do not forget that you are to be his wife, so their opinions do not matter. You must cease this train of thought. It will get you nowhere."

"I am in need of a distraction if I am to banish these thoughts."

"Oh?"

Rebecca sat beside her again. "Your lips," she breathed. "I could think of nothing else when we kissed. If we tried it again, perhaps I might earn a respite from my worries."

"We cannot kiss here!" Emily jerked away from her. The ducal gallery had been daring enough, but in public! At the theatre!

"Perhaps our lips cannot touch, but I can kiss you with my fingertips. If I may modify the great bard's words—oh, then, dear saint, let *hands* do what *lips* do."

Rebecca leaned closer to her, and Emily closed her eyes. What sweetness this moment held. How had every sense sprung to life? The velvet on her chair was soft and plush beneath her thighs, the lights were bright and hot against her eyelids, and the scent of oranges wafted up from the pit where the masses devoured them.

Everything felt fresh and novel tonight.

Rebecca touched a finger to Emily's back. It was hardly more pressure than a breath against her skin, but her heart began to pound as Rebecca traced a line between her shoulder blades and dipped the tip of her finger beneath the lace at the edge of her gown. Her touch was gentle but undeniably seductive.

It marked her.

It claimed her.

It was so intimate and private that she felt naked here in her seat. She would have willingly pulled down her gown for Rebecca's exploration to continue, if they had been anywhere else.

"There are so many people watching," Emily whispered.

"They may watch what they like. What do you think they see? A woman touching her friend's shoulder as they gossip?"

But it was more than a touch. And they were more than friends. And these heated words were nothing like gossip.

"Let me hold your hand, Emily. Only we shall know that it is a holy palmer's kiss."

Rebecca took her hand and pressed their palms together. An ache, rooted in the space between her thighs, grew loud and relentless inside her as Rebecca threaded her fingers through Emily's and then squeezed her hand. Their fingers slid against each other in a shockingly intimate rhythm as Emily ground the heel of her hand against Rebecca's palm. The kidskin leather of their gloves was so thin that their hands could have been bare, the heat between them bringing a flush to Emily's face.

How could a touch feel so much like scandal?

"Perhaps we will never be free of each other," Emily said, looking away. It was unbearable, and yet she wanted more and more.

"Who could wish to be free of such sweet torment?"

"We are to be married."

They fell silent, staring ahead of them instead of at each other, their hands still joined.

"But even though it might be wrong, or it might be folly—it might be a thousand things that I cannot even begin to comprehend, or to say—I want to see you." Emily swallowed. "I want more than this."

She clutched Rebecca's hand tighter as if she could save her, and the ache began to pound as their fingers tangled together again.

"You know where my family lives. You may call upon me anytime." Rebecca's eyes sparkled.

"That is different than seeing you alone."

"We are not alone here." She moved her thumb against Emily's palm and then pressed it against her wrist where her pulse fluttered.

"But here, we can pretend."

Oh, she could pretend a thousand different scenarios than the one that she had freely chosen for herself.

If only she had been brave enough to have waited before she agreed to wed.

But how could she have known that there was anything like this worth waiting for?

Instead, Emily sat under the avid stare of a hundred eyes, in a theatre decorated for enjoyment on a beautiful summer evening, next to the warm and inviting embodiment of forbidden female passion.

CHAPTER SEVENTEEN

Rebecca's brothers were waiting for her when she returned home from the Theatre Royal. Avenbury had escorted her in his carriage, in the company of his cousins. Lady Henrietta and Lady Elizabeth were chaperones in name only, given how little they cast their eyes over her all evening. She could have flirted with a dozen men without their noticing, and who knew what else she could have done with Emily before the barest suspicion of bad behavior arose?

She didn't want to think of a future without chaperones. The idea of jostling in silence after an evening's entertainment with no other company save for sarcastic and taciturn Avenbury shriveled her soul. What manner of man was he truly?

Henry was lighting a cigar as she took her shawl from her shoulders.

"What are you doing that for?" Marvin batted at his arm. "The smell will wake up Mother. You know she cannot abide cigar smoke."

He rolled his eyes and jostled him back. "Let's take this outside, then."

"I bid you good night," Rebecca said, and started up the stairs.

Her head was filled with thoughts of Emily, and she wanted nothing more than to pore over her memories of tonight, sifting through each touch and every word as she gazed at the starlight from her bedchamber window.

"Wait." Marvin grabbed her hand. "We stayed in so we could talk to you."

"We could have been anywhere else tonight," agreed Henry. "Could have gone dancing."

"Could have gone to Vauxhall."

"Or elbowed our way into a gaming hell."

"You could have accompanied me to the theatre and said your piece there." But Rebecca followed them to the back garden.

The grass was damp with dew, so she stayed on the pavestones until she came to the drawing room window. She perched on the windowsill ledge and propped her feet on a sturdy stone flowerpot to prevent her slippers from getting wet. The glass was cold against her back, and she wished she had kept her shawl. Her brothers wrestled for the bench beneath the birch tree, with Henry winning the bout and Marvin pacing the grass with his hands shoved in his pockets. Henry puffed on his cigar, and after a minute, lit one for Marvin, too. Rebecca waved the smoke away from her face.

Rebecca was brought back to her schoolgirl days in Montreal, when her brothers, newly grown into adulthood, regaled her with stories. She would laugh at their exploits as they boasted of the music halls and the eating establishments, the gambling and drinking and a dozen romantic entanglements that went awry, as none of her brothers were ever lucky in love.

"You say that," Arthur, her eldest brother, had told her once, "but you don't understand. We are very lucky in love. *Very.*"

Henry guffawed. "We don't keep love for long, is all. A night or two suffices."

Maybe she too wasn't meant to keep love for long. Was that why she had tumbled in and out of it so often?

Maybe this experience with Emily was not so unlike her past, even though this fever ran deeper than ever before.

"So why did you not come to the theatre tonight?" she asked.

"That's why you're marrying, remember? Someone else can take you to the godforsaken theatre now and listen to actors mumbling their way half-drunk through their soliloquies."

"I do not recall such poor performance at any play you brought me to." She glared at him. "These are respectable actors, performing for respectable people."

"Are they though?"

"Respectable people, we mean."

"Of course they are. I was there with Avenbury and chaperoned by his cousins. Lady Emily and Lord Danfield were there too. It was a family affair. My new family."

"That's who we meant when we questioned their respectability," Henry said.

Marvin frowned. "Don't forget we will always be your family."

"We were here first. And if it comes to it, we'll be here last, too."

Rebecca narrowed her eyes. "What is that supposed to mean?"

"Father told us about the dinner last week. The duels and the women and whatnot."

Rebecca felt a mild panic whenever anyone spoke about that dinner. There was so much that had happened that was altogether private.

"Dashed shame about that old bird wanting to break up your engagement."

"But is it though?" Henry puffed on his cigar. "Would it be such a bad thing?"

Rebecca could hardly comprehend him. "Father would duel with me himself if I tried to cry off. This business deal is everything to him."

"Business does all right though, doesn't it? And we're here now and getting on fine. I don't know that we need a duke in the hand, and all that."

"Seems like we could get a decent business going on our own. I've been to all the bank meetings. I've met some of the lords. I don't know that any of them would turn their nose up at a good gin."

"The duchy would like nothing better," Rebecca said. "The whole family wants me to break the engagement." She was no longer certain if it was a warning or a threat.

"What does Avenbury want?"

"I don't know. I heard only his grandmother's words," Rebecca said slowly. "His own behavior is a mystery."

"What do *you* want?"

No one had really asked her that. Or she supposed if they had, she had been too intent on insisting that she was in love, and so was Avenbury.

"I want to be happy," she said, laughing a little. "I know that may be a foolish wish."

"Nothing foolish about it. Would a cigar make you happy?" Henry offered one to her. "Not that it's ladylike, but you're still some weeks off from being a proper marchioness. We won't tell anyone."

She smiled and shook her head. "I leave that to you gentlemen."

"Gentlemen!" Marvin rose and ruffled her hair, almost dislodging her from her perch on the windowsill. "Gentlemen! Here in this garden, we're your brothers, and don't forget it."

"We aren't too gentlemanly to forget how to protect our family."

"Our manners aren't as nice as some of the gents you see here."

Maybe she didn't need her shawl after all, for a curious warmth stole across her heart with the scent of smoke and flowers and the laughter of her brothers. They may be in a different country, but this was as familiar as life itself.

How could she ruin their dreams? They thought they understood how to bring business to the nobility because they knew that their product was one of the best. But having rubbed elbows with enough lords and ladies, Rebecca knew better.

The real power and the real money, the ranks of which the dowager was trying to forbid her entry, were a different breed altogether. There was a realm of fabulous wealth, guarded jealously by rules and customs that maybe none of them could ever understand.

But she understood one thing.

Their pride would not allow them to survive if she did anything to embarrass them. It didn't matter that they *wanted* her to cry off. The minute she did, they would squash her family's business without a second thought, and all the expense—passage on the ship, their wardrobes, the house, the time they were investing, the warehouse her father was leasing—all of it would be a waste.

And that would be Rebecca's fault.

This was far worse than kissing a girl in Montreal and being hurried away to New York. Her parents would be so furious this time that they might well cast her off entirely.

She laughed. "I love my marquess."

If she repeated it, one day it might come true.

She waved at her brothers and skipped into the house and up the stairs to dream of Emily.

When the banns were cried, Emily wondered how much attention she would draw to herself if she burst into tears. Would the wide brim of her bonnet cover any wetness on her face? She managed to restrain herself by clutching her hands into fists and staring ahead at nothing in particular. This moment would pass, and the next one might come easier.

An illicit thrill ran through her at the sound of her name and Rebecca's in the same sentence, although of course they were linked forever now to Lord Danfield and the Marquess of Avenbury. In four short weeks, she and Rebecca would stand at the front of St. George's, facing away from each other and toward the men in their lives. It would be exactly as Emily had dreamed at the beginning of the Season.

But now, it all felt horribly wrong.

The next day at breakfast, Papa was talkative. "Danfield is as decent as they come. But if you ask me, he could take a lesson from his brother. Defending one's honor is one of the best things a man can do. It speaks well of a man's character in my eyes."

Lady Calloway darted a look at Emily and then patted Papa's hand. "You are right to value honor. But I would say that Danfield is as calm and good-natured as any young woman could ask for. He will not go looking for trouble with pistols at dawn."

"Forget I said anything," he boomed, his face softening as he looked closer at Emily. "My wife is right, as she always is. Danfield will provide for you. Do not forget the family you are marrying into!"

Almost royalty." He puffed out his chest. "My daughter, marrying the younger son of a duke."

His pride made her misery more acute. How could he be so happy when she was so distraught?

She stared at her plate. "I forgot that I have ordered the carriage," she lied. "I must collect my reticule and be gone."

The carriage was a great expense, and she ought not be taking it for frivolous purposes, especially when she had no purpose at all beyond a wish to leave the house.

The idea of setting up one's house was the great draw of marriage. Doing so on behalf of a husband became less appealing by the day, but Emily's dreams of leaving had started the day that Papa had married Lady Calloway.

Her maid sat in silence across from her as the carriage trundled through London. As there was no point to the excursion, there was equally little pleasure in it. She had exchanged staring at the ceiling for staring out a small window at the multitude of Londoners going about their lives, heedless of her observation. Children shrieked in the street and people plied their trades from market stalls amid the endless clopping of horse hooves on cobblestones.

What did it matter to any of them who she was? She wanted to be a good daughter, a successful debutante, and a worthy bride. The people through the window might see her carriage and think a fine enough lady sat inside of it, but the people who scrutinized her in society were more rigorous in their examination. At any moment, they could find her lacking in any indiscernible way.

Judgment could come from any corner. Lord Danfield. The dowager duchess. Papa. Lady Jersey. Society was filled with eyes and people who had nothing more important in their lives than the leisure to observe.

And yet was she not the same woman, whether she was in her carriage in a simple day dress with her hair in braids, or when she was wearing hoop skirts at court and curtsying to the queen?

She had thought the façade that she had donned at the start of the Season would become second nature to her the longer that she lived in the role. But instead, it was starting to feel like a costume at a fancy dress party, and the cost was more than the price of clothes.

Her very skin felt too tight sometimes, as if she were a moth about to be born anew from the caterpillar's mortal coil. But if she were a moth, her fate was to be drawn to Rebecca's dancing flame.

Her breathing slowed.

Emily knew where Rebecca lived. Hadn't she invited her to call when they had been at the theatre? Her palm tingled with the memory of Rebecca's hand pressing into it, her wandering fingers as wanton as her thoughts.

She rapped on the roof of the carriage and gave Rebecca's address to the coachman.

The Tremblays did not stand on ceremony, for she was admitted to the house as soon as she arrived, and shepherded to a small but charming drawing room.

When Rebecca entered the parlor, it was like feeling the first raindrop after a long drought.

This was what peace felt like.

Emily's mind was clear and empty, her heart beat strong and free.

Should she not embrace the magic that worked its way around them and accept that Rebecca was her lodestone? Why did she need to question this longing to understand this mystery?

"What a wonderful surprise," Rebecca said, settling herself onto the sofa beside her. Emily's breath caught in her throat at the touch of her body against her own, hip to hip. "I am delighted to see you in our humble abode."

"I hope I am not interrupting. I know it is an unfashionable hour."

"We can set our own fashion, meant for an audience of two."

"An exclusive contrivance."

Emily allowed herself to sink into the sofa. Rebecca's eyes were warm and mischievous, and her wide smile was irresistible. Emily leaned forward.

"Ah! Lady Emily! A proper lady paying us a call. We're honored."

Emily jerked back. She had met Rebecca's brothers briefly before but was surprised anew at their exuberance as they entered the drawing room.

"We're glad you'll be there for Rebecca when she marries the Marquess of Avenbury. It's good to have a friend wherever one goes, and she'll need it."

"And what do I need it for?"

"Are you or are you not subject to comportment lessons?" Mr. Henry Tremblay laughed. "I doubt Lady Emily here needs to be told how to hold a teacup."

"I know how to hold a teacup," Rebecca fairly growled.

"Perhaps you do, but you are as liable to break it over a fellow's head as to sip from it."

"That's a falsehood if I ever heard one," Emily declared, her eyes narrowed. "No one would bother to waste a teacup on you when it's clear that only an anvil would fell such a thick head."

There was a silence, and then the brothers guffawed. "Danfield is a lucky man to nab you!"

"I consider myself fortunate to align myself with the ducal family, and even more so to have earned as valuable a friend as your sister."

Rebecca gazed at her with shining eyes.

"I am here to collect my dear Rebecca." She fixed her eyes on Rebecca's and tried to sound severe, but it was difficult when such joy was straining against her composure. "Or have you forgotten that you promised to accompany me at half two?"

"I did forget," Rebecca murmured, her lips twitching at the lie. "Please allow me to change my dress and I shall return in a blink."

After Rebecca left the room, there was a shift that Emily almost attributed to the weather, but she could see from the window that the skies remained blue instead of cloudy gray.

Neither brother was smiling anymore.

Mr. Marvin Tremblay eyed her with suspicion. "You need to look out for her, Lady Emily."

"Your sister is a capable woman."

"You have known her for long enough to take her measure. Our sister cries at rainbows and befriends anyone who looks at her and falls in love in less time than it takes to blink."

"She has been in love before?" Emily was quiet for a minute.

"All the time! Seems to only take a dance or a kind word before she loses her heart."

"She could be taken advantage of at any turn. Why, what if she meets with a lady's relief society and promises away her fortune to them once she's a marchioness?" Mr. Henry Tremblay pummelled his fist into his palm, his face drawn with worry.

"She's a soft touch. It's just the type of thing she would do!"

"You speak of finances, but is that not for Avenbury to guide her?"

"Ah, he won't be too concerned. You're sensible and responsible. You'll look out for her, won't you?"

"We can trust you? Or can we not?"

Emily looked up at the broad-shouldered men with Rebecca's brown eyes but none of her softness or her sweetness. What would they think of her if they knew why she was really here? She was yearning to kiss their sister, to dissolve herself into her essence, to commit adultery of the heart if not in the eyes of the law. Emily was here because her heart pulsed for Rebecca and because she dreamt of cleaving to her.

It was far from sensible, or responsible, or respectable.

She sat in silence, unable to articulate any of the truth.

"We *can* trust you?" Mr. Marvin Tremblay sounded almost menacing.

Emily forced herself to smile. "Your sister is perfectly safe with me."

That, at least, was the truth. Emily would not allow her to be harmed.

"Because we know what our sister is." The brothers exchanged looks, which left Emily confused.

"She doesn't *know* we know. But we know."

Mr. Marvin Tremblay sat beside her and looked in her eyes. "Do *you* know?"

Emily did not know how to reply. "An heiress?"

"Hmmm. She doesn't know," Mr. Henry Tremblay said to his brother. "This is a bit murky."

"Know *what*?" Emily could not fathom the direction of their conversation.

"I'm ready!" Rebecca said brightly.

Emily was grateful to escape the interrogation.

"You are awfully quiet," Rebecca said to her in the carriage. "Is there a problem? Is that why you appeared with no reason at my doorstep and pretended we had a prior engagement?"

The whole problem was that they had prior engagements, but Emily didn't say it. "I was having a difficult day…and I thought seeing you would make it better."

The smile Rebecca gave her proved that her suspicions had been correct. Rebecca had the power to chase away her doldrums and replace them with simple joy.

"Where are we going?" Rebecca asked.

"Anywhere you like."

Emily knew she would be happy, as long as she was by her side.

Chapter Eighteen

"The British Museum," Emily repeated, after Rebecca gave the address to the driver.

Rebecca grinned. It was wonderful to have a carriage at her convenience and a friend who gave her carte blanche to choose their destination. "I expect you have already been before, but I do hope you don't mind. I have scarcely had time to examine the sculpture gardens and the library. There are a great many things I long to see!"

With Henry as her escort, she had only ever managed to coax a half hour from him before he crammed his hat on his head and insisted that they depart for more interesting sights than marble and stone and swirls of paint.

"It will all be new to me. I have never stepped foot in it."

"You, who have lived in England all your life, have never paid pilgrimage to this shining monument to nature and mankind?"

Rebecca had known that they were not perfectly alike, but this gave her pause.

"Before you wield your power as a future marchioness to lock me up in the Tower, I beg of you to please have mercy on me."

Rebecca laughed. "I promise I will exercise clemency."

"It reminds me of Northelm Manor," Emily remarked as they walked up the sprawling staircase to the second floor, where they were told the fossils and curiosities were kept. Her maid trailed behind them. "But I suppose that is apt. It was a duke's mansion before it was a museum."

Rebecca ran her hand along the railing, carved with painstaking detail. The hallway featured soaring ceilings, beautiful molding around the doorway, magnificent marble columns with ornate carved tops—and there were still greater rooms ahead. "Do you think someday I would be able to convince Avenbury to sell the manor and transform it into a tribute to knowledge, instead of a shrine to the family?"

"With such blasphemy, now it is you in danger of being hauled off to the Tower of London."

Glass cases lined the walls, filled with every wonder. Rebecca rushed from one novelty to the next, while Emily studied each placard and explained the details to Rebecca once she caught up to her.

The first room was filled mostly with fossils and bones and animals. Rebecca was delighted to discover coral samples from the ocean she had crossed and examine shells from faraway beaches.

"I have never seen coral outside of my jewelry box," she said, peering at the pale orange spikes and protuberances in the box in front of her. Their form was fascinating. It was undulating and mysterious, with edges that looked to be hard as stone. "Some of these fragments look almost like honeycomb, and others look like little trees."

Emily checked the card attached to the case. "It says here that coral can cure poison. How intriguing. My mother always told me it was good luck. I have several pieces from her. Two hair pins set in gold, and a beaded necklace." She fell silent, her chest rising and falling beneath the thin fichu tucked into her bodice.

"Have they brought you luck?"

"I do not recall. I put them away when she died." Emily turned away from the coral and crossed the room.

Rebecca hurried after her. "Wearing them in her memory may bring you peace."

"I think it would." Emily blinked, and her breathing slowed. "I should wear them again and take note if luck follows me."

"You seem to have trouble with the past," Rebecca said, studying her as if Emily herself was under glass. "Sometimes I wonder if you are scared of the present."

"Whatever do you mean?" Her tone was short.

"I do not mean to offend you. But you do not always look like you are paying attention to your surroundings. And whenever you are faced with difficulty, your first thought is to turn to your smelling salts."

"I use them to clear my head." She scowled. "Besides, here I am surrounded by nothing but the past, which I think disproves your argument that I do not think of it."

"What are you thinking about right now?"

"We are in a museum, are we not? Paintings." She gestured vaguely. "Art."

Rebecca gazed at her. "We are looking at coral and *fossils*."

Emily bit her lip. "I was wondering which gown I have not worn yet to Almack's. The duchess will be in attendance tomorrow."

"If you are not enjoying yourself, we can depart right now."

Rebecca wanted to give her each moment of pleasure and entertainment as it unfurled like a flower in bloom. She wanted to breathe the same air and to share the same experiences. She would follow Emily anywhere, at the merest crook of her finger.

She didn't want to examine the depth of such emotion.

"But I do enjoy being with you." Emily lowered her lashes and looked away, gripping her reticule. "These times with you have been the best part of my time in London. But there is so much to do, and I am always so busy." She sighed and met Rebecca's eyes. There were lines set deep around her mouth, and she straightened her shoulders. "The truth is that I always need to be prepared for what comes next. Since Mama died, and Papa remarried straightaway, I cannot trust anyone but myself. I must remain vigilant to the next moment, and the next, until I have sailed safely through them all."

"But for what purpose are you are living through any of them if you are always in anticipation of the next? You are grasping at stars but paying no mind to the beauty of the sky around you. Once you get anywhere, there will always be something else to chase."

Rebecca moved to the edge of the room and sat down, then patted the bench beside her. "Come, rest with me awhile."

Emily hesitated a moment before she followed, settling her reticule to one side as she sat with an inch to spare between them.

"Think of me, and listen to me," Rebecca murmured and was encouraged when Emily closed her eyes and tipped her head back. "You do not need to concern yourself about anything beyond our time together right now."

Rebecca wanted to remove each worry from her mind and to kiss the reminder of them from her brow. If she could give Emily one afternoon of peace, she thought she would truly know what happiness was.

❖

"Breathe deeply."

Rebecca's voice was quiet but commanding, and Emily wanted to do whatever she instructed. She pressed her back against the wall, the plaster cool beneath the muslin of her day dress.

"It smells musty. Like old books." Emily sniffed again. "This room could benefit from a thorough dusting."

Rebecca laughed. "What else do you smell?"

The almond scent you use in your hair. The violet perfume you applied to your neck. I wonder if you dabbed it anywhere else on your body. Emily could never say such things. Her eyes were closed tight, but she knew people still roamed the room. She heard taffeta skirts swish as ladies walked by them, and the creak of the wooden floorboards beneath the men's leather boots. Although she felt alone with Rebecca, she knew they were far from private.

She focused again on the air, letting it fill her lungs. "I smell crisp linen and old paper."

"What do you feel?"

This was easy. "The padding on this bench could be thicker. It is not uncomfortable, but it does not invite a lengthy stay." She shifted, but it was to press herself closer against Rebecca. She heard her giggle, and she lowered her voice. "I would be most pleased to have a longer stay on a softer surface with you."

The illusion of privacy invited confessions to spill from her lips.

She yearned, she wanted, she *craved*.

The spell could be broken in a moment by opening her eyes to the bright reality of the museum, but Emily was surprised by how much she wished to linger here in a secret world with Rebecca, with her voice as her guide.

"What do you feel when you think of what you saw in this room?"

Pain echoed through her heart as she remembered the orange coral, the exact color of the beads in her hairpins. Mama's laughing face flitted across her mind. Emily commanded the memory to stay, at least for one more instant so that she could stare at her brown eyes and blond hair, to remember the warmth of her arms around her. She could almost smell the roses that she would bring into the parlor by the armful on sunny afternoons.

"I feel happy," Emily whispered.

Tears welled against her closed eyelids. She was so full that she might burst, struggling to breathe, but she didn't want the smelling salts. She wanted to *remember*. Her mama could always be with her, and her grandfather and her grandmother too, if she pushed through the pain of remembrance and thought of its joys instead. There were so many years to look back on, bright and wonderful, and she could access them at any time.

She did not need to forget the past and its pain, only to worry of a future that may never unfold the way she planned.

The past was a gift, and she could reopen its wrappings any time she chose.

Emily opened her eyes. "Thank you."

"Every minute with you brings me happiness," Rebecca told her, squeezing her hand.

"You have an astonishing optimism," Emily said. "You are so confident. So certain of happiness. I doubt everything."

Rebecca's eyes were shadowed. "Happiness is something I can possess without fear of it being stolen from me. It costs my family nothing, and yet to hear them complain about me, one might think that my moods are expensed to their account. I thought maybe having a cheerful daughter would reconcile my parents to me."

"I worried you had lost your optimism at that awful dinner at the manor. I had never seen you so bereft."

"I admit it suffered a blow the size of a cannonball. But you removed the wreckage from my soul, and brushed aside the debris with your embrace and your kindness."

"Me?"

Rebecca sighed and looked at the painted ceiling. "You have listened to me. You have accepted me for who I am, from our first stroll around a ballroom. You never laughed at me, nor mocked me. You do what you say you will do." She moved away from her on the bench, crossing her arms across her chest. "I cannot rely on many people. My brothers are eternally late and they serve themselves in all things first. My parents consider me an afterthought. My friends at home called upon me when they wanted to be invited to parties through my parents' connections. No one asked after me when I was unwell or out of sorts. No one sought to comfort me when I had been crossed in love. Only you have committed to every engagement we have made. At every turn, you have been there. And you have cared."

"I was angry at first that the dowager had tied our fortunes together, and I regret the words I said to Juliet when you found me speaking with her. I can become frustrated when I do not feel like I am in control of my surroundings." Emily was ashamed of her behavior. How self-righteous she had been! How snobbish and self-indulgent.

"One outburst cannot be weighed against the measure of so many kindnesses."

Emily felt a weight lift from her shoulders. "This is the most meaningful friendship I have ever had."

"Friendship?" Rebecca stilled beside her.

"Friendship," she repeated quietly. It could be no more than this, could it?

Rebecca stood and shook out her skirts. "I would love to see more of the museum now. Perhaps I shall purchase a subscription to a journal on natural philosophy. The Empyreal Fellowship could suggest one to me. Or I could patronize a committee and commission scientific demonstrations myself. I suppose I will have the wealth to do such things."

"You will have all the wealth you could ever dream of. The future is yours, to do with what you will."

But when Emily was in bed that night staring at the ceiling, all she could think of was Rebecca's admission that she had been crossed in love. It matched what her brothers had said to her before they had left for the museum. Had Rebecca loved a man? Or another woman? Had there been more than one? Did such a thing even matter?

Had she liked their kisses as much as she liked Emily's?

The questions gnawed at her, but she pushed them away. Sometimes the past truly should remain in the past, locked and forgotten, where it could do no harm.

For Emily was alarmed at the feelings that overwhelmed her when she was with Rebecca. She recognized the pulse of lust, familiar to her now over recent weeks. But what was this more urgent sensation, throbbing in her chest like an open wound?

Could a woman love another woman?

Such an idea filled her with terror, for love was at the root of danger. Love uprooted lives and passion destroyed peace. She need look no further than Avenbury, dueling with innocent men over his lust for their wives, or her own father, rushing to marry Lady Calloway so soon after Mama had passed.

Love was a power she did not ever wish to yield.

Since Emily's visit to the museum with Rebecca, she tried to be mindful of the present and to enjoy it, for soon enough she would be a bride, and her time would not be her own. She cherished the moments she spent with Rebecca, from sitting side by side at musical performances in the afternoons, to strolling arm in arm around the edge of a ballroom. Each encounter was thrilling, even if they were rarely alone and could not express themselves as they wished.

The temptation of more kisses led her into reckless behavior. At any ball they attended, Emily found an opportunity to pull Rebecca into the retiring room for a passionate embrace, startling whenever she heard footsteps beyond the door. They kissed outside in gardens, shielded by hedgerows and statuary, and once Emily was emboldened by privacy to brush her hand across Rebecca's breast atop her fine muslin frock.

There was never time to explore further than kissing and tasting and touching, though Emily ached for more.

Accompanied by Emily's maid, they attended the Empyreal Fellowship again. Rebecca chose to embrace the mystery and intrigue of the demonstrations, while Emily was surprised at her own impulse to close her eyes to what she thought she knew, and to believe in something else entirely.

Soon after they entered the salon, Emily slipped away from Rebecca to discuss palmistry with an enthusiast who promised that she could divine the future with no more than a few glances at her hand. But when the lady peered at her palm and pronounced that her near future would be an unhappy one, she snatched her hand away and went to sit beside Rebecca to watch a presentation on automatons, held by a Swiss clockmaker who had brought several of his pieces on a tour across England.

One of them was a mechanical bird in an ornate gilded cage, whose movements were so lifelike that Emily was enthralled. Birdsong erupted from its open beak as its head moved from left to right. When it stopped, Emily and Rebecca joined the crowd in thunderous applause, and the clockmaker wound the key at the base of the cage again so that they could watch for a second time.

"It's uncanny," Rebecca breathed. "I know it is nothing more than metal and gold and clockwork, but I have never seen its like."

"To witness something that is not alive, going through the motions of pecking seeds and stretching its wings—it's almost sad to see the mimicry of realism, and to know that such movements are futile." Emily stared at the bird as its movements slowed and its song stopped, and the clockmaker twisted the key yet again.

"It's beautiful to witness such artistry. How marvelous to be so talented to create such a thing! And how lucky we are to see it." Rebecca nudged her arm. "I am glad that we came here today."

"So am I," Emily whispered.

But her heart ached. After their marriages, would it be possible to find time to escape to the salon? No matter how much she tried to embrace these stolen moments with Rebecca, it felt hopeless. It was an illusion of happiness.

Nothing they reached for together could be real.

CHAPTER NINETEEN

The Tremblays were delighted when the Duke and Duchess of Northelm requested them to visit the ancestral seat of Castle Beaufort in Hertfordshire.

"It is a mark of great favor to be invited." Mother adjusted her bonnet half a dozen times after entering the carriage, as if the ducal family could appear before them at any moment instead of awaiting them half a day's journey away.

"Of course we are favored. We are to be family," Rebecca said. It was fatiguing to remind her parents at every turn that her upcoming marriage was facilitating their good fortune. "Lady Emily and her family will be there as well."

Emily had sent her a note the day before. Rebecca had pressed the scrawled missive to her lips before tucking it into the folds of her handkerchief, which held pride of place in her reticule. Her presence would make the visit bearable.

"Good river transportation in that part of England," Father said. "Easy enough to get goods to and from London. I am keen to see the canal on the Lea. If conditions are so favorable, it might be ideal to build another distillery right there. Could be another business venture with the marquess."

Rebecca wished she could have stayed behind in London with her brothers. She was dreading to see the estate where she would spend her future days.

The land itself was all pastoral splendor, lush and luxurious, with an abundance of wild marjoram blooming along the road. From the carriage window, Rebecca saw a village of well-maintained cottages, a beautiful stone church with two spires, and the woods that the dowager had told her was forbidden to enter unless one was of noble Beaufort blood.

She shrank back in her seat as the carriage trundled toward the estate, the walls looming farther above and longer across than she had imagined. The painting that the dowager had shown her in London had given her little indication of its true scale.

Someday it would be her responsibility to maintain what had flourished here for generations, and to offer her own body to produce the next generation to continue the work.

On and on, the dukedom would go, unbroken and inexorable.

Welcomed or not, upon her marriage she would forever belong to these people and to these grounds, until she was laid to rest and turned to dust beneath them.

Such thoughts brought her little comfort.

She hoped Emily was at the estate already. There were but two weeks before they married the brothers. But after the wedding bells had rung, would Rebecca be swept back here alone?

Her throat closed, and she spluttered.

Later in the afternoon, she was instructed to meet the marquess at the front of the estate. Avenbury waited on the steps outside, looking every inch the duke he would one day become, tall and broad-shouldered and casually majestic. His boots shone with gloss, his collar was starched and pressed against his jawline, and his cravat spilled forth like his good fortune. He didn't look at her as she approached him.

"I am to give you a tour of the grounds." He puffed on his cigar and inclined his head an inch in her direction.

"I expect that means that the dowager is in residence and has provided her usual instructions, my lord?"

"Grandmother knows no other way but to dictate, but no. My esteemed parents are here instead."

Rebecca breathed in the clean country air and wrapped her thin wool shawl tightly around her shoulders. She could be cordial. It was in her nature to be curious, and there was ever so much to explore.

If only her heart was not as heavy as an anchor.

She gestured before them. "What a glorious time you must have had here as a young boy, my lord! I see a pond that looks marvelous for fishing. Did you and your brother climb that gnarled oak over by the water?"

The elements were all present to have cultivated an ideal boyhood for a gentleman, except for the horrible conditions within the castle itself. How could he and his twin have thrived on such a lack of love?

"I supposed I was happy enough." His voice was short.

"I would like to see anywhere that had special meaning to you. As your future wife, I ought to know all about you."

If Rebecca knew him better, she could cast aside her doubts about their marriage. She hoped that once upon a time he had been a happy child, laughing and playing and eating too many scones with jam that he had begged from the kitchens. Her heart ached at the thought that it might not have been so.

"You are most persistent."

Rebecca chose to take it as a compliment and tucked her hand in the crook of his elbow. "Thank you. Shall we explore together?"

He did not need to know that she wished it was Emily beside her. Emily would have leaned against her and laughed as Rebecca waved and greeted the sheep in the neighboring field. She would have waited patiently as Rebecca stopped to pluck a cornflower from the side of the path. Instead, Rebecca was the recipient of Avenbury's disinterest as she spoke of her love of apple blossoms and hyacinth and told him of her experiences skating on the frozen ponds at home when she spied the rushing river to the east of the estate.

When they encountered the villagers, a somewhat different man emerged from beneath the cloud of cigar smoke. This Avenbury was every bit as proud as he was in London, expecting to be served in an instant as was his due, but gone was the sarcasm in his voice. People fawned over him, and he greeted them all by name as he brought her to each of the shops along high street.

Rebecca would have even described him as *pleasant* as he purchased an iced current bun for her from the bakery. He insisted that someone buy her a new handkerchief from the general store to catch the icing that dripped from the bun and slipped a sovereign to the girl who rushed to procure it.

"Thank you, my lord." Rebecca took a bite of the best bun she had ever tasted on British shores. This was a promising development.

"He's a good one, my lady," the baker said earnestly, bobbing his head. He was eighty if he was a day, stooped and wrinkled and thin as a rake, and he beamed at Avenbury as if he were his own child. "We are right pleased that he is marrying. And to such a pretty lady, if I might add!"

"You are kind," she told him, and took another bite. "I am sure I shall come here often."

Avenbury pulled a sheath from his leather belt, encasing a blade the length of his forearm. Rebecca froze and almost dropped her pastry. There was no cause *here* for a duel, surely? But a duel could not be held by such a knife? And what shameful cad would duel with an elderly man?

"You always looked out for me, Sam," Avenbury declared, and held out the knife, the handle turned toward the baker. "Do protect me from any footpads who might have followed me from London, will you?"

Sam cackled and grabbed the knife. Rebecca could tell when he pulled it from its sheath that it was worth twice as much as his bakery. "I would do that and more for you, my lord! This is a pretty enough gift for an old man."

"You are a generous man," Rebecca said to Avenbury as they walked away from the village.

"These are my people."

Had she been wrong about him? She wanted to ask about the duels but could not push the questions past her lips. Everyone had their flaws. Was she so perfect that she could judge another?

Could she someday fall in love with such a man?

But how could she even entertain such a notion? The truth was that her heart was locked up and chained to Emily's. The links between them were feather-light and delicate, made up of little more than fancy and unfulfilled yearning, but they bound Rebecca as if they were made of iron.

If she were a man, and Emily belonged to another, would the strength of her feelings be enough to drive her to violence? If Danfield accused Rebecca of trespassing against his property—she shuddered to think of Emily as *property*, but such was to be their fate as wives—would she accept his accusation and meet him at dawn?

God help her, but she did not know.

By the time they returned to Castle Beaufort, Emily had arrived with her family, and Rebecca then knew from the joy that seeped into her bones what her answer would be.

Ready would be her sword, and primed would be her pistols, for Lady Emily Calloway should be hers and hers alone.

Dinner that night was a stilted affair, but Rebecca had never been so pleased for awkward conversation. The previous occasion that the three families had dined together had left explosive revelations seared into her mind. Tonight, her parents pressed the duke for details about the land. Emily's father had little conversation beyond Napoleon and the ongoing war. Whenever a lull fell over the table, Emily's stepmother asked the duchess about the kitchen gardens and preserves and praised the variety of dishes brought out to the table.

Avenbury and Danfield limited their quips, but the glares that they exchanged spoke volumes. Danfield made several remarks about his felicity in marriage that Rebecca thought were meant to goad his brother, and certainly paid Rebecca no compliments.

"I will cherish my bride beyond measure. She is an elegant addition to my household. There are no others who possess her grace." Danfield rocked back in his chair and smirked.

Emily said nothing. Rebecca could tell from the twitch at her lip that she was uncomfortable, and she longed to hold her hand and soothe her.

Avenbury raised his glass. "Remind me to gift you a bottle of Tremblay's finest so that I may toast you on the happy day."

"It will be your happy day, too."

"And one celebratory sip of such fine gin will lead me merrily into my cups." He smiled at Rebecca, with no warmth behind his eyes. "I will be beside myself with joy, darling. And of course my wife's love is not the only riches I will be blessed with."

"Commerce at the table is an unwelcome conversation to the ladies." The Duke of Northelm glowered at his son. "Propriety and decency are the greatest riches of all."

Father, who appeared chagrined at the reminder that perhaps his own conversation about the canal had been unwelcome, started talking to the admiral about naval defenses, and the moment passed.

After dinner had ended and Rebecca had endured the tedium of drawing room discourse and a rubber of whist, after glasses of sherry and tea had been consumed, after she had donned her linen nightgown and lain down on her bed and found that she could not sleep, she pulled on her night wrapper and slipped to the room across the hallway.

"I hoped you would come." Emily's eyes were shining.

Her hair was braided and her face was freshly scrubbed, a towel in her hand as she stood by the wash basin near the window. The breeze fluttered the lace edge of her chemise, the cotton so sheer that Rebecca could see the outline of her body.

Here, she knew that she was welcome.

Rebecca joined her and stared out the window at the shadows in the garden. Someday, somehow, the sprawl outside was destined to be hers. Every passing day brought her further from believing it.

Emily curtsied, the back of her long neck exposed as her braid slipped over her shoulder. "May I be the first to honor the future Marchioness of Avenbury, here in her own abode?" She rose and took Rebecca's hand, pressing kisses between her knuckles and along each finger. "And eventually, Her Grace, the Duchess of Northelm."

"I cannot fathom it."

"You will make a magnificent marchioness and an even better duchess." Emily's eyes were bright. "You are unlike anyone I have ever known."

"I am no better than anyone in this castle."

Rebecca could not believe herself to be *in* a castle, let alone be its future inhabitant. Such a thing was for princes and princesses, not for the daughter of a gin distiller! The dowager had been right to force those lessons on her, knowing that there was not enough time before the wedding.

There would not be enough time even if she practiced for years before she became a duchess.

She was not worthy of the role.

"I don't want to think about the future," Rebecca whispered. "All I want is here, right now. I will find a way to be content later with the rest of my lot in life. Let tonight be for us and for happiness."

Emily cupped her face. "That optimism of yours. It makes me believe that anything is possible."

"I want—I need—"

"What is it? What do you need?" Emily leaned forward, staring into her eyes with an intensity that almost shocked her. "Tell me."

"I need *you*. I need your body on my body. I need to know every inch of you, and I want to honor each part with my lips."

The words were plaintive, even desperate. But God help her, if she could not slake this awful lust, she might well die.

"Is it safe to do such a thing here?"

"I am certain of nothing. But I must *believe*. I cannot promise you anything beyond the fact that I desire you, and I want you more than anything I have ever wanted in my whole life."

"But the weddings—"

"Could anyone blame us for anticipating our wedding night? Enough women do such a thing that only true sticklers would raise a brow."

"I think we are meant to anticipate it with the groom, instead of another bride."

Rebecca's eyes darkened. "Let tonight be our true wedding night."

CHAPTER TWENTY

Emily melted as easily as candlewax, helpless against the intensity in Rebecca's eyes. If she could look forward to enough nights in Rebecca's arms, then maybe she could gather enough joyful memories together to endure the long days of her future as Danfield's bride.

"I promise to honor." Rebecca kissed her cheek. "And to cherish." She pressed her lips against her other cheek. "And to adore."

Her own lips, as yet untouched, ached.

"Is this what you want?" Rebecca breathed, standing so close that their breasts were almost touching.

"I want whatever you can give me. Whatever I can get."

Emily had thought she was well prepared these days for kissing. Surely, after so much practice and a hundred rehearsals in her mind, it had been burned into her senses. But to her shock, it was nothing of the sort.

It was as new and fresh as if it were the first time all over again.

Was this how it would be *every* time? This wildness that clamored in her heart? This frantic flutter of her pulse? There was a sizzle and a spark and a potency that she craved as their lips came together and her mind went blank.

Rebecca's sighs and the press of her body took her away from the castle to another place entirely. A place where Emily could allow herself to be soft, to unbend, to take pleasure for herself.

For it was undeniable that this was pleasure. Emily grasped hold of Rebecca's waist as if she would perish if she let her go. She kissed her with a fervency that almost unnerved her, pressing hard little kisses along her cheek and jaw and collarbone, astonished that she was caressing another woman with such carnal intent.

It was beautiful, and pure, and joyous.

Would it ever be enough?

Emily had not thought much further than kissing. She had thought she could be content with the electric touch of her lips, but she was jolted into speculation. Because there was more to earthly desire than this, was there not?

The extent of her tutelage was a vague instruction to allow a gentleman whatever liberties he desired once they were secure in the confines of marriage.

This was no marriage between herself and Rebecca. And yet there was also no gentleman present, so did such a thing even count as a liberty if it was between women?

Despite what Rebecca had assured her, Emily worried that they were the only women alive who wanted such a thing, let alone actually had *done* such a thing. If they were not the first two women in all of eternity to have kissed with such tender passion, then Emily could have well believed it to be true.

How could anyone have experienced this rush and *not* shouted about it for all to hear? Would she not have heard of such a marvelous thing, if other women that she knew had experienced it?

"Have you done more than kissing?" Emily asked, leaning back.

"No. But I have an active imagination. And in my dreams, I have done things that my waking self would consider most unimaginable."

She swallowed. "Oh? Like what?"

"My waking self has thought of touching you here." Rebecca trailed her hand over Emily's breasts and caressed her nipple, ruched and straining against the cotton of her chemise.

"And your dreaming self?" Emily heard her voice crack.

"My dreams are set rather lower." She brushed her hand gently against the top of Emily's thighs.

"*Oh.*"

"I have given much thought to the palmer's kiss." She cupped Emily's sex in her hand through the cotton. "I think it can have another meaning."

Emily's gasped, then gripped Rebecca's shoulders to steady herself. "The study of Shakespeare is a noble pastime."

"Do let us learn."

Rebecca tugged the chemise down her body, baring her breasts and her belly and her legs. Emily shivered in the breeze.

Rebecca kissed her neck and moved her lips across her collarbone. "I have wanted to kiss that little freckle there for weeks."

Emily slid Rebecca's night rail off, and they stood naked together for the first time. She understood the appeal of sonnets rather better now, for if she had the talent, she could have composed a dozen in praise of Rebecca's body. The curve of her waist invited her fingers to dip into it, and the slope of her shoulder inspired her lips to touch it. Her breasts were full, her nipples tight and jutting upward, and Emily pressed a kiss in the valley between them.

There could be nothing wrong in the pleasure they took from one another. Not when it felt like this. Not when Rebecca worshipped her with her eyes and touched her so reverently that she felt royal.

She was lost in a haze of kisses and caresses and was surprised when she felt the mattress beneath her. They had tumbled onto the bed and she had not even noticed.

Rebecca moved on top of her and slid her hand down her belly. She slipped her fingers against her damp center. "This is the palmer's kiss I have been dreaming of ever since that night at the theatre." She eased a finger inside and ground her palm against her delicate nub.

Emily let out a strangled sound and buried her head against Rebecca's neck, straining against her, aching with need and the press of her palm and the fullness she felt inside. New sensations stole her breath and thundered through her body.

"I want you to feel."

The sheets under her back were fine linen and rumpled as she moved with restless abandon. Rebecca's skin was smooth and warm, and the muscles of her arms were firm as Emily held on tight while she thrust again her.

"I want you to taste."

Rebecca kissed her, deep and hot, her violet perfume in Emily's nose. She tasted of mint and honey, and her skin smelled like rosewater.

"I want you to come apart under my hands."

Emily cried out, twisting her hands in the sheets, her pleasure reaching feverish heights before it broke in a stunning wave.

After she had gathered herself together again, she splayed her hands across Rebecca's lower back, then clasped her bottom. "I want to please you, too." She arched up and kissed her, pressing their hips together.

"Anything you do will please me."

She shifted until their legs were tangled together, and her upper thigh connected with Rebecca's center. Emily tilted upward, and Rebecca shivered. She rocked their bodies together and slid one hand through Rebecca's hair to pull her lips against hers, tasting her again.

She moved her other hand between them and touched Rebecca, softly, then more urgently as her hips bucked, listening to the sounds she made and the way her breath caught and then became shallow.

It didn't take long before she shuddered and collapsed in her arms, gasping.

After a long moment, Rebecca pulled the linen sheet high above their heads. "The air grows so cool here at night."

Emily laughed. "I cannot see you now. We are like foxes, hiding from the hunt in hollow ground."

"To me, it is more like hallowed ground." Rebecca held her hand, linking their fingers together, then raised her hand to her lips and kissed it. "Anywhere with you is sacred."

After some time had passed, Emily sat up and rummaged through her reticule. "I have something for you." She hesitated with her fist clenched around the smooth silver ring before holding it out to Rebecca.

"What is it?" Rebecca plucked the ring from her palm and held it to her eye. "Oh!"

Emily thought of it as a talisman, to protect her and to bind them together. She knew it was silly. She did not believe in such things, and yet being with Rebecca made her believe anything was possible.

She and Rebecca existed, tangled together, and for what ultimate purpose she did not know. Perhaps it was all right not to seek understanding, but to hold tight to this precious time.

"I went to the jeweler before we left London and have carried it with me in case we had a chance for intimacy. I wanted to be ready."

"Of course you did. You like to be prepared."

There was a plait of her hair in the center of the ring behind a thin glass, set with pearls all around it.

"This is the most intimate gift I have received in all my life." Rebecca slid the ring on her finger and held her hand out, admiring it. "It is beautiful."

"Now a part of me can be on you, anytime you wish." She felt bold and daring, reveling in the dancing candlelight. "Now that we have had our wedding night, it is fitting that you wear my ring."

"The ring is meant to come before the wedding."

"I don't care that we have it all backward. I would do it all again, the exact same way."

"You, who cares so much about order?"

Emily kissed her hand. "I only care that we are placed next to each other. Not how we got here. Not what comes next, nor what came before."

Rebecca was delighted when she entered the parlor at breakfast and saw Emily in her pale pink morning dress, sipping tea with Lady Calloway and the admiral. Her feelings were so strong that she could only steal glances at her, afraid that if she looked her fill, her face would reveal every intimacy that they had shared the night before.

Warring with delight was despair.

She nibbled on a piece of toast as Father and Mother spoke to each other about the castle. Although they refrained from mentioning the value of each amenity and innovation, she knew that she would hear no end of their financial speculation during the trip back to London.

If she could have chosen to ready the horses that instant and leave the estate after her perfect night with Emily, she would have been at the stables consulting with the coachman. To play-act for three more days in front of everyone was going to be difficult.

Rebecca traced her finger over Emily's ring, wishing she could stroke her lover's hair instead of gazing at it beneath glass. She wanted to steal each night for them in secret bliss. But the days stretched long before her, as if in penalty for daring to touch another man's betrothed.

Oh, but she would choose such pleasure again and again and again.

"What delights do the day have in store for us?" Lady Calloway asked.

The Duchess of Northelm sipped her tea. "You were so inquisitive about our gardens that I have arranged our housekeeper to take you for a tour."

"How generous! I would very much enjoy such a thing, Your Grace."

"I would love to see more of the estate," Emily said. "The view from my bedchamber window is so charming that I would like nothing more than to walk to the riverside. Perhaps Miss Tremblay would care to join me?"

"What an excellent idea," declared the duchess. "Miss Tremblay, you must familiarize yourself as best you can with the estate. These people may need time to accept you, as we ourselves strive to do. They are good and loyal folk, and you will not be displeased with their manners."

Rebecca nodded. "I will endeavor to be lovable, as per your expectations." At a sharp look from Mother, she added, "Your son squired me around the village yesterday and everyone I met was delightful. This is a most agreeable part of England."

"Agreeable." The duchess smiled. "Yes, our efforts here have resulted in a thriving estate and a growing community, and it is all very…agreeable."

Rebecca's face burned. She had been trying for a tone of neutral pleasure, as the dowager duchess had lectured her time and again to temper her enthusiasm, but clearly, she had erred too far on the side of caution.

After the tea was finished and they had their fill of toast, Emily and Rebecca strolled toward the village, arm in arm. Rebecca wanted to remember forever the angle of the sunlight that dappled through the straw bonnet onto Emily's face and catch the scent of grass and flowers and the faint trace of her perfume in her lungs, and to hear the birds chirping as they did in this moment when she could still lay claim to happiness.

Rebecca's chest ached for all that she would lose in in a fortnight.

"Last night was more than I ever could have dreamed," Emily said. After tossing a glance over her shoulder, she slipped her hand in Rebecca's. "I will cherish the memory."

"I would like to make new memories tonight."

"No matter how often we may find our way to bed together, and I hope it *will* be often, last night will always be special in my heart."

Oh, her heart. Her tumultuous heart, struggling to escape her chest with its frantic rhythm.

"I see you are wearing my ring." Emily's smile was shy.

"It is my treasured possession."

Rebecca supposed people might wonder whose hair was embedded in the ring, but she did not care. *She* would know that it was Emily's. She knew it meant that she was hers.

A woman rushed up to them, straightening her mobcap as she approached. "I hope our future duchess will look kindly on a curate's wife who wishes nothing more than to wish her happy. We are so delighted that you will be the marchioness!"

She curtsied to Emily.

Emily untangled her hand from Rebecca's and gestured to her. "It is my dear friend here who will be your marchioness. May I present to you Miss Rebecca Tremblay?"

"Oh! Begging your pardon, my lady! I saw such elegance and thought—oh, but I assumed so wrongly! I am so sorry."

Of course any onlooker would think Emily, the epitome of an English rose, would be the marquess's bride.

"It is a reasonable error," Rebecca assured her, raising her up from her second curtsy. "Lady Emily does have every grace that one would expect of a future duchess. I am lucky to have her soon as my sister-in-law."

It was cruel fate that such a relationship was all she could ever claim to have.

"You are to marry our dear Lord Danfield! We will look forward to having you visit our village," she said to Lady Emily. "Would you care to—oh, but I *am* being forward today!—would you like to visit our general store? We do not have London's extravagances here, but we would be honored for your patronage."

"It so happens that I have urgent need of a length of ribbon," Emily said. "Do bring us to the shop so that we may spend our pin money wisely."

After they had bought too much ribbon and were each sucking on a twist of candy, they walked toward the river that gurgled at the edge of the village.

"I feel like a sacrificial offering." Rebecca gestured at the fields beside them. "I am here to exchange my fertility for financial gain. How many women before me made the same bargain to possess these hills and valleys?"

There was so much history soaked into these fields and stones, heavy with ancestry and blood and tradition, and rife with ghosts. Rebecca shuddered.

"You think so much of the past, but not enough of the future." There was concern in Emily's eyes. "These coming weeks and months will be terrible for you if you do not prepare yourself."

"What do you mean by that? It is no surprise to me that I do not love Avenbury. My family will gain, and I will have lost, but this is nothing that I am unfamiliar with."

"You fear the future. You live so joyfully that it inspires me." Emily sighed. "When we are together, it is like we are in a container made of glass. It is a beautiful life, fragile and delicate and wondrous for being apart from the world. But these are pockets of time, and you are heedless of their consequences because you will flee before they catch you."

Rebecca sucked on her candy. "I do not always flee."

Emily caught her gaze and held it. "Have you not run away from me each time that things have been complicated? You plunged out of a window when you thought the duke might catch us in his study. You left me on the terrace after our first kiss. You left me at dawn this morning, aching and alone after we experienced bliss that I hardly thought existed. Where will you run after your wedding vows?"

The dowager had told Rebecca that the duke was magistrate of the village, but it appeared that Emily was its chief inquisitor.

"I will have nowhere to run." Rebecca tossed a rock into the river and watched it sink. "The cold bleak truth is that I will be alone here, as isolated as if I were locked in the Tower for my crime of marrying a man I do not love." She looked up at Emily. "And you will be several counties away, in his brother's embrace."

"Never his embrace."

"I know you too well for mistruths. You will never refuse your duty."

"But it is duty only. There will be no tenderness."

The future was a yawning chasm, longer than the river that churned before them.

"If I have tried to hold onto happiness while I still had time to run and catch it, is that such a terrible thing?" Rebecca swayed, fatigue settling into her bones. She sat on the riverbank with her back against an oak tree. She had little enough sleep last night, but more than that, she was exhausted by the weight of expectation that she had been carrying for months. When would she know peace?

"No." Emily sank down beside her.

"I thought my force of will would allow me to love Avenbury and his family. But maybe they are not loveable. Or if they are, it is by their own kind. I am not one of them, and so I cannot love them."

Perhaps Emily would not understand. Emily, who should be the marchioness, beloved already by the Beauforts and the villagers. She swallowed the envy that she would need to learn to live with for the rest of her life.

"Have you lost your optimism at last? Have you given up on love?" Emily's voice was quiet, and she was staring into the river.

"Never," Rebecca whispered. "I will never give up on love."

"Then let that be enough."

But did Emily know that Rebecca loved her? She was far too afraid to break the spell and say the words.

CHAPTER TWENTY-ONE

The Duchess of Northelm presided over the drawing room like a queen. On the table before her was spread a ransom in glittering jewels, from coronets to necklaces to brooches to arm bands. The soft light from the windows gave them a rich warm lustre where they were nestled into the length of purple cloth.

Emily had seen fine jewels before. She had admired plenty of rubies and sapphires and opals adorning the fine ladies of the *bon ton* during the course of the Season, in the ballrooms and the theatres.

But these were of a different caliber.

Rebecca pressed her hand to her mouth. "These are gorgeous! Have you worn all of these, Your Grace? On what occasion would one wear *that*?" She pointed at a three-strand necklace of enormous emeralds. "I would choke if I had such a thing around my neck."

"No, I have not worn everything that the dukedom possesses. You may try, Miss Tremblay, but you would wear yourself ragged in the effort. The fear of being robbed for your riches grows when you wear jewels the size of a goose egg, and keeping a brigade of footmen to escort you everywhere grows tiresome." Her eyes lingered on Rebecca. "Besides, many of them will not suit."

Rebecca cast her eyes downward.

"We are honored that you have seen fit to show them to us," Emily said, trying to draw her attention away from Rebecca.

"It is no favor. This is why we invited you to Castle Beaufort. I decided that you must choose your wedding jewels from the ducal vaults. I will not have anyone at St. George's think that either of you are paupers." She took a deep breath, as if to steady herself. "After all, you will become cherished new members of our family."

Avenbury and Danfield entered the room, arguing in low tones but stopping when they saw their mother.

"We are here as summoned," Danfield announced.

Avenbury peered at the table. "Ah, you have taken the swaddling clothes from the safe. Well, Miss Tremblay, you are to be given leading strings of pearls and diamonds to tie you to the duchy, and eventually you will grow up to earn your very own bonnet sewn of velvet and trimmed with ermine. The coronet shall fit you well at the next coronation, I think."

"I could never," Rebecca protested. "I would not dream of wearing such a thing."

The duchess gazed at her. "You will become comfortable with it. There are many girls who would do a great many things to wear the strawberry leaves."

"I thought we were here to discuss our weddings, and not the future coronation? Prince George may not have such a happy event so near in the future to be planning such a thing today." Danfield leaned over the table. "I think those rubies would suit Lady Emily."

Emily bowed her head in assent. "Every piece is beautiful, my lord. I would be proud to wear any of them by your side."

But it was Rebecca she thought of, standing in the church beside her, reciting her vows. *I promise to honor, and to cherish, and to adore.* The words that Rebecca had spoken to her last night in the sanctity of her bed rang in her ears.

"Diamonds for Lady Emily," the duchess decided. She picked up a thin chain of sparkling jewels, with a half a dozen diamonds clustered on its pendent. "They will be beautiful against her golden hair."

"I would be happy with pearls," announced Rebecca.

Pearls. The symbol of tears. Rebecca clenched her hand into a fist, the pearl-studded ring with Emily's hair visible on her finger, and Emily's heart ached for what they could not have.

"No, Miss Tremblay. You will wear the ruby heirloom."

It was a collar of wrought gold studded with rubies, square-cut diamonds nestled between each one. It was heavy and old-fashioned, and nothing like what would suit Rebecca. But it was undeniably ducal.

"Ah, so I was given the illusion of choice?"

Avenbury laughed. "I wonder that you did not choose it straightaway. It is clearly the most luxurious piece on the table."

"I am not such an expensive woman."

"If you are not now, then you must become one."

"Mother, do let me know if this is the final choice and I will arrange for a diamond tiepin to be made up in London," Danfield said. "We must be a matched pair."

"I don't care what you deck me in." Avenbury picked up a necklace and let it run through his fingers. "Gold is gold, isn't it?"

"We will consult with Northelm. There are more jewels in the safe in his study. Come with me."

The duchess left with her sons.

"How convenient it is that there are no chaperones necessary when two ladies are left alone together. And even more convenient that they have left us with these riches." Rebecca tapped her chin. "Do you suppose we would make it far if we were to stuff our reticules and leave by the back garden?"

"We would be caught before we left the room."

"I wonder if we would be caught if we were to do anything else scandalous in this room."

"Anyone could come in." Emily's argument was half-hearted. Rebecca's eyes held the same longing that Emily felt deep in her bones.

"That is true of most of our encounters. You must simply believe that they will not."

"I did first see your legs in a duke's study," Emily remarked.

Rebecca blinked.

"I saw your bare thigh as you scrambled out the window the night we met."

"Oh! I didn't realize."

"I would rather like to see it again, this time in a duke's drawing room."

"Such a thing could be arranged."

How much more could she take, with secret kisses being their sole respite?

Nothing was far enough, nothing was deep enough, not even when Rebecca's fingers touched her soft center and then filled her.

What was enough, when there was no man to tell them to stop?

Was it when Rebecca's lips replaced her hand and brought Emily near to tears on the settee?

Was it when Emily knelt before Rebecca in reverence, breathing in her essence and tasting her like fine wine?

They did not have the luxury of time, but they made good use of what little amount they could spare.

"Her Grace seemed more taken with you today," Emily remarked as she tidied herself afterward.

"She likes me more than she did, but I am not sure that is saying much."

"She favored you with that ruby necklace. I gathered that it was a mark of great honor."

"I am to be the marchioness. It is nothing more than that. Come now, you do not mean to tell me that you are jealous?"

"I am marrying the younger son. I must accustom myself to thinking I am second best." Emily shoved a pin into her curls. "When I am with you, I can forget the whole world. But our secret life will grow smaller and smaller, until I am forced back into the world with memories for company. Our lives will change soon."

"And then what comes next?" Rebecca asked her. "I mean, after the wedding. You asked me to think of the future, but what do you see in your own?"

Emily's fingers tangled in the strings of her dress as she tightened the gathers on her skirt. "We will be married, and go to balls and soirees, and someday have a child or two."

"And what will you speak of? Will you laugh in the carriage on the way to the ball? Will you tease him with your fan and cajole him for a kiss?"

Emily struggled to imagine it.

"Because I know how it could be. With *us*." Rebecca's eyes were warm. "There is no lifetime long enough for me to tire of talking to you. There are no corners of London that I do not wish to drag you into so that I may tease a kiss from you. You could *never* be second best to me."

The return to London was difficult. As little as Rebecca had wanted to go to Hertfordshire, by the end of the third blissful night in Emily's arms, she could have been persuaded to stay another week or month or year. She would never forget those sweet hours of exploration between the sheets, committing Emily's lips to memory, and discovering every part of her body and learning its rhythm. Now that she had indulged in a taste of true happiness, sleeping alone was a bitter tonic.

The ruby necklace was like shackles awaiting her in two weeks' time. All the way to London, she stared at the ring that Emily had given her. A symbol of promise, of hope. But could their clandestine indiscretions be enough?

She accepted the first invitation she could for the chance to see Emily again.

Rebecca loved taking a turn about the room with Emily, cherishing the opportunity to converse with her in private. She had never been enthralled by another woman's stride before, but the way Emily moved her legs and glided across the wooden floorboards was as graceful as a bird in flight.

The way Emily did *anything* fascinated her.

She relished in the press of Emily's arm and the occasional brush of her hip when Rebecca broke their rhythm as they turned the corners of the room. Emily knew what she was doing and gave her a look, but Rebecca simply grinned in return. This was the most they would see of each other tonight, as Emily was so popular that she always danced every set.

But not yet.

For in the space of this precious perimeter, Emily was still hers.

"You are going to Almack's tomorrow?" Rebecca wished she wouldn't go. She had never been granted a voucher, so it meant she would not see Emily until the day after next.

"I go every Wednesday. You know that."

"Why do you like it so much?"

"It brings me peace. And I do so love to dance."

"I don't love to see you in a man's arms," Rebecca said softly.

"I wish they were your arms. But they cannot be. Society does not change. Its predictability is its beauty. I know where I belong."

But Rebecca thought Emily could belong anywhere. She was more than a perfect debutante, more than an automaton whose movements were preordained. Away from London and from society's hard gaze, Emily shone brighter than the stars.

"I can think of many more satisfying places to be."

"The salon?"

"My bed," Rebecca clarified.

"We cannot live our lives from bed."

"I know. But it's a lovely place to dream, and I like nothing more than dreaming of you."

Emily's smile was her reward, but Rebecca's heart was heavy. She could count the steps from here until they rejoined Emily's stepmother. There was but a quarter of the room before they must part.

"I tire of only catching glimpses of you across the dance floor."

"And yet our main purpose here is to dance." Emily laughed.

It was too much to bear.

"Give me your fan," Rebecca said.

"Whatever for?"

"I am overly warm."

"You do not have one of your own?"

"Yours is larger."

Emily fished it out of her reticule and handed it to her, her brow creased.

The fan was beautiful, painted with wildflowers that matched Emily's pastel blue dress. Its ivory sticks were unblemished. Oh, it was selfish of her, but Rebecca wanted to leave her mark.

She fanned herself and slowed her pace. She had been honest about being warm. The fan stirred much-desired air across her heated cheeks, and it brought Emily's perfume closer to her, so she could pretend that she had touched the oil to her own wrists and anointed her own neck with Emily's essence.

"May I have my fan back now?"

Rebecca flicked her wrist again and enjoyed the breeze. "In a moment."

She picked up the slim pencil that was attached to the guardstick of the fan and studied it.

"Why have we stopped?" Emily tapped her foot. "I must return to Lady Calloway."

Rebecca succumbed to temptation. She gripped the pencil and wrote her name with a bold flourish on the last ivory stick, pressing the lead tip as hard as she could to leave as dark a mark as possible.

Emily gasped. "Whatever are you doing?"

But her voice was delighted, and when Rebecca peeked at her, her eyes were sparkling and her lips were parted in wonder. Emboldened, she wrote her name on the next stick. Then again, and again, and again, until each one bore *Miss Rebecca Tremblay* across it.

Emily took it from her as carefully as if it was more expensive than the ducal heirlooms. "I would accept each and every dance from you. If only I could."

Rebecca took her hand. "If I could hold you in my arms all night, I swear that no one could pry me from you. I would dance with you through supper, I would dance until the servants doused the candles. And then I would dance as the sun rose so I could seize the opportunity to start my day anew with you."

Emily sighed and squeezed her hand. "Oh. That is the most beautiful thing anyone has ever said to me."

"By dancing with no one, will you stay next to me?"

She withdrew her hand and lowered her eyes, but not before Rebecca caught a glimpse of tears. "You know I cannot. I wish I could lose myself in the dream, but we are not alone. Lady Calloway would question me and everyone would see me refusing to dance and it would be so unusual. Danfield expects me to dance with him and his friends. I cannot be so unpredictable."

Emily slipped the fan in her reticule and stepped toward her stepmother, then turned back to Rebecca. "But I promise you that

I will keep this fan forever. And I will never forget the beautiful dream it represents."

Rebecca knew Emily was dutiful. She could have predicted that Emily would react this way. But watching her polite smile as a gentleman wrote his name on a borrowed fan twisted her heart in a way that she had not thought possible.

She told herself that she was grateful to share whatever scraps of time they could find to be together. After all, Rebecca knew Emily truly intimately, and that was worth more than a thousand dances.

She could not bear to think of Danfield soon possessing what she had so reverently worshipped.

She must banish such thoughts before she did something regrettable.

The weddings were a week away, and Emily's head was filled with nothing except thoughts of Rebecca. The way she laughed at things that Emily would never have thought twice about until Rebecca marveled at them. How she rushed into a room, impatient and ready to be delighted by new experiences. The shape of her lips when she smiled, and the change in her eyes when she leaned in for a kiss.

The next seven days would be over before Emily could catch her breath. All she wanted was to pause the flow of time and to steal more of it by Rebecca's side.

But tonight was Almack's, and she knew she would not see her there. Emily sent a note to Rebecca, requesting to spend the afternoon with her. She was willing to return to the British Museum, or anywhere else she might suggest. But she received a note in return with Rebecca's regrets, as she was occupied with her family.

Emily was quiet for the space of half an hour. Differing emotions fought for her attention. Regret at accepting the betrothal, discomfort that her father had paid for its offer. Joy that her fate would soon be twinned with Rebecca's, despair that they would be linked through their husbands and not to each other.

Yearning for a love she could not have.

Love.

She was in want of occupation, if her thoughts were so unruly as to run in such a direction. Emily shook her head clear and picked up her reticule from the chair where she had discarded it the previous night. She emptied the contents on a table near the empty fireplace and moved her lip salve and silver comb to one side, which she would bring with her again tonight in case she had need of them in the retiring room.

Emily hesitated when she saw last night's fans strewn on the table. One had been borrowed from Lady Calloway and was filled with gentlemen's names for each dance. The other was a precious relic that she would revere forever. She spread the fan open and traced her finger across the scrawl of Rebecca's name, each letter so very dear to her. How she had wanted to fling her arms around her last night and kiss her, right there in the ballroom! It had taken every ounce of fortitude that she possessed to turn from her and rejoin her stepmother.

They could hardly find a moment alone for such passion. It would never do to scandalize high society by indulging in a public display, despite how much she wished they could.

She kissed each signature on each piece of ivory, in place of the woman she wished to hold close.

Emily retrieved her keepsake box from under the bed. She creaked open the lid, and the aroma of lavender filled her nose from the linen sachet that she kept tucked among her treasures. There was the fan from her first London ball, the coral hairpins from her mother, and handkerchiefs that she had embroidered with clumsy stitches when she had been a girl. A shiny rock that she had picked up in Bath during her finishing school days rested in one of the corners, though she could no longer recall its significance. There was a pressed rose from the grounds of her father's house in Somerset, its petals faded and crumbling, and a scrap of silk torn from her dress the night she had tumbled out of the duke's study after Rebecca.

She placed the fan in the box. After a moment, Emily retrieved her vial of smelling salts from where it lay on the table with the rest of the contents from last night's reticule. She rubbed her thumb over the worn metal filagree as she had done hundreds of times. The idea of revival had brought her such comfort this Season, and the bracing shock of the salts had steadied her when she had most needed it.

But she relied on them too much, instead of on herself. It was time to put the vial away in the box, to become a memory instead of a crutch.

She then attempted to busy herself at her wardrobe, riffling through her ballgowns in search of what to wear to Almack's, but she did not see any of the beautiful silks and linens and muslins in front of her.

Love was a danger. To entrust one's heart to another opened the path to heartbreak. How would she survive her marriage to Danfield if anything rent her relationship with Rebecca?

It was best to keep their affair friendly, and physical.

It puzzled her still, these feelings and desires that she had for her fellow woman. How could they be strong enough to have changed her life? She had become a different person since meeting Rebecca.

Was such a thing as love even possible between women?

And it if was possible, could there be a cure for this spell that bound her so helplessly in love?

The answers she sought could not be found in her wardrobe, so Emily left the bedchamber. Who in the *bon ton* could she possibly ask? Not Lady Jersey. She could only imagine the look on Lady Calloway's face, even if she asked in the most roundabout manner.

Not even Juliet could be trusted with such a question.

She needed to consult someone with more worldly experience.

CHAPTER TWENTY-TWO

When Emily arrived at the Empyreal Fellowship an hour later, she paid no attention to the lecturer in the parlor. She was here to learn of other things. It was the first time that she had ventured through these doors without Rebecca, and she was astonished at her daring. But she needed to understand her own mind.

And her own heart.

She remembered her introduction to the older gentleman from her first visit to the salon, and found him sitting in an armchair by the window with a pipe and a newspaper. She had her suspicions that he might be able to help her. Had he not said once that there might be questions that he could answer?

"Mr. Boyd! It is good to see you again."

"Ah, Lady Emily. To what do I owe the pleasure of your company?"

"Do you know much about the study of classicism?" she asked brightly, perching herself on the chair opposite to him.

His brows lifted. "I think of myself as an erstwhile scholar, yes. Are you interested in such things?"

She wasn't particularly, but she knew not how to proceed. Could she ask him straightaway what she wanted to know? She fidgeted as her courage shrank. She should never have come here alone! Rebecca would have been happy to investigate such a thing. She had no trouble engaging with anyone about anything.

But she could learn from Rebecca's example, couldn't she?

"Are you wanting to know about something specific, Lady Emily?" Mr. Boyd's face was so kind, and they were in such little danger of being overheard.

"Recent circumstances in my life have me curious about the relationships between man and…well, his fellow man. I thought perhaps the past would be a good place to start to learn about such things."

"I am not so old that I myself was around in the age of antiquities, but I know a few things." He smiled. "We have many writers who attend our humble salon. I am happy to share what little wisdom I have. Are you thinking of writing an article? Could I offer to connect you with a publisher?"

"No, thank you." She struggled to find the right words. "I have more of a personal interest."

"I am all for serving one's personal interests. What is it about history that has captured your fancy? Man has always been at war with other men. One can hardly make things simpler than that as a starting point."

"War holds no fascination for me, sir. We experience far too much of it in the present."

Mr. Boyd eyed her and folded up his newspaper. "Man is also bound to love his fellow man."

"Oh?" Emily feigned indifference, but this was much closer to what she wanted to talk about. She resettled her skirts around her and looked down at the carpet.

"Is that not what the Bible preaches? And besides, do we not have peace between as many nations as we have war between others?"

"That is an excellent point about the general way of things. But I suppose I am wondering about the feelings that an individual man may have for another man."

"Or woman?" he asked gently. "There are many lovely ladies in the world. They do not much interest me in that way, but their charms are undeniable. I have wondered about you and the friend that accompanies you here."

Had Emily been so obvious? Had *Rebecca*? Had she let down her defences because she foolishly felt more comfortable here, away from anyone they knew? She could ill afford such lapses.

"I am sure I do not know what you mean by that," she lied. "I am interested from a purely philosophical perspective."

"There are many of us who claim to be students of such esoteric knowledge, only later to admit that what we want is to understand ourselves. And if that is the goal, may I recommend making an intimate study that requires no books and no lectures, if you can imagine such a direct learning process? In such a way, we may perceive ourselves, and in turn, be perceived."

Emily's face burned. She had indeed studied Rebecca most intimately! And as a result, Rebecca understood her in a way that no one else ever had.

"I do not count myself among such a multitude." Emily paused. "But *are* we speaking of multitudes? Or does there exist a mere handful of such people? I seek to satisfy my intellectual curiosity, of course."

"Multitudes," he confirmed gravely. "Definitely multitudes."

"May I be so bold to ask how you know?"

When Mr. Boyd grinned, the smile spread wide across his face and he looked much younger than his snowy hair belied. "I have made independent studies for many, many years. I have discovered beyond a shadow of a doubt that man indeed loves his fellow man, and in such places as France, Spain, and certainly here in London itself."

Could such a thing be true? But there would be no purpose to him spinning falsehoods.

She lost herself in thought until he spoke again. "Have I satisfied that curiosity of yours?"

"I fear it can never be satisfied," she whispered.

"If you would accept another suggestion from an old man who has wrestled with such things... There is no wisdom better learned than by experience. You are a young woman, Lady Emily. You have many years ahead of you. Chase after knowledge and live through the mistakes you will make along the way. You will be the happier for it."

"I am not certain I should be seeking such wisdom."

"What is the harm in knowing a little more than you do now?"

She thanked him and left the salon, her mind a mess of thoughts on the carriage ride home. Could such experiences be so common? Or was Mr. Boyd so *uncommon* that he was able to attract other uncommon people such as herself into his sphere?

Perhaps it didn't matter.

He had answered her question. Love existed, and love persisted, as unusual as it might be. There was hope that their love could grow and bloom among the thorns of their marriages. Hope would have to be enough.

Emily had thought she was in search of a cure. But if indeed a charm existed to reverse the spell of love, she found she no longer wanted it.

❖

Rebecca was in a beautiful room on Picadilly Street, filled with beautiful fabrics, with one of the best dressmakers in all of London cooing over her as if she were the most beautiful woman in the world.

She knew she wasn't. That title belonged to Emily, with her cascading blond ringlets and sparkling blue eyes and that dear freckle on her collarbone. Oh, if only she were here. It would be far easier to tolerate this with Emily beside her, while she was adorned with expensive trappings that served to bind her closer to the dukedom.

Instead, Mother had accompanied her as she tried on her wedding dress one last time for the hem to be altered. She perused the fashion plates while the dressmaker knelt and plied her needle.

Rebecca sighed and smoothed her hands over the cream silk. She was no more interesting to her parents now than she ever had been, and there was no indication that they would think any differently of her as a marchioness.

"You have nothing to sigh about," Mother said, turning a page.

"Does my happiness matter to you?"

She looked up. "Of course it does. But you are always happy."

"It is an effort to appear happy when one is miserable."

"Is it effort to be handed a king's ransom in clothing? Is it misery to marry a marquess and have every luxury one could imagine? We have very different ideas of labor."

Rebecca tried to rein in her frustration. "I do not claim that my situation is anything close to the workers in the distillery or the docks."

"Then what are you complaining about? You are ungrateful."

"I am not ungrateful!" she cried. "I am sacrificing my happiness for this family, so that the business will thrive. Yet I have received no encouragement from you or Father. You criticize me daily."

Mother dismissed the dressmaker, who bobbed her head and hurried out of the room.

"Are you expecting the Duke of Wellington to present you with a medal of bravery? Marriage is not a sacrifice. It is a blessing. I hope you remember it when you are in that beautiful castle with nothing on your mind besides which champagne to serve for your supper."

"This is not the life that I want."

"Regardless, it is the life that you chose."

Rebecca threw up her hands and stepped from the pedestal. "*Father* chose it. He presented me with the betrothal, and I have tried and tried to be happy to please you both. But there is no pleasing you!"

Mother's lips thinned. "Your father and I have always wanted the best for our only daughter. We have done all we can for you. It is you that failed yourself. If you did not have such *inclinations*!"

"Which inclinations?" Rebecca held her breath. They had never spoken of it.

She thrust aside the fashion plates and strode to the window as if she could not even look at her. "Rebecca, you know what happened in Montreal." There was a long pause, then she whirled around. Her face was white and there was an intensity in her eyes that alarmed her. Her chest was heaving beneath her heavy brocade dress. "You kissed another woman! A *woman*! How could you have done such a thing to this family? Do you know what would have been said about you if anyone had discovered the truth? You are lucky that we had the means to leave the city with no whisper of your shame. And then you rewarded our generosity by tumbling in and out of unwise engagements over the space of half a year. How could you expect that we would trust you with your own future when you clearly did not know your own mind?"

"I knew my mind." Rebecca's voice was low. "I have no regrets about my actions."

"Then do not be upset at your situation, for the consequences of those actions are what brought you here."

Rebecca had always wondered if her mother would be softer to her if she could only explain that the kiss in Montreal had not been about rebellion, but about passion. Here she had the answer, for Mother turned from her before she could speak and summoned the dressmaker again.

She was not interested in Rebecca's experiences as a person.

Anger pricked at her heart like dozens of the dressmaker's pins. Why had she denied herself and worked so hard for her parents' love and approval when it could never be earned? Why was she continuing this sham of an engagement that no one else wanted?

She did not wish to marry Avenbury. He was disinterested in the prospect of marrying her, using her instead as a pawn to goad his father. Not one member of his family had a kind thing to say to her.

What was the point of this wedding?

She plucked at her dress, wanting more room to breathe, but the dressmaker tugged it down again with a frown.

Mother snapped her fingers. "Dry your eyes, Rebecca. Here are the boys with the carriage. We must be gone."

Rebecca's distress must have been evident during the drive home, because after they entered the house, her brothers ushered her straight into the garden.

Marvin scanned her face. "What's the meaning of all these tears? Will you miss us so much when you become a marchioness?"

Rebecca did not wish to talk. "I am unwell. Let me go to my room, please."

"I'll fetch you a tincture as soon as you tell us what ails you."

"You're unsteady on your feet. Sit down." Henry tugged her onto the bench.

Rebecca collapsed as if she were a pile of discarded linens. Her bones had no strength, her muscles were weak. She curled up against the hard metal, the slats pressing into her cheek, and wiped at her eyes. "There is nothing to be done."

"There's always something to be done," said Henry. He flexed his arm. "I've had my share of bruises to prove it."

"Is it the marquess? Has he upset you?"

"No, of course not." She hiccupped.

Marvin glowered. "We know where his club is. We can get the truth from him if not from you."

"He must be used to blokes finding him and issuing a challenge."

Rebecca sat up. "What do you mean? You cannot duel with him. Do be serious!" She paused. "What weapon would you choose?"

"No need for a duel." Marvin exchanged a look with Henry, who nodded. "We want to talk to the man. If you are having last minute wedding worries, then maybe he can ease them."

"We want to be sure he will be good to you."

"And it would be fisticuffs," Henry said, jabbing at the air. "If he is a cad, he deserves a proper thrashing."

"That's not proper at all, no man would accept it. It would be pistols, Becky, never fear." Marvin took imaginary aim at a tree branch. "Aim for the knee, nice and low. None of us want to kill a man."

Rebecca swallowed. They loved her. Her parents would forever find fault with her, and she would need to learn to accept that there would be nothing but disapproval from them—but her brothers loved her.

And she loved them right back.

They were carefree and happy and shrugged off any misadventure that befell them.

This was the life that she wanted, with Emily by her side.

Marvin cracked his knuckles, then beckoned to his brother. "Come on then, let's go find the marquess."

They got to the front door before Henry turned around. "Becky, are you coming?"

She grinned, at last feeling like one of them. "Of course."

It didn't take long to bring the carriage round and to jostle their way through London to Brook's. Marvin rapped on the door and asked a servant to bring out the marquess, if he so pleased, to attend the Tremblays at his leisure.

"I cannot be rude about it," he grumbled to Henry when he jabbed his shoulder. "I'm not forgetting that he's to be a duke."

Avenbury came outside and they hustled him into the carriage.

"We thought it would be best if our chat was private," Marvin said.

"Are you abducting a peer of the realm?" he asked. "Do you mind if I light a cheroot, or will that disrupt your mayhem?"

"Of course we are not abducting you," Rebecca said. "That would be absurd."

"Such a word describes my life very well these past few years, unfortunately."

"We want to know a few things, is all." Henry leaned forward, his elbows on his knees. "Are you going to be a good husband to our sister?"

"I highly doubt it," he drawled.

"Are you going to be a good business partner to my father?" Rebecca asked, her voice small.

He lit the cheroot and took a puff. "For as long as I have need of him. But once I have your dowry, the connection means little to me."

"Are you truly the Murderous Marquess?"

Avenbury gave her a mocking bow as best he could from the confines of his seat. "Imagine what you will."

"None of this is satisfactory." Marvin exchanged looks with Henry. "Sounds fairly damning." He cracked his knuckles again.

Avenbury sighed and gestured with his cheroot. "We could have rubbed along together tolerably well, I think. But I beg of you, Miss Tremblay—cry off, and we can all be done with this melodrama."

Chapter Twenty-three

D id you hear the news, Em? Our Becca has cried off."
Juliet came bustling into Emily's parlor. Her long black hair was loose under her bonnet, as if she had done no more than run a brush through it before hurrying over.

"What did you say?" Emily reeled. She opened her mouth, but no more words came out.

"The Marquess of Avenbury is the catch of the decade, and Rebecca Tremblay cast him aside like a fishwife discarding the offal!" Juliet was more animated than Emily had ever seen her. She sat down across from her, then gripped the arm of the chair to lean over it as she spoke to Emily. "Apparently, she did it last night, right before he attended a private dinner. Everyone was most upset about it. He will lose a good deal of money, after all, and though the family didn't wish to dabble in commerce, they were not disposed to look too unkindly at her fortune."

"How do you know this?" Emily asked slowly.

Was it possible that Rebecca had told Juliet? But then why had Rebecca not told *her*? She had not missed a note from her today, had she? She resolved to hunt down the butler at the earliest opportunity, once her heart had stopped racing and Juliet had departed.

"Oh, you know how gossip makes its rounds far quicker than any could ever guess."

"I cannot imagine the family gossiping about such a thing. Lord Danfield has not come to tell me." Emily shook her head. "You must be mistaken."

"Perhaps he will call on you later. It is still unfashionably early. As to the news being bandied about, perhaps a servant caught wind of it." Juliet averted her eyes.

The scales fell from Emily's own. "*He* told you."

"Who?"

"The Marquess of Avenbury."

Juliet spluttered and almost knocked over the lamp on the table beside her.

Emily sagged back in her chair, her mind swimming. Juliet had insisted on turning down every proposal, and making sure everyone knew of it. She had tried to dissuade Emily from marrying Danfield. She had asked for gossip about Avenbury at each turn.

"You cherish a tendresse for the marquess, don't you?"

"I cannot believe that you are accusing me of such a thing." Juliet sniffed.

"For God's sake, tell me everything! Or are we not friends?"

Were they not indeed? Had it all been a ruse? Juliet had befriended her only after Danfield's attentions had been remarked upon.

Juliet sighed and clasped her hands around her knees. "You are most perceptive. I am glad you have found me out, for I have so longed to tell you!"

"Tell me *what*?"

"We were never so far advanced in our affections to be affianced, but you are right. I harbored hope that he would ask me to his bride. I met my dear Avenbury during my debut Season a few years ago. Oh, it seems an eternity now." There was a soft look in Juliet's eyes that Emily did not recognize. "We danced, and we talked. He has such an acerbic wit! I have never met anyone like him, neither before nor since. As no man can live up to his measure, I have spurned any other attachment."

"You were not engaged?"

"No, but we were near enough. I must admit that I allowed him to write to me."

"To write you letters!" Emily was shocked. To permit such a thing was scandalous with no engagement between them.

"I was brought low by love, Em. I was felled by my own desires. I would never have stooped to such a thing, but he left London at once after the scandal. I could not live without him committing pen to paper and giving me such news as he saw fit for my tender heart."

Emily's mouth was dry. "And what news was that?"

"Avenbury never fought those duels."

She stared at her. "Now you speak nonsense. The accusations against him cannot be false. Why, his own family admitted it to me."

Juliet picked at a loose thread at the seam of the armchair. "They think it was him. I cannot tell you more than this. I cannot. Do not twist my arm, my friend, for you shall not like the answer."

Dread crept into her heart.

Danfield. Oh, *Danfield.*

If Avenbury was innocent…had it been his own twin brother with his pistol on the heath?

"And now that Becca has cried off and the field is clear, I can once more see myself as dear Avenbury's bride! It does not matter that he will lose her fortune, for he will gain mine." Her eyes were bright. "And you and I shall be the very best of sisters-in-law."

"I must go."

Emily didn't want the smelling salts that she had locked away in her keepsake box, even though her lips were numb and her ears were ringing. What she needed was Rebecca. How fast could she call the carriage and be by her side?

"Wait! Are you not happy for me?" Juliet's face was shining. "Finally, I have the chance to get everything I ever wanted."

"I wish you well as the new luckiest girl in London. May you enjoy it more than I ever did."

❖

Emily rushed through Rebecca's house after a confrontation with the Tremblay brothers, who eventually relented and told her that Rebecca was in the back garden. Rebecca wore a simple white day dress that was cut low on the shoulder with long flowing sleeves, the sheer Swiss dot fluttering around her ankles as she arranged a pile of cut flowers into a vase. She looked up when Emily strode up to her.

"Why did you do it?"

Rebecca put down a rose. Her face was sober, her eyes clear. "I did it because I love you."

"But I cannot do this without you!" Emily cried. "If you love me, for God's sake, why could you not *marry him*?"

Now she faced decades alone with Danfield, with no Rebecca to embrace her or console her. What would become of her?

"I cannot love you while I am married to another. It is not right."

"Then you will stay in London." Emily sank to the bench, her knees trembling. She could arrange to be in London as often as she needed an escape. Being a perfect bride would surely earn her a respite every now and then, and of course like most of the *ton* she would be in town for the entirety of the Season. Why, she could see Rebecca almost as often as she could wish. *Often* would have to suffice, if she could not have her *always*. Her breath came easier.

"Will you marry Danfield?" Rebecca gazed at her.

"Yes."

"Then I cannot stay in London."

Panic stole her breath again. Emily tried to shake her head clear. "This is absurd. I love you." With trembling hands, she pulled Rebecca down to sit with her. "Is that what you were waiting to hear? I love you. You have my thoughts, my acts, and my very heart. All of it is at your disposal. There is no part of me that can exist without you by my side."

"Then why must you marry?"

She stiffened. "The wedding is next week. Everything is settled with my father. You know I must marry Danfield."

"Danfield is the adulterer." Rebecca said it gently, stroking her thumb over Emily's knuckles. "Avenbury told me."

"Juliet said as much to me," she whispered. "But as long as I do not love him, I do not care what he has done."

"Can you really marry a man you do not respect? Emily, he seduced married women and killed their husbands. And then he said his own brother was the villain. Is this the man that you want to wed?"

"Of course not! But who else will marry me, if I refuse to honor my engagement to Danfield? No one would believe the truth even if I dared reveal it. He is seen as the consummate gentleman. A lady's prerogative only goes so far in the eyes of common sense."

She would lose the social standing that her mother had always wanted for her. She would no longer be welcomed at Almack's. She would be forced to continue living with Papa and Lady Calloway, and to be silent about her beloved Mama.

And yet, Emily was no innocent. Was her desire for adultery any different from Danfield's? Emily shuddered to think that she was anything like him, but she knew that her marriage vows would never keep her from Rebecca's bed.

The difference was that it could not matter to anyone else if she sought pleasure in Rebecca's arms. They harmed no one, as long as her heart was not engaged with her husband's. There would be no duels, no breach of honor if it was another woman that she loved. There was no possibility of children from such a union.

But was she simply excusing her sin?

"Come with me." Rebecca's voice was low.

Rebecca had become a necessity, like tea in the afternoon and church on Sunday. She was open and earnest and more valuable than any coronet. She was the real heirloom, greater than jewels, more valuable than velvets and silks and cloth of gold.

She was simply Rebecca.

The love of her life.

"These feelings are dangerous." Emily had known it her whole life. To love was to be vulnerable, and she felt the truth of it in her cracked and bleeding heart.

"Unfamiliar, perhaps. I would grant you that. But there can be no danger in the way I feel when I look at you."

"When I look at you, my world collapses."

"Then hold on to me and let everything else fall away."

But Emily shrank away. "What if all we ever share together is the shadow of real life? If we go together...we will never have the protection of marriage. How would we live? On what income? In which house? I cannot take such a risk."

"It is not a risk if you love me."

"And what if you fall out of love?" It was her greatest fear. To be forgotten, discarded. To be seen forever as second best, unworthy. Her vision wobbled, and she blinked hard to clear the tears from her eyes.

"I would never do that." She held her hand out. "Look, I still wear your ring on my finger. Is that not proof of my dedication to you?"

"Your brothers told me that you fall in love as easily as anything."

Rebecca's lips tightened. "And you would take their word over mine?"

"Is it true?"

Rebecca stood and paced the length of the garden. "I admit that this was not my first engagement. It was my fourth. None of my betrothals lasted more than a few weeks. I ended each one when I realized that I didn't love any of them. I *couldn't*. And then I thought I loved my friends, beautiful girls who smiled at me and turned my heart to jelly. But now I know it was not love at all, because it pales in comparison to how I feel when I am with you." Her eyes were wide. "Emily, I love you, and only you."

"But what can we have together?" Emily gripped the bench, her head reeling. "If I marry Danfield, we have opportunities ahead of us. We will have my pin money, and protection from scrutiny, and most of all—we will have *time*. Our whole lives are ahead of us to figure out how to make this work. And you want to throw this away?"

"You would rather stay in a loveless marriage and forego the greatest love you may ever know? May luck be with you, Emily. If you marry Danfield, I will not change my mind. I will not stay in London. I will not seek you out." Rebecca's face was white and her eyes were filled with tears.

This time, it was Emily who fled.

She had nothing left to grasp on to. Not her silver filigreed vial. And not Rebecca.

Chapter Twenty-four

Rebecca's toast was wet with tears each morning, and the pillows in the drawing room had to be changed out daily due to her habit of sobbing on the sofa. At least when she was in the back garden, she could think that she was helping to water the flowers. Instead of sitting on the bench where she had last seen Emily, she tucked herself on the lawn beneath the birch tree next to the Sweet Williams. What did it matter if there was dirt on her gown when she had no desire to leave the house again?

Society could rot for all she cared.

Her parents were arguing inside the house, and she could see them as shadowy figures beyond the gauzy white curtains of the open window. Closing her eyes, she tried to listen to the birds instead of their words, but it was of little use.

"She deserves all the unhappiness she gets," Father snapped. "She has ruined this family's golden opportunity. I should have known she would never change her ways."

Oh, but she had changed. The problem was that her parents had never bothered to understand her, so they could not see how different she was from when they had embarked on their journey to England.

Mother came outside to continue the lecture that had not ceased these last three days.

Rebecca opened her eyes. "Would you have married Father if you thought he was a murderer?"

She had not told them that it was Danfield who shot those men. She owed no loyalty to the Beauforts, but felt little inclination to tell her parents the truth when they refused to really listen to anything she had to say.

"A duel is a different sort of thing altogether than murder, and we have all known about this for weeks. Why would you cry off now, Rebecca? After all the effort we have all spent. The voyage here. Leasing this house and renting the curricle and the carriage and hiring all these servants. Your dresses, and your brothers' gambling debts."

"I cannot be held accountable for gambling debts!" This was a new accusation. Was there to be no limit to being blamed?

"If we were not in London, there would not be such temptation."

"New York had temptations on every corner. I cannot believe you think otherwise."

Mother's lips pursed.

"We can go back home, as if none of this ever happened. Our friends in New York will treat us no differently. When will Father book the voyage?"

London had been a glorious adventure, but her time here had been a series of slides fitted into a peep show box for the entertainment of others. Now, it was time for another setting that would suit her rather better.

"Go back? Why would we do that?"

"I wish to God you were not so flighty!" Father roared from the door that led to the garden. He was silhouetted against the frame, his arms folded across his chest. "If you had only been a fourth son, you would have been more use to me."

"We aren't going home?" Rebecca's chest tightened and she shrank against the birch, its bark digging into her back through her thin dress.

"I have sunk too much money into this endeavor. There are funds tied up in the banks. I have leased land for a warehouse, and I've talked to interested buyers. With or without your pretty marquess, we are bringing the Tremblay gin to England."

"But if you have set everything up so well here, we should return to oversee the business."

"Henry will go back and make the arrangements. Your mother and I are staying here and will continue our work with Marvin. Unlike you, we honor our commitments. We stay when faced with a challenge."

"Does my happiness matter?" Rebecca asked, though she already knew the answer.

"With time, you would have become a duchess. No girl in New York City would ever have turned that opportunity away."

"I do not love him."

"Love has nothing to do with commerce, so forgive me if I neglected to include it in the betrothal contract."

He stormed away, and Mother followed him.

The garden was peaceful in their absence, but Rebecca's heart was untouched by the tranquility. She was chilled despite the sun and yanked off her bonnet to tip her face toward the light.

If only Emily would break her engagement! Then there could be a reason to stay.

But she had to admit that the future was less certain than she had imagined it to be if Emily was free from Danfield's yoke. Unmarried, she would continue to live with her father and stepmother, and like most of society, they would leave London soon for the country. Rebecca would not see her for months, until the Season began anew.

And then what would happen once they did return to London? Emily would become someone else's betrothed. Eventually, she would marry a man and earn the security she so desperately wanted, regardless if it was Danfield or someone else.

Under which circumstances could their fragile affair continue?

Rebecca pressed her forehead to her knees and began to sob again. It would have been better never to have met Emily, and certainly to never have had the pleasure of her lips against her own, now that it begat such torturous memories.

There could be no future for them.

Rebecca could not stay in England. But for once, she didn't think she was fleeing. She was not being flighty, and she was through running from consequences.

It was time to close this chapter of her life and to begin anew. She rose and went in search of Henry.

❖

Emily stood at the periphery of the ballroom of Almack's, fanning herself. Once she thought she would have liked nothing better than to stroll the length of this room on Rebecca's arm, enjoying the fact that they were lucky enough to be somewhere so exclusive. But now she was glad that Rebecca had never been inside. She would have wrinkled her nose and rolled her eyes, and she was better off having never breathed its stuffy air.

"Are you certain you do not wish to dance?" Danfield blew out a breath and raked a hand through his hair. "I came because I know you like it here, but what is the point if you do not dance? I could have been at White's."

Each stick of Emily's fan was empty. She had refused every offer tonight, despite plenty of invitations to grace the floor.

"There are other pleasures to be had here than dancing."

They were few and far between, but the truth was that she could not bear the idea of him touching her, holding her close as they waltzed, her skirts flowing between his trousered legs as they turned and twirled. As she could not dance with other men and deny her betrothed without publicly slighting him, she had chosen to dance with no one.

He had kissed Emily's hand when she had arrived and pretended as if nothing was amiss. Did he not realize that she knew of his misdeeds? She could not forget what she had learned. There was darkness lurking behind the ducal façade.

This was the life she had told Rebecca that she had wanted for them both. Here was security and reliability. There was very little comfort to it, despite its grandeur. The promise of a glorious future was tarnished, and she could no longer believe in it.

Danfield left her with a curt bow and stalked toward another young woman, who willingly followed him to dance.

There, but for the grace of God, the other debutante went. It could have been her that Danfield had proposed to. It could have been any other woman.

Why did it have to be Emily?

Why had she wanted so badly for it to be her?

Lady Sefton and Princess Esterhazy were across the room, talking to one another with a glass of ratafia in hand. Gentlemen glided across the dance floor with elegant ladies in tow, turning in long-rehearsed and familiar movements. Emily had danced to the same music for so long that her feet were restless in her slippers, aching to join the herd of the nobility.

These were her people, were they not?

Didn't she belong here, as she always had?

But she felt different. Rebecca had not only marked her name on the ivory sticks of her fan. She had written it on every bone of her body, claiming her from the moment of that very first kiss.

Everything around her was familiar and steeped in tradition. Her organized mind loved the predictability, but her traitorous heart beat against the rhythm of the violins and the harpsichord.

She was changed.

Emily hadn't known where she belonged until Rebecca had shown her that it was by her side. She still had uncertainty and doubts, but the part of her that now believed in magic and hope was growing stronger each day. Whatever her future held, it was not cradled here between these staid and stately walls.

She told Lady Calloway that she wasn't feeling well, and she gave her excuses to Lady Jersey. The truth was that her mind felt clearer than it ever had. She had sought peace and comfort here for so long, but no more. As she sailed through the front doors, she knew that she would never return.

Emily's family dined at Northelm Manor one last time before the wedding. Emily felt dull and dispirited and tried to concentrate on each dish as it was served. It was preferable to think about the presentation and taste of the guinea fowl and salmon than to listen to the conversation around the table. Her shoulders ached, as she could not relax amidst this company.

She missed Rebecca and the glances they used to share across the table. Her presence had made these dinners palatable. Now she was replaced by Juliet and her mother, at Avenbury's insistence. Juliet's preening was almost as difficult to digest as the praise showered on her by the duke and duchess, who made no pretense that she was a much preferred candidate for marchioness than Rebecca had ever been.

Each slight against Rebecca felt like a blow against her battered heart. They had never valued her. They had not known the treasure that they had let escape.

Emily hoped that Lady Calloway would not wish to linger over tea in the drawing room later. She could hardly bear much more tonight.

If only she could escape now, between the offerings of fruit and cheese. She wished she could duck beneath the footmen's arms and run from this place. As she reached for an almond, she noticed that her hand was trembling.

What if the allegations about Danfield were untrue? Could she then be contented and settle into her life as his bride? If Avenbury had not duelled with those men, it did not necessarily mean that Danfield must have stood in his place. Perhaps no one had killed anyone.

But that was the unlikeliest outcome of all.

After dinner, Danfield and Avenbury escorted Emily and Juliet outside on the terrace for some air. Avenbury leaned his hip against the low stone wall and lit a cheroot. Emily stared. That wall was where she and Rebecca had sat the night of their first kiss.

Now it was desecrated.

Avenbury glanced at her and gestured with the cheroot. "Are you looking for one of your own, Lady Emily? I have plenty."

She started. "Oh, of course not. I apologize, I was lost in thought."

"I will take one," Juliet announced, and plucked his from his hand. "Do try it, Em."

She thrust it at her. Emily took an uncertain puff, then coughed. "I am unused to such things."

Juliet took it back and blew a perfect smoke ring. "It takes practice, but it is not difficult."

Avenbury lit another. "My engagement is in shambles, but I am free at last."

"Free and broke." Danfield laughed. "You are the heir, but you have no fortune now."

"Whatever do you mean? He's to be a duke." Juliet frowned at him.

"Our parents were shrewd when Avenbury's duels were discovered. They were aghast, as any decent member of society would be. Our father moved the money out of the entail, so my brother will inherit vast amounts of land, and castles." Danfield smiled angelically. "But the money will be in my own coffers."

"They believed my brother's word," Avenbury said. He flicked the ash from his cheroot. "But soon enough, they will believe *me* instead. I thought I needed the Tremblay fortune to catch their attention, but I was mistaken. Grandmother thinks highly of me again, as I had a very interesting conversation with her this morning about certain past events that she had not understood correctly. She will have much to say to Father. And then who do you think will be without wealth? My poor—*poor*—younger brother."

"At least I never was known as the Murderous Marquess," Danfield ground out.

"I may never be free of that blasted moniker. And you may never gain a title, so there shall be no delightful witticisms at its expense. But the truth has its ways of revealing itself. I would not rest so comfortably on your borrowed laurels, brother dear."

Emily was numb to the arrows that the brothers flung at one another. Whether they were truth or lies, she could not bring herself to much care. Everyone was awful, and everything was tedious, and the one person she had liked at any of these gatherings was gone.

Her cheeks burned as she stole another glance at the wall where they had kissed, and then she looked over near the orange tree where they had fixed each other's dresses on the night that they had met.

Her desire and her love and her yearning were overwhelming, but so was the pain of loss and regret.

It had been worth it to know what love truly was.

It was nothing to be feared.

It was the peace and comfort that she had been looking for her whole life.

Love was not here tonight, with Danfield yawning with boredom and Juliet simpering on Avenbury's arm. Had she understood anyone correctly? She had not seen Danfield for who he truly was, and she had not seen Juliet for who she truly wanted.

"I do not waste emotion where it is unwarranted," Avenbury said gently. "I do not care that you lied, nor that you schemed, nor even that you killed. You will always be my blood. And there may be some day in the future when we need to stand together. There are always wolves at a duke's door. So I will not cut you down where you stand, even though you deserve it for being a dastardly dog. Only our family need know the truth. I will not cry out to all of society your misdeeds and your murders."

"They were affairs of honor," Danfield snapped.

"They were affairs of other men's honor, not your own. You should have had the decency to delope. You should have slinked home with your tail between your legs and you should never have done it all over again and besmirched the honor of another lady. You certainly should never have pinned the blame on me and ruined my reputation. You underestimated me if you thought I would never return."

Danfield laughed. "Do not pretend to be an innocent lamb."

Avenbury smiled. "The important thing is that I never was caught in any of my crimes."

"I would be happy to marry you, no matter what you have done," Juliet declared. "Ours is a love for the ages."

"Then we all shall have our happy endings, for I am to wed the pious and gentle Lady Emily this very Sunday. If she cannot cure me of my misdeeds, then perhaps no one can. But I have faith in her capabilities."

"Em is the best of all the debutantes to emerge in society this year! She will do you much credit." Juliet beamed at her.

Emily swallowed. "I will not."

"I beg your pardon?"

"I will not marry you, my lord."

It was curious how simple it was, when the dilemma had loomed so large over her for so long. Could life be so easy? If she was unhappy and unwilling, could she not choose to leave?

She turned her back on them. She heard Danfield spluttering, and Avenbury laughing, and Juliet crying out to her to stay, but she ignored them all and walked back into the house in search of her family.

She had no more to say.

She was free from the confines of the role that she had chosen to play since the start of the Season. She felt like an actress no more, dancing to everyone else's fiddle.

Now she needed to find Rebecca and tell her how she felt.

CHAPTER TWENTY-FIVE

It was not difficult for Rebecca to convince her family to book her passage home with Henry. Now that she was something of a disgrace, her parents were happy enough to wash their hands of her. She packed her belongings with the help of her maid, lingering over the dresses she had worn when she had been with Emily. The memories might lose their power faster if they were tucked away.

As she looked out the window at the moon, she marveled that it was the last time she would ever see it from London. The moon in New York was the same, but it was with a different heart that she would gaze up at it.

The return voyage was better than the first one, when she had been trying so hard to impress Avenbury and earn her parents' love. Now Henry was her only companion, and there was far less stress to their daily routine. They played a good deal of cards, they dined with the other passengers en route to America, and they strolled the deck together each night that the seas were calm enough.

It reminded her of walking around the ballrooms with Emily, arm in arm as they whispered their hearts to each other.

She sighed.

"Ah, so you had your heart broken, Becky. We have all been there. You more than most. You spent plenty of summers moping about someone or another back home, and now you can add an Englishman to your list."

It had been an Englishwoman, but she did not correct him.

"You do not think me foolish?"

"No more than anyone in love is. You're still plenty young. When your hair is gray and you are nursing an aching knee by the fireplace, you will look back on this summer with great fondness."

"Will I?" It was difficult to imagine it.

"How many girls can say they spurned a duke's heir? That's a grand and tragic thing. And really, between you and I, Avenbury was a right bastard when he wanted to be. Selfish prick."

"Mother would be aghast at the language."

"It will help harden you heart to him. Say it with me now. Selfish prick."

"I cannot!" Rebecca looked around them in horror, but they were alone on the deck in the dusk.

"Think of it like a dram of whiskey when you're trying to cure a cough. Might be nasty in the mouth for a moment when you're not used to it, but you'll feel better afterward. Say it now." He was laughing, and it was healing her heart.

"My former fiancé was a selfish prick," she whispered.

"There you go! Now shout it over the railing so all the birds and fish can hear it. Avenbury has dominion over the land but he's got no power out here, has he?"

She leaned over and took a deep breath of clean sea air. "The Marquess of Avenbury is a selfish prick!" she shouted into the wind.

Henry hauled her back. "Not too far, we can't have you toppling into the sea. That's enough for today, but don't you feel better?"

"Much."

It was true, though it hadn't been the marquess who broke her heart.

She swallowed hard. "That was a kind thing you just did. I never thought any of you cared much for me, you know."

He blinked. "You're our little sister! We looked out for you all the time. We chased away plenty of ne'er-do-wells on the nights you sneaked out to parties."

"You *knew* about those?" She thought she had been so careful.

"Of course we did! One or another of us would go after you so that you came to no harm. We took turns."

Rebecca pressed a hand to her heart. "I never knew."

"Well, it doesn't surprise me. You traipse through life going after what you want and pay no mind to what else might be happening. You are more of an open book than you might think."

She had some secrets left. He could not possibly have guessed at the nature of her relationship with Emily. But had she been so focused on herself and her choices that she had not considered the pressure that Emily was under? Rebecca could return to America, and these past months would fade like some strange dream. But Emily would have had to give up her entire life, and to remain in England where her choices would haunt her.

Maybe it hadn't been fair to expect Emily to end her engagement.

Maybe Rebecca should have stayed. Maybe they could have found a way to be happy together if she had given it a little more time.

There were days when Rebecca wanted to beg the captain to turn the boat around and return to England. But weeks had already passed, and it would be weeks still before they docked.

Would Emily have forgotten about her?

For all of her tears and heartache, she came to the same conclusion time and again. She did not want to be with someone who did not want her enough. Emily had worried about feeling second best, but had not seemed to realize that she was treating Rebecca the same way when she made her commitment to Danfield.

Emily had never been willing to put Rebecca first.

She did wish that she had taken the time to say farewell. When Emily had broken her heart and fled, she had no intention of it being the last time they ever saw one another. Rebecca had thought she would be in London longer before returning to sea, but the ship had been booked much faster than she had expected.

She could put her unsaid feelings into a letter and post it as soon as they docked. But what did she want to say? What more was there to explain?

Should she include a lock of her hair to remember her by? Would Emily want such a thing?

At least she still had Emily's ring.

❖

"I wish to speak with both of you," Emily announced to Papa and Lady Calloway at breakfast. She had explained nothing the previous night, claiming only that she was unwell.

"No need to stand upon ceremony." Papa tossed aside his newspaper and propped his elbows on the table, moving them off when Lady Calloway swatted at him. "I like nothing more than a good yarn with my morning coffee."

"I would prefer that we speak at Kelligrew's."

A muscle near Papa's eye twitched. "The tea emporium?"

"I always enjoy a fine cup of tea," Lady Calloway said. "I am unfamiliar with the establishment. Is it new?"

Emily did not take her eyes off Papa. "It is an old shop, but respectable. It has a good variety of tea and sweets to please most anybody."

"It sounds charming. Shall we arrange to have luncheon there?"

"No reason not to," Papa said, his voice thick. He cleared his throat and rose from the table. "I shall join you when the carriage is brought round at noon."

When they arrived at Kelligrew's, Emily insisted on sitting at the table in the corner, remembering that her grandparents had always preferred it there. From the way Papa wiped at his brow, she thought he was remembering it too.

"This is a trifle different than I was expecting," Lady Calloway said as they were brought tea and soup. She eyed the cracks in the wall and the faded velvet on the chairs. "I suppose this is the last time you will see somewhere like this after you marry Lord Danfield!"

Emily folded her hands in her lap. "I will not be marrying Danfield."

Papa dropped the bread he was in the midst of buttering. "I beg your pardon?"

"I have decided that we will not suit."

"For what reason?" He looked ready to call for the ships of war on her behalf, and she tugged him back down in his chair.

"He is not a good man, Papa."

"If you are talking about this business with his brother, there is no more to be said about it. Debts of honor must be paid." He tore at the bread and a shower of crumbs fell to the table.

"Avenbury is innocent." She explained what she had learned. "I cannot marry Danfield knowing what he has done."

Papa's jaw slackened. "He is a blackguard! To have put the blame on his own brother is beyond the pale."

"What infamy you have escaped." Lady Calloway's eyes were wide.

"I am lucky that it is over now," Emily said. "I discovered the truth before I was brought to the altar and bound to him forever."

She didn't add that she would have decided not to marry him anyway. There could be no happiness without Rebecca.

"What remarkable fortitude, when you have lost so much. You would have been so beautiful, standing there in St. George's!" Lady Calloway dabbed at her eyes with her handkerchief. "Forgive me, but I did want this for you. It was a wonderful opportunity. And he was so handsome." She crumpled the linen square in her hands. "You would have had such beautiful children."

"Thank you," Emily murmured.

She squared her shoulders. "Well. There are other men out there, Emily. Better men, just as fine in appearance. This will not be the last opportunity you have."

"I may not want another man," Emily said, choosing her words with care. She had no intention of ever revealing to them what lay in her heart for Rebecca, but she wanted to prepare them that she may never wed. "This experience has soured me on matrimony."

"You will sing a different tune next Season. We will return to Somerset, and you can lick your wounds." Papa reached across the table to pat her hand. "London will await you when you are ready."

"I am prepared to meet my future, whatever it may look like."

"Your calmness is admirable. You inherited that from your mother."

"I loved coming here with her," Emily said, looking him in the eye.

She thought that he would be gruff or agitated. She had steeled herself for the harsh words that they might exchange. Instead, there was a softness around his mouth, and a tear in his eye as he gazed around the room.

"I came here a time or two with her before we married. It's gotten shabbier over the years, but I remember it when it was fresh plastered and painted. I kissed her hand over at that front table during our courtship." Fine lines crinkled near his eyes as he pointed. "Ah, those were different days."

Lady Calloway cleared her throat. "I understand she was a wonderful woman."

"Did you know about her?" Emily asked.

"I beg your pardon?"

"We never talk about my mother. Do you know anything about her?"

Papa's face was troubled. "Emmy dear, I am afraid that is my doing. It hurt to speak of her, so I refused to say her name for a long time."

"You removed her portrait from the drawing room." She had stared at the empty wall every night for a year.

"Forgive me. It tore at my heart to see her face. And I thought it a kindness to my new wife to put the painting in the attic. I was not sensitive to what you might think of it. I loved your mother. I have never forgotten her."

"I would be happy for you to return the painting to its rightful place of honor," Lady Calloway said. "There is no question that you should talk about your first wife. I never intended to replace her. You are a good man, Thomas, and you raised a conscientious young woman who questions what she thinks is right and proper. Those are good qualities to have, Emily." She paused. "But if I may say so… your father is honorable and kind. What you thought of him was half-truths clouded by your assumptions. I think we all have things in our past that are difficult to explain when they are hidden away."

Emily thought of Rebecca. She would never be able to explain the nature of their relationship. If others drew their own erroneous conclusions, she would be forced to accept them.

But she would always know in her heart that her actions were sown with love.

"I love you," she said to Papa, her voice cracking. "I did not understand your decisions. All I wanted was to hold on to my memories of Mama, and the life we shared together."

"You were so devastated that I thought I was sparing you pain by avoiding to talk of her, but I see now that I added to your suffering. I am sorry, Emmy."

They shared a smile, and Lady Calloway dabbed again at her eyes.

"So what do you say? Shall say we retire to Somerset next week and rehang the portrait straightaway?"

Emily had lain awake in bed all night thinking of what she wanted next. "I want a new beginning. I want the adventure you have so often spoken about, Papa."

"A lady's adventure is marriage," Lady Calloway said. "That is your new beginning."

Papa leaned back in his chair. "What is it you are thinking of?"

"I would like to see America," she said slowly. "Wouldn't it be wonderful to see it for ourselves? We could spend the winter there. All three of us, together."

"I never say no to a sea voyage," Papa said. "It sounds like a grand adventure indeed."

"It would be good to have a change of scenery." Lady Calloway smiled.

Emily could not wait for the future.

New York was a sprawling city of shouting voices and tall brick buildings, and although Emily had been prepared to find London infinitely preferable, her heart was captured as soon as she walked off the boat and onto the docks.

She breathed deep, her first lungful of air in a different country. Rebecca had been at this very port and had walked this very path. How strange to think of it, as she knew her only as she had been in England. Would she be a different sort of woman in her own homeland?

"You did well for a first-time seafarer," Papa told her, patting her shoulder. "I'm proud of you, Emmy."

She stood straighter, pleased with his praise. "I am grateful it was a calm passing."

Stepmama pressed a handkerchief to her lips. Her face had a greenish tint that had not left her since their departure. "It is not an experience I am keen to repeat with any hurry. Do tell me that we will stay here for a while."

Six weeks at sea was long enough for Emily, too. Her legs felt strange as she walked across gravel instead of shipboards, without the need to adjust her gait to the swells.

"Maybe it is an indication that I am growing older, but I am happy enough to be on land again myself." Papa squinted at the people bustling around the port, loading goods onto vessels in barrels and trunks. "There are plenty of cities to visit if New York doesn't suit. We are in no hurry, are we?"

Emily wondered if any of those barrels contained Tremblay gin. She was indeed in a hurry, but Papa couldn't know it. How soon could she discover for herself what lay inside the city? She had been sincere in her wish for fresh scenery, and she had grown closer to both Papa and Stepmama during the voyage. She finally considered them to be a proper family. It had been good for them all to talk without the heaviness of the past surrounding them. No matter what happened with Rebecca, she would always be grateful for this time with them, and profoundly relieved to have left her broken engagement behind her in London.

But her purpose now that they had landed was singular.

Emily had wanted change, but had chosen to come here for Rebecca's sake. Somehow, she would find her. She was her lodestone, and Emily would never again resist her pull.

Their accommodations were grand, as they were staying with one of Papa's friends from his naval days. Mr. Fletcher was also a retired admiral, and a fine gentleman. He lived in a beautifully furnished brick house with his wife and three sons, each of whom he tried to push toward Emily as prospective husbands.

But Papa smiled and told him that Emily was on leave from husband hunting and would take up the sport another time.

Emily sat at the window in her bedchamber on her first night in New York, braiding her hair and looking down at the city. Was Rebecca sitting in her own bedchamber somewhere out there, readying herself for bed too? Did she wear her hair the same way, and did she have the same night rail?

Was she alone?

Or had she fallen in love with someone else?

It had been months since they had laid eyes on each other that afternoon in the Tremblay's garden. It was now October, and Emily knew she had been lucky to make the crossing before spring. She didn't like to think of the passage of time, because it reminded her that they had been apart longer than they had known each other. Perhaps she was a fool to think that their love had been as meaningful to Rebecca as it had been to her.

Perhaps she was the sole initiate in her devotion.

But she had crossed an ocean on behalf of love and renewal, and by God, she would not give up her faith now.

CHAPTER TWENTY-SIX

Rebecca had settled into a peaceful routine with Aunt Mary and Henry and Arthur. Arthur had remained behind to handle the daily Tremblay business, and Rebecca had been so happy to see her oldest brother again that she cried into his lapels for almost ten minutes.

"Have you developed a habit of waterworks since being so long at sea?" he asked, laughing. He took her by the shoulders and tipped her chin up. "I don't recall you being so quick to cry."

Arthur looked the most like Father of any of her brothers, but his face was kinder, and Rebecca's shoulders hunched again as her lip trembled.

"Our Becky has had a tough time of things," Henry told him. "Prepare yourself for dramatic tales of British high society, and be grateful that you stayed in New York."

For weeks, Rebecca regaled them with stories at dinner. With each passing day, the pain of Emily's loss ebbed, and the tales of the *bon ton* became familiar and funny instead of heart-wrenching. She was able to turn her embarrassment on its head and laugh with her family over the snobbery of the fine ladies and gentlemen, and their faces began to fade with time.

Aunt Mary indulged her whims, and subjected her with as many remedies that the physician saw fit to prescribe.

"A girl needs some pampering after being crossed in love," she said comfortably. "Here is another posset for you. You've grown thin, and I want to see you healthy again before winter arrives."

Her appetite had suffered along with her broken heart, and she had not eaten well on the ship. The food in England had been different enough to render her especially grateful for the familiarity of dishes on her aunt's table. Shellfish, corn chowder, and asparagus soup were pressed upon her as strengthening meals, and she relished the taste of home in each bite. There was no overcooked mutton to be found here.

Rebecca discovered that she had little enough taste for the parties and the theatres and the gaiety that she had once enjoyed. Her former friends did not visit her, and Rebecca did not care to enquire whether it was because she had not married the marquess after all. Was she considered damaged goods? Or did she hold no social power to interest them anymore?

She was still an heiress so there were polite invitations extended her way, but she ignored them all in favor of cards with her aunt's friends, and visits to the lending library, and strolls through the neighborhood parks.

Why had she yearned so much to leave, when it was so pleasant here?

She did not even envy her brothers when they stayed out late and came stumbling home reeking of cigar smoke and brandy. She had become content with routine, and habit, and the quiet bliss of watching the leaves change color on the trees as the squirrels busied themselves in preparation for winter.

She had healed, and she was proud to tell Henry that she thought herself happy again.

"That's a funny statement, because you don't seem happy," he said.

She sighed. "You live to be contrary, do you not?"

"I do not. I stand by what I said. You are missing something. You are quieter than you used to be. Where's your spark, Becky?"

"I have been told all my life to be less rash, and now you fault me for learning it at last?"

"Those words might have come from Father and Mother, but not from me! You are meant to be high-spirited. A quiet life is good for a spell but won't interest you for long."

She could not find the energy to argue.

❖

Society in New York turned out to be as small as that of London, for Mr. Fletcher knew who Emily was talking about as soon as she found the courage to bring up Rebecca's name at dinner.

"The Tremblay family? The gin distillers? Of course I know of them. They have a huge fortune and are active in some of the charities here in town. A friend of mine is the captain of a merchant vessel who transports goods for them. He says they are not stingy with their wealth."

"The sign of a good family," Papa declared. "I thought that Mr. Tremblay was a fine enough fellow."

"They are acquaintances of ours," Emily said quietly. "I should like very much to visit them."

"It is no trouble for you to have the carriage. Please, feel free to call on them tomorrow afternoon."

Emily almost spilled her wine across her dinner. Tomorrow? Was it possible that she would see Rebecca so soon? What dress could she have pressed and readied? Which earbobs should she wear? Did she have time to curl her hair?

She excused herself after dinner, knowing that she would be poor company and hardly capable of more than an absent-minded murmur. Hope had buoyed her for so long, and it terrified her to think that tomorrow could be the end of it all.

She could not banish the memory of Rebecca crying in the garden. There was every possibility that she would not want to see Emily again, and she would need to learn to live with devastation.

Emily could not have done the short drive in the carriage the next day without Stepmama. She noticed but did not comment on Emily's agitation and remarked upon the view in a way that did not necessitate any reply. Had Emily been alone, she would have commanded the driver to return, or to circle the block once they arrived, for her thoughts were scattered in every direction.

The sturdy buildings were not so different from London and yet entirely unfamiliar. Emily trailed behind Stepmama to the door. This was where her dear Rebecca had spent her autumn! She could imagine her walking along the street, with a smart wool pelisse to protect her from the weather.

It was safer to stay outside with her thoughts, but Stepmama beckoned to her after the butler opened the door. They were brought to a drawing room where a kindly older woman sat with her knitting. When they introduced themselves as friends of the Tremblay family from England, Mrs. Richardson rang for tea and told them that her nephews were elsewhere on business or they should have been happy to see the Calloways.

"Where is Miss Tremblay?" Emily blurted out.

Mrs. Richardson peered at her. "She is at the lending library. Are you well, Lady Emily? You seem distressed."

Stepmama smiled. "We have been traveling for some time, and it is natural for a young woman to seek out her friends. We have few acquaintances as yet here in the city."

Friends.

The word gnawed at her. Would they be sipping their tea and speaking with such banality if they knew they were talking about torn-apart lovers?

But of course they did not know.

She gripped her teacup with shaking hands. It would be rude to overstay her welcome, but what if she left before Rebecca returned? She would be forced to wait for Rebecca to repay the call, but it would allow her to spurn the overture entirely. She could not bear to sit in Mr. Fletcher's parlor day after day, her face pressed to the window, awaiting a knock that never came.

Emily was willing to plead and to beg. But first she needed to be granted an audience.

When she heard footsteps in the hallway, the hair on her arms rose like she was at Vauxhall with the electricity machine. Although she recognized the way Rebecca walked and heard her beloved voice call out to her aunt as she approached the room, Emily was still unprepared to see her again.

Rebecca stood in the doorway, her lips parted as she gasped and stepped backward, her hand pressed to her throat. Her brown curls were longer, and her cheeks were thinner. She wore a long brown woolen dress with a red shawl around her shoulders, and her cheeks were a becoming shade of pink from the brisk October air.

Emily could not stop herself from rising and taking a step toward her. But her vision blurred, and she felt hot all over. Although she tried to steady herself on the back of a wooden chair, her knees went weak and she collapsed.

Rebecca was on her knees in an instant. "Emily!"

There was no time to wonder at her appearance in New York. She grasped Emily's limp hands in her own. "Do we have any smelling salts, Aunt Mary?"

"Emily always carries some with her. She is prone to fits of the vapors, poor dear, though I have never once seen her fall." Lady Calloway rummaged through Emily's reticule, then blinked. "Oh. She must have forgotten them. I have never known her to be without her vial."

Emily was pale, and her lashes fluttered against her cheeks. Rebecca tried to swallow her panic. "We must call for the housekeeper."

The housekeeper and an army of maids crowded the parlor, bearing compresses and tinctures and laudanum, but no salts could be found.

"Vinegar should do the trick," Lady Calloway said. "Anything with a strong scent." She stroked Emily's hair and patted her cheek. "Is it overly warm in here? Perhaps a window could be opened?"

Emily stirred, and Rebecca's heart leapt. "Emily," she whispered, rubbing her thumb over her knuckles. "Wake up, Emily."

Her eyes opened, and the sight of her beautiful blue eyes would have brought Rebecca to her knees if she had not already been on them. "Oh! Rebecca! What happened?"

"You fainted," Lady Calloway told her.

"I do not remember." Emily struggled to sit up.

Lady Calloway motioned her to remain still. "Pray do not exert yourself. You are unwell."

"Lady Emily is welcome to stay here as long as she needs to recover," Aunt Mary declared. "We have plenty of room. I would never turn away a friend of my niece."

Emily's cheeks turned red. "I do not mean to impose." She stared up at Rebecca, her brows halfway up her forehead.

"Do not be foolish. Aunt Mary is right. You must rest." Now that Emily was out of danger, Rebecca was flustered. How had Emily come to be here? *Why* was she here?

Arrangements were made for Emily to stay the night so that she could rest without the undue stress of being jostled all the way home in the carriage, and an invitation was pressed upon Lady Calloway to bring the admiral the following evening for dinner.

In less than a quarter hour's time, Emily was propped up in a guest bedroom in one of Rebecca's thick flannel night rails, with a hot cup of ginger tea on the bedside table.

"I did not plan this," Emily assured her, then bit her lip. "Or rather, I did plan to visit you. That must be obvious. But I had no intention of fainting! I am so embarrassed."

"There is nothing embarrassing about it," Rebecca said, and she sat on the corner of the bed. "I was so worried when you fell. I thought you might have hit your head."

"I take it I was less than graceful. But I am as well as can be expected, truly. I feel much better now."

"What are you doing in New York?" She hesitated. "Where is Danfield? Is he with your father?"

"Danfield?" Emily blinked, then laughed. "Oh, of course. You left England before the gossip rags were printed. I didn't marry him. I just couldn't."

"Thank God." Rebecca flopped down. "I hated the thought of you with him. It tore at my insides to imagine you by his side."

"I hate the thought of me with anyone." Emily swallowed. "Anyone but you."

Rebecca smiled. "I underestimated how sweet it would be to see your face again."

"I would understand if you were angry, instead." Emily pulled the blanket higher and folded her hands on her lap. "It was not well done of me to leave you as I did. I am so sorry. I should have stayed and we should have talked. I have learned that hiding a wound only helps it to fester, and I do not want that for us. I want there to be openness and trust between us. Always. And forever." She took a deep breath. "I still love you, Rebecca. I should have said it until my lungs were sore, and then I should have written it a thousand times until your eyes were tired of the words. I love you, I love you, I love you."

"I love you too." Rebecca's heart was overflowing with joy. "I never stopped loving you."

"I am glad, for I have crossed an ocean to find you. It was no small feat."

"What was your plan once you found me?"

"My plan was to tell you every day of our lives how lucky we are to love one another."

She threaded her fingers through Emily's, delighted at the idea. "And where shall we live in this grand plan of yours?"

"My father and stepmother have agreed to winter here in America, but I admit that I do not know what the future holds."

"How do you feel about not knowing?"

She paused. "I am not worried any longer about what will come. Life is never free of hardships or struggle. That is the nature of being alive. But now I am confident that we will find our way through. Even though right now I confess that it appears to be a garden maze with no exits."

"I would rather like to be stuck in a garden maze with you, secluded from view. We could do most anything in a maze. Perhaps you might sit upon the sundial and I might lift your skirts."

"We would find our way out together and find a proper bed," Emily said firmly. "That is what we would do."

"Oh! It seems we are in precisely such a proper bed now."

"Are we indeed?"

Emily's lips curved into a smile and she leaned forward. The feel of her lips after weeks of absence brought memories that overwhelmed her. Rebecca's eyes filled with tears, and Emily pulled back, her brow furrowed. "I did not mean to distress you."

"I am not distressed. Oh, my love, it is just that I cannot believe you are here." Rebecca touched her cheek. "I am so happy. I had not imagined this could be possible."

Emily gently kissed the tears that had gathered at the corners of her eyes, threatening to spill. "All things are possible with love."

EPILOGUE

Emily wiped the crumbs from the last table after she latched the door and closed up the Calloway Tea Emporium for the day. She had opened the establishment six months ago with an investment from Papa and was beginning to think that it would truly be a success.

They had sold all of the Savoy cakes that had been baked that morning and most of the meringues. A new order of tea had arrived from England last month, and they had gone through a goodly amount of it already as the weather had turned cool and people sought to warm themselves indoors.

"Thank you, Mama," she murmured, pressing her fingers to her lips and waving them at her mother's portrait. Papa had been kind enough to send it from Somerset, and it hung above the mantle where she could see it from where she stood most days at the counter.

Her staff was small, but dear to her heart. They comprised mostly of men and women she and Rebecca had met through the local literary salon, and who had stories to tell that reminded herself and Rebecca of their own.

Rebecca came out of the back room and snaked her arms around her waist as she stood behind her. She kissed her neck. "Another good day?"

"Every day is a good one with you." Emily clasped her hands around Rebecca's.

"I could not agree with you more."

"It is growing dark. Henry will be wondering where we are."

"He knows where we are," Rebecca said, nuzzling her cheek.

After their first winter in New York, Papa and Stepmama had returned to England. When Emily had elected to stay behind, Rebecca's aunt had insisted that she stay with them as she was such a devoted friend to her niece.

The arrangement suited them all for another year, and Emily and Rebecca had relished the long afternoons strolling arm in arm through the city, and the long evenings spent in each other's arms. But when Henry married and moved to Montreal, he invited both Rebecca and Emily to live with him, and they had been delighted by the offer. They had their own bedchamber and their own sitting room, and though Emily had feared that they would be an imposition, they were treated as honored members of the family.

Though the nature of their relationship was never remarked upon, Henry had indicated early on that he had always known about Rebecca's sapphic indiscretions in Montreal, and that he had well enough suspected of their love affair while they had been in England.

"I do not relish going outside for the walk home." Emily had been here for three years now, and she didn't think she would ever become accustomed to the bitter wind that watered her eyes and stole her breath and froze her fingers if they were not well hidden under thick woolen mittens.

"Only think of how I will warm you up once we are at home." Rebecca squeezed her waist.

"I suppose I must have patience. One day, the season will turn again, won't it?"

"Hope springs eternal."

"Hope has already given me everything I ever dreamed of." Emily gazed at Rebecca's face, so dear to her, and so precious. "Without hope, I would never have followed you across an ocean. Without hope, I would never have thought we could have any kind of happiness together."

"Then let us never be without it, nor without each other, for we have built something wonderful that many would envy." Rebecca kissed her with a tenderness and sweetness that left her breathless. "Now, let us go home and enjoy our life together."

About the Author

Jane Walsh is a queer historical romance novelist who loves everything Regency. She is delighted to have the opportunity to put her studies in history and costume design to good use by writing love stories. She owes a great debt of gratitude to the local coffee shop for fueling her novel writing endeavors. Jane's happily ever after is centered on her wife and their cat and their cozy home together in Canada.

Books Available from Bold Strokes Books

Brooke Takes Queen by Alaina Erdell. Brooke Staley faces personal and professional upheaval when Elizabeth Bettancourt, the emotionally scarred new owner of the resort she works for, considers selling. (978-1-63679-886-8)

Coda by Anna Gram. Parker is intriguing, magnetic, impossible to ignore—and completely wrong for Hannah. But sometimes love's melody refuses to end. (978-1-63679-926-1)

Secrets Under the Junipers by Suzie Clarke. Who killed Hallie Lynn Peeples? Cecilia McConnel needs to know. Bitsy Hanover holds the key. Can love uncover secrets? (978-1-63679-845-5)

The Debutante Dilemma by Jane Walsh. Two debutantes are engaged to wealthy and titled brothers…but discover they only have eyes for each other. (978-1-63679-896-7)

The Love Book by Gun Brooke. When literary agent Rowan Cross receives an anonymous manuscript that deeply resonates with her, Verity realizes she has accidentally sent her own manuscript, complete with her very real feelings for her boss! (978-1-63679-850-9)

Traveling Toward Forever by Erin Dutton. When almost-strangers take a road trip through America's national parks, love may be the final destination. (978-1-63679-894-3)

Beautiful Things by Emma L. McGeown. A warmhearted romance of missed chances, undeniable chemistry, and a stubborn love that maybe, just maybe, can find its way back. (978-1-63679-934-6)

Love Takes a Village by Karis Walsh. As Lena Preiss struggles to manage a busy restaurant in the Bavarian Christmas village of Leavenworth, Washington, chocolatier Devin Meyer brings an unexpected richness into her life, along with her delicious desserts. (978-1-63679-902-5)

Secrets of the Heart by Jenny Frame. When a beautiful stranger starts asking questions about Nikki Sharkey, head of an infamous crime syndicate, Nikki will stop at nothing to protect her daughter Isla. (978-1-63679-653-6)

Talon and the Songbird by Julia Underwood. In a world where survival depends on strategic alliances, Makayla and Talon must navigate not only complex politics but also the dangerous territory of their hearts. (978-1-63679-970-4)

The Great Popcorn Romance by Georgia Beers. Opposites attract, and Riley Shaw stands no chance of resisting Hannah Kramer's magnetic pull. But opposites know just how to drive each other crazy… (978-1-63679-910-0)

Three Blissful Days by Dena Blake. Kendall Jackson attempts to make her ex regret dumping her by announcing she's dating beautiful park ranger Ivy Patterson. But there's nothing fake about how attracted Ivy is to Kendall. (978-1-63679-707-6)

Chasing Her Scent by MJ Williamz. When Sheridan Rousseau walks into Lisette Mouton's charming little bookstore in Quebec City, she unknowingly holds the key to a mysterious box hidden in a secret room. (978-1-63679-900-1)

Heart's Run by D. Jackson Leigh. Hoping to recover an escaped racing mare, stock transporter Tobie Mason locks horns with local wild horse advocate Maggie Wilkes. (978-1-63679-825-7)

Scandalous by Kris Bryant. When a Hollywood actress trades places with her twin sister, everyone's in an uproar about getting duped, but Lindsay's more concerned about finding out which twin she made out with. (978-1-63679-874-5)

The Art of Love by Ali Vali. When Mimi and Bianca both set their sights on Jolly, sparks fly, loyalties are tested, and hearts collide as they navigate the unpredictable nature of their hearts (978-1-63679-719-9)

The Other Side of Forever by Kel McCord. Will Kenzie and Rachel be able to make love work when Rachel's cozy suburban dream feels like Kenzie's worst nightmare? (978-1-63679-812-7)

The Secrets of Rhydian Hill by Ronica Black. A doctor in need of a new start. A woman running from a killer. A love story that could end in tragedy. (978-1-63679-880-6)

Feeling Lucky by Krystina Rivers. What happens when, despite suddenly having enough money to buy almost anything, Lucy and Tanner start to discover that maybe all they need is each other? (978-1-63679-876-9)

Iceberg by Gun Brooke. When Lady Arabella hires Zandra, she never expects to find love, especially not as a disaster looms on the horizon. (978-1-63679-908-7)

It Happened One Semester by Aurora Rey. After a Pride night hookup, can eager new Assistant Professor Hudson Greene and Dean of Advising Callie Shaw overcome the odds and ace falling in love? (978-1-63679-814-1)

It's Kind of a Bad Idea by Sarah G. Levine. What happens when an emotionally unavailable serial dater meets the one woman she can't help but fall for—who happens to be the one woman who told her not to? (978-1-63679-920-9)

Thankful for You by Tagan Shepard. Everyone deserves to find their person, maybe Karen has finally found hers? (978-1-63679-884-4)

What Happens on Location by Nan Campbell. How can Helen produce a successful movie when its director is the woman responsible for the demise of her marriage? (978-1-63679-904-9)

When Love Comes Around by Radclyffe and Ronica Black. Can Maya Sanchez and Nolan Wright trust each other enough to build something real, or will the past tear them apart? (978-1-63679-930-8)